A SUMMER WEDDING FOR THE CORNISH MIDWIFE

JO BARTLETT

Boldwood

First published in Great Britain in 2021 by Boldwood Books Ltd.

Copyright © Jo Bartlett, 2021

Cover Design by Debbie Clement Design

Cover photography: Shutterstock

A CIP catalogue record for this book is available from the British Library.

Paperback ISBN 978-1-80048-951-6

Large Print ISBN 978-1-80048-950-9

Hardback ISBN 978-1-80048-949-3

Ebook ISBN 978-1-80048-953-0

Kindle ISBN 978-1-80048-952-3

Audio CD ISBN 978-1-80048-944-8

MP3 CD ISBN 978-1-80048-945-5

Digital audio download ISBN 978-1-80048-948-6

Boldwood Books Ltd
23 Bowerdean Street
London SW6 3TN
www.boldwoodbooks.com

other people's outfits, when his own taste in clothes was definitely questionable. Good-natured teasing was a big part of family life and their house had always been filled with laughter. Watching her parents together, Anna couldn't help smiling.

'Are you sure you two don't want me to bow out, so you start having trips on your own? You've waited nearly twenty-two years to get your freedom back.' Even as she said the words, she mentally crossed her fingers that her parents wouldn't take her up on the offer. When she thought any distance into the future and the idea of starting a family of her own, she couldn't separate that out from being with her wonderful parents, who'd already been in their forties when she came along. She pictured a camper van of her own, trundling along in convoy with Vanna, her husband and children every bit as excited about a trip away with Nanny and Granddad as she was. But if they needed a decade of freedom between now and then, while she established herself in her midwifery career, then she wasn't going to be too selfish to let them have it.

'Having you never meant giving up our freedom. Having you meant we got what we wanted all along.' Maggie smiled at her daughter, tears making her eyes glassy, as Colin nodded in agreement.

'I didn't know just how much until the day your mother put you in my arms.' He slid his arm around Anna's waist again. 'But if we don't get a move on, you're going to be late for your graduation photos and your mother's planning on buying the biggest size they've got to put up above the mantelpiece. We can talk about our trip to Ugley Green later and the first thing I'm going to pack is this tie!'

'Over my dead body and you're not taking those hideous sandals you bought either!' Maggie gave her husband a gentle nudge, and took his arm on the other side of Anna; the three

musketeers off to mark a special day in the history of their little family. One day, if Anna got her way, that family would be twice as big, with a partner and at least two children of her own. But the three musketeers would always be at the centre of her world – she couldn't imagine it any other way...

1

EIGHTEEN YEARS LATER

'This is a crazy idea, isn't it?' The suffocating feeling sweeping over Anna was only partly down to the wedding dress designed for someone at least six inches shorter, which made it impossible to move her arms.

'What? Trying to find a dress in the only bridal shop in Port Agnes, instead of going into Truro?' Her best friend, Ella, raised an eyebrow, but Anna shook her head.

'No. Well, yes… but not just that. Trying to choose a wedding dress that's going to fit whether I'm five months pregnant by the wedding, or still the same shape as a slightly lumpy ironing board.' If someone didn't unzip the itchy lace on the back panel of the dress soon, Anna was going to rip it off. 'It's bad enough tracking my temperature and jumping on poor Brae every time there's the remotest possibility that I might be ovulating, but I had no idea planning a wedding could completely take over your life too. Now I know why most people give it at least a year!'

'First of all, you do not look like an ironing board and no one says you have to wear a traditional wedding dress.' Ella gave her a

level look. 'Brae would marry you in your underwear. In fact, he'd probably like it and I bet he likes being jumped on too!'

'Don't even joke about the underwear thing. I've been having anxiety dreams about walking down the aisle naked as it is!' Anna laughed. However horrifying the thought of displaying her lumpy bits in public might be, Ella was right; Brae wouldn't give a damn what she wore and she felt the same about him. Not only that, she had Ella with her every step of the way too, and she couldn't have asked for a better bridesmaid. Or a better friend. When Ella had joined the midwifery unit that Anna headed up, they'd immediately hit it off, and it was Ella who'd set her up with Brae in the first place. Port Agnes had been a haven for both of them, when they'd needed it most.

'As long as you don't want me to go naked too. You know I'd do almost anything for you and Brae, but I've got to draw the line at that!' Ella grinned and Anna laughed.

'When you agreed to be my bridesmaid, I promised I wouldn't make you look like you were dressed as one of the sweets from a tin of Christmas chocolates, or put you in layers of orange tulle. I'm hoping that when Susie gets back out here, she'll have something both of us can live with.' As Anna moved, the bones sewn into the side of the bodice dug into her flesh. 'In the meantime, can you unzip this thing for me, before it brings me out in a rash?'

'No problem.' As it turned out, Ella had to give the zip a pretty hard tug. Susie, who owned the wedding dress shop, had insisted that most of the samples would fit Anna and that would make it relatively easy to find her a dress she could take home straight away; if she didn't mind having one that had been tried on and probably rejected by every bride-to-be in Port Agnes. Although if the fit on this first dress was anything to go by, Anna wasn't holding out much hope of finding anything. Even Susie had furrowed her brow after the first couple of dresses, describing

Anna as '*unusually long in the torso even for someone so tall*' and disappearing to find something more suitable for her apparently freakish dimensions. None of it was doing much to build up Anna's confidence.

'I keep wondering if I'm too old to wear a proper wedding dress anyway. I'm nearly forty.'

'Who gives a stuff, even if you were ninety-nine?' Ella was having none of it. 'You should wear exactly what you want to wear, whether that's a pair of jeans, or mountains of silk and a train I can barely help you down the aisle with – it's your day.'

'I wish Mum hadn't lost her dress.' Anna swallowed hard against the lump in her throat. Maggie should have been there. Sitting on one of the chairs covered in crushed velvet, staring at Anna with tears filling her eyes every time she came out of the changing room, even if the dress she was wearing was a monstrosity. It was such a rite of passage for mothers and daughters and the ache that never left Anna intensified as she caught sight of the empty chair again. Shaking herself, she turned back towards Ella. 'It was Nanna's before hers, and it would be right on the vintage trend now, but it got lost in the last move before they...' Even after so many years, Anna found it hard to finish the sentence, to admit out loud that *both* her parents had gone. Every time she thought about walking down the aisle she pictured another empty space, but this time it was next to her, where her father should have been.

'You might not have the dress, but you'll be sharing your mum and dad's wedding day.' Ella's tone was gentle. She knew exactly why Anna had chosen 6 July for the wedding. Anna's parents had got married in 1966, just before the start of the football World Cup, where her father would be working as a groundsman at Wembley Stadium and her parents had spent a two-day honeymoon in a London guest house, before her father started his new

job. Anna's mother had returned home without her new husband and had always said that she'd married him accepting that his greatest love would always be football – but all that had changed when Anna came along. From what they'd said, the wedding had been very low-key, but wearing her mother's dress would have been really meaningful. So even if Susie miraculously found something that would fit Anna's apparently outlandish upper body, it could never measure up.

'Okay, I've got three more dresses for you to try on.' Susie smiled as she came back out into the shop, with the dresses draped over her arm. 'And four for Ella. You said you didn't have a specific colour theme, didn't you?'

'Uh-huh, we're just going with the flowers the hotel has on display and we're going to personalise our own centrepieces for the tables. We couldn't really expect them to do anything extra when they're doing us such a big favour by squeezing us in.' The Red Cliff Hotel on the outskirts of Port Agnes was in an old manor house and they'd booked the ballroom in the west wing. The fifth and sixth were the only days in July when there wasn't another big event booked in. It meant that they had to do all the setting up on the fifth, but with less than fifty guests it was doable. By the time the seventh rolled around, Anna would have a family again for the first time in years. That was a million times more important than the dress, the venue or any other detail that *Brides Monthly* might insist was essential to the perfect wedding.

'Fantastic.' Susie smiled again. 'I'll leave you girls to try the dresses on and let me know what you think.' Thankfully she seemed to have picked up on the fact that Anna didn't want an audience, or anyone to try and convince her that something looked okay when it obviously didn't. It was different with Ella, Anna trusted her implicitly and there weren't many people in the world she could say that about.

'Okay. You go first and when we've found something for you, I'll see if I can find anything halfway decent. If we find anything you like, I'll see if she can order something in the same colour for Jess and Toni.' Anna channelled her inner bridezilla and hustled her best friend into the changing room. She might not hold out a lot of hope of finding the right dress for herself, but Ella would look brilliant in anything. At least one decision was going to be easy. Her other bridesmaids were midwives at the unit too, but bringing all three of them, and hoping they'd all like the same dress, had felt like asking for trouble.

'I think this one looks like a wedding dress, especially as it's ivory.' Ella emerged from the changing room in the last of the four dresses, screwing up her face in the process. 'It's also a really similar cut to my own nearly-but-not-quite wedding dress.'

'I can see what you mean, but the colour wouldn't have bothered me if you'd wanted to wear it.' Anna scanned the younger woman's face, searching for any hint that she might be upset. Less than two years before, Ella had been very publicly jilted by her fiancé on the day of her wedding, and worst of all it had been caught on film and become a viral internet sensation. If it still bothered her, even in the slightest, she was doing a very good job of hiding it.

'I like all of them, apart from this one, but if it was down to me I'd go for the grey dress. It's the perfect colour and I actually feel quite slim in it.'

'Grey it is then.' Anna breathed out. 'I suppose I better try and find something now.'

'I wish I could wave a magic wand and give you the dress you really want, but just keep an open mind and give me a shout if you want some help.' Ella waited outside the changing room and Anna took the first dress off the hanger. She didn't even bother to ask Ella to zip it up, before pulling it off again. There were big

flowers decorating the waistband and shoulder straps, and it couldn't have been more wrong. She felt like a fairy on top of a Christmas tree, and an ancient one at that. Her dad wouldn't have been able to stop himself saying 'Are you really wearing that?' if he'd been there. She could still remember the time she'd channelled her inner Britney Spears and worn a denim cap and low-slung jeans, with a tiny crop top. Her father had looked her up and down for a moment and disappeared without saying a word. A minute later he was back with a big overcoat, which he'd insisted would improve the outfit no end, and the truth was he'd been right. But not even a giant overcoat would save this one. Pulling on the second dress, she couldn't help shaking her head, even as she tried to listen to Ella's advice and keep an open mind.

'Do you want me to zip it up for you?'

'I suppose so.' Anna drew back the curtain and Ella quickly zipped up the dress. Stepping out, she just hoped it would look better in the soft lighting of the shop. If anything, it looked even worse. 'Do I look as uncomfortable as I feel?'

'The dress is fine, but it's not you, is it?' The puffy skirt would have looked cute on someone short, but it made Anna feel like a drag queen with none of the glamour.

'I hate it almost as much as it hates me, judging by the static shock it gives me every time I move.' Anna pulled a face. 'At least there's one more to try. I just need to get this monstrosity off first.'

'What's it like?' Ella's voice was tentative before she came in to zip up the last dress.

'I don't know yet, but it already feels a lot better than the others.'

'Well if the front is half as nice as the back, I think you're on to a winner.'

Stepping forward, Anna could see how the dress really looked for the first time and she actually felt like doing a gameshow

hostess twirl. The dress was vintage style and it was by far the closest to the one her mother had worn. She could almost hear her mum whispering in her ear that this was the one. Turning around to face Ella, she smiled. 'So, what do you think?'

'It's perfect.' It was Ella who said the words out loud, sniffing hard. 'You look so much like your mum in the photos you showed me.'

'I know it sounds stupid, but it's almost like I can feel her here when I'm wearing it.'

'It's not stupid.' Ella slipped an arm around her waist. 'And Brae is going to think he's gone to heaven when he sees you walking up the aisle towards him.'

Anna nodded, trying not to think again about the fact that she'd be walking up the aisle alone. Losing both her parents in such quick succession had been like someone pulling the rug out from under her feet and she wasn't sure she'd have survived if she hadn't been able to bury herself in her job. Her boyfriend at the time – who she'd met just after leaving uni – had been sympathetic in the beginning, but in the end even he'd told her that she needed to get over it. Did you ever really get over losing the people you loved, though? Anna had learned to live with it, like anyone who'd lost someone had to. It had probably been inevitable that she'd lose her parents sooner than most people – her father had been forty-four when she was born, and her mother had just turned forty – but facing her wedding day without them had brought their loss right back to the surface again, even after all this time.

Her mother had died from pancreatic cancer which had swept through her body like a forest fire, taking her from her beloved family less than six months after the diagnosis. Her father had been completely devastated and, when he'd died of a heart attack three weeks later, Anna was convinced it was because

his heart had been broken by her mother's death. The only comfort was that both her parents were no longer suffering. As an only child, losing them both had left her rootless, but her work had got her through. The first few years were a blur of taking as many shifts as she could, but accepting a job in Port Agnes – her dream job, heading up the new midwifery unit – had turned out to be the start of slowly piecing her life back together. Now she was engaged to a man she adored and who she was certain her parents would have loved, if they'd only got the chance to meet him. She'd never be able to replace her mum and dad, but having children of her own and recreating some of the memories and traditions that had made her childhood so wonderful, might just lessen the ache. She wouldn't be alone in the world any more then either; there'd be people who shared her DNA, and that of her parents. Family meant the world to Anna, more than ever since she'd lost hers, and she desperately wanted to have one again.

'Oh my God!' Ella jumped as a crack of lightning lit up the shop, followed a split second later by a rumble of thunder. A storm wasn't just coming, it was right overhead and it had come out of nowhere.

'I hope that's not an omen.' Anna wasn't normally superstitious, unlike her mother, who had looked for signs in everything that happened. But with the rain already coming down so hard that it was bouncing back off the pavements, and the sky such a dark shade of grey that it looked almost black in between the flashes of lightning, it was hard not to feel a sense of foreboding.

'My dad always says a thunderstorm is a fresh start; a way to clear the air and wash away your problems. So I'd take it as a good omen.' Ella suddenly shivered despite her words. 'I just hope the boys got the boat back into the harbour before it started.'

'Surely they'd have seen the storm coming from across the water, long before we did?' Anna jumped as a gust of wind rattled the shop door, making it sound as if someone was desperately trying to get in. 'I don't know why Brae's got this crazy idea into his head about catching the fish for the wedding breakfast anyway.'

'Because he's an old romantic.' Ella laughed at the look that must have crossed Anna's face. Most people wouldn't put fish and romance together, but Brae was different. He'd spent years in the Navy before taking over his parents' fish and chip shop in Port Agnes when they'd retired to Spain. So, one way or another, the sea was in his blood. With Ella's boyfriend, Dan, acting as Brae's best man, he'd also been roped into a series of fishing expeditions to catch the sea bass that Brae had persuaded the head chef at the Red Cliff Hotel to serve for the fish course. They'd started early so that they'd stand a good chance of catching enough and storing it until the big day in a freezer he'd bought and put in the garage especially. Anna just wished they'd settled for something from the hotel's usual supplier, or even some fish fingers; anything as long as Brae and Dan weren't out at sea in a storm like this.

'I'll just give him a call to make sure they're okay.' Anna picked up her phone. The call went straight to voicemail, but she told herself that didn't mean anything was wrong; even if she'd much rather have heard Brae's reassuring voice instead of an automated one at the other end of the line. However difficult a day had been, just speaking to him could always make it better.

'No luck?' Ella didn't look worried and Anna swallowed down the panic that she knew would rise in her chest if she let it. She had to stop thinking that things could go wrong at any minute. Just because her whole world had collapsed before, it didn't mean it was going to happen again. And if she spent all her time worrying that it would, she was going to miss out on so much.

'It's fine. You know Port Agnes is filled with places where it's almost impossible to get a mobile signal. I'll try again later, if we don't hear from them first.'

'How are you getting on, girls?' Susie stepped back as she caught sight of Anna. 'Oh that's the one. Please tell me you've chosen that?'

'I have.' Anna had almost forgotten she was wearing the wedding dress. The street outside the shop was already looking more like a river than a road, and another crack of lightning lit up the shop, making the lights flicker.

'Ooh, I haven't seen a storm like this in years!' Susie didn't seem remotely concerned, even when the lights flickered again before going out altogether. But then the person she loved most in the world probably wasn't out at sea in a ridiculously small fishing boat in the middle of it all. 'It's so dark I can't even double-check the price. But, whatever it is, I'll be taking seventy-five per cent off.'

'That's way too generous, you said fifty per cent for one that's been used as a sample, but this is in pristine condition.' Anna tried to look at Susie, but her eyes kept being drawn back to the sky outside, which had grown even darker. An old-fashioned street light mounted on the wall of the shop opposite, suddenly came away from the brickwork and smashed down into the road. 'Did you see that? The storm's getting worse!'

'It'll pass soon and, don't worry, I'll call Adele, who owns the shop opposite, and ask if she needs a hand clearing up the glass.' Susie's voice had a sing-song tone as she brushed off Anna's concerns. 'As for the discount, fifty per cent is the reduction for the sample and the other twenty-five per cent is because you delivered Maisie. Jennie said she couldn't have got through it without you and that little girl is the light of my life.' The older woman smiled as Anna finally turned to look at her.

She'd overseen the delivery of Susie's granddaughter six months earlier. It had been an unexpectedly rocky delivery for a home birth, but thankfully everything had turned out okay in the end.

'I'm really more than happy to pay what you charge everyone else.'

'I won't hear of it.' Susie crossed her arms. 'And the same goes for Ella's bridesmaid's dress.'

'And they say the only reward of midwifery is the job itself. Who knew we could get all this discounted stuff? We've been missing a trick!' Ella laughed and Anna felt her shoulders relax. No one else seemed concerned about Brae and Dan. It was coming up to the anniversary of losing her mum so maybe she was just being silly, letting the time of year get to her the way it always did. The least she could do was be gracious about Susie's offer.

'If you're really sure, thank you so much.' Anna stepped forward, as Susie enveloped her in a hug and a cloud of Chanel N°5. It was the same perfume her mother had worn and it seemed like another good sign, even to someone with as few superstitions as Anna.

Before Susie could reply, the door of the shop was flung open by a woman who looked like she was in her late fifties, letting in a gust of wind that lifted up the skirt of the wedding dress, like Marilyn Monroe standing over that infamous subway grate.

'I'm sorry, Susie, I know I'm more likely to sprout wings and loop the loop above the Sisters of Agnes Island than get wed again, but I've got to come in before I get blown straight back down the high street and into the harbour. I thought I was never going to make it up the hill as it was.'

'Don't be daft, Janis! Come in and shut that blessed door. You don't want to be out in this. I'll light one of the gas rings out back

and boil some water to make us all a cuppa. We can all wait it out here until the worst of the weather passes.'

'Now you're talking.' Janis took off her coat and shook herself like a wet dog might have done and with the same complete lack of self-consciousness. 'If you can muster up some biscuits to go with that tea, I promise that if I do ever find husband number four, you'll be top of my list to buy a frock from for the big day.'

'I'll see what I can do. As long as you promise not to scare Anna off with tales of your divorces. She's just about to embark on her one and only wedding, God willing, and the last thing she wants to hear is that all men are useless.'

'I think both you girls would be better off assuming that, then anything else would be a bonus. All this hearts and flowers stuff Susie peddles is just setting you up for a lifetime of disappointment in my opinion.' Janis made eye contact with Anna and dropped a perfect wink. 'Although whoever he is, he's a lucky fella.'

'She's marrying Brae, from the chippy.' Susie imparted the information and Janis shrieked in response.

'Ooh, I love him! He batters the best fish in Cornwall, and he always gives me a few chips to get started on while I'm waiting for my order. You'll make a handsome pair and your kids are bound to have red hair too, I'll bet, with both of you being ginger. They won't have to ask anyone to reach up and get them an item from the top shelf either, will they?'

Anna couldn't help laughing and everyone joined in. It was a compliment of sorts and she always loved hearing how well-liked Brae was. Not that she'd ever doubted she was making the right decision, but without the possibility of gaining her family's approval, it somehow meant a lot.

'I'm definitely hoping we'll have a family one day.' Anna had to keep reminding herself that it wasn't a given and that, if it

didn't work out that way, she was still incredibly lucky to have found Brae. She didn't need to be a midwife to know that starting a family at almost forty wasn't what Mother Nature necessarily had in mind, but the fact that she'd been a late baby – and somewhat of a surprise to her own parents – also gave her hope. After years of nothing happening, Anna's mother had assumed she was going through the menopause before she'd discovered that a baby was finally on the way. Anna had to believe it would happen for her too – that there'd be a little girl she could call Maggie, or a boy who'd just have to put up with the fact that his middle name was Colin, even if it seemed a ridiculous name nowadays to ever assign to a newborn baby. 'I don't mind if they're tall, short or somewhere in between, but I've got to admit that I'd love them to have Brae's red hair. Mine is mostly out of a bottle these days.'

'And his sunny nature, I'll bet?' Janis tilted her head. 'Although I've warned him more than once not to keep whistling in the shop when he's serving. It's unlucky, and if any of the fisherman hear him, they'll be blaming him for all sorts. Even this storm.'

'I thought that was just if you were on board the boat?' Susie pulled a face. 'It's all stuff and nonsense anyway.'

'Try telling that to the lads caught out in this weather.' Janis wagged a finger. 'My old dad spent his life on the boats and he said whistling encouraged the wind to get stronger. He'd cuff my brother and me around the head if he ever heard us doing it.'

'I think it's more likely to be down to global warming.' Ella's notion was about as unromantic as they came, and Janis sighed.

'I don't know about all that malarkey, but when I rounded the harbour, a wave came right across the top of one of the boats that was moored there. If anyone had been on deck, that's the last we'd have seen of them. I just hope there's no one out there.'

'Brae and his friend, Dan, went out fishing earlier, and we've not heard from them yet.' Anna whispered the words.

'I'll try and call them again.' Ella picked up her phone, shaking her head a few seconds later. 'It's still going straight to voicemail.'

'They'll be in the pub, I'm sure of it.' Anna was trying to convince herself, but the hairs on the back of her neck were standing up all the same.

'Oh your Brae's a big, strong lad. He'll be right as rain, you mark my words.' Janis reached out to squeeze Anna's arm, and a split second later a mobile phone started to ring. Realising it was hers, Anna rummaged in her bag, silently willing it to be Brae's number illuminating the caller display. When she finally located the phone, the call was from an unknown number.

'Is that Anna Jones?' It was impossible to gauge anything from the man's tone of voice, but that didn't stop her pulse thudding in her ears.

'Speaking.'

'My name's Gary Warner, I'm calling from the coastguard. We had a distress call from a boat that's registered to Brae Penrose, and your name and contact number were listed on the record.'

'Yes, he's been out fishing in the boat today.' Anna was struggling to get the words out; she didn't want to ask any questions she couldn't handle the answer to.

'We've located the boat.' The man's tone was still deadpan, but Anna was weak with relief as she shot a smile in Ella's direction.

'That's great, and Brae and Dan are okay?'

'That's just the problem. When we found the boat, there was no one on board.'

'But that can't be right! They're both experienced at navigating the waters around here, they wouldn't just leave the boat.

They'd wait until help came.' Her words were tumbling over one another and, even as Ella reached out to take the phone, it slipped from Anna's hands. She couldn't lose another person she loved, and she absolutely couldn't lose Brae. She loved him so much, she would never survive it.

The fact that news spread like wildfire in Port Agnes could be a blessing or a curse, as Ella knew only too well. The small seaside town was built on a labyrinth of narrow roads which rose up from the harbour and clung to the cliffs, like the limpets in the rock pools on the wide stretch of sandy beach and the hidden coves just beyond it. By the time Ella and Anna had made it back to her parents in the bakery opposite the harbour, they'd already heard the news that Dan and Brae were missing; one of the crewman from the lifeboat station had texted her father.

Ella couldn't cry. If she did, it would set Anna off again and one of them had to hold it together. When she'd taken the phone from her best friend, the coastguard had explained that Brae and Dan's boat had been taking on water when they'd found it. And fast. With the storm still lashing Port Agnes with a terrifying power, it might have seemed crazy for them to abandon the boat, but the coastguard said it was probably the right decision if they had some other means of making it back to the harbour. The trouble was, Ella and Anna knew exactly what they'd had to use as an emergency escape raft: a two-man kayak.

danger of dislodging the mortar board that her mother had helped her pin in place just moments before.

'The three musketeers are forever. Always have been, always will be.' Anna's decision to choose the university closest to home was so she wouldn't have to spend any length of time away from her parents. It probably seemed an odd thing for a twenty-some-thing-year-old to do, but, as the only child of two only children, they really were one another's whole worlds.

'I was thinking we ought to take Vanna out for a trip to cele-brate your graduation and I've found just the place!' Colin grinned, his whole face lighting up with excitement, the way it always did when he was planning a trip in the old ice cream van he'd converted into a camper – just after Anna started secondary school – that they'd christened Vanna. In between their annual summer holidays in Port Agnes, on the beautiful Atlantic coast in Cornwall, the three of them took it in turns to plan road trips. They'd pick out weird and wonderful place names from the well-thumbed map book that only ever left the glove compartment of Colin's car when they were planning one of their adventures.

'Where is it this time?' Anna raised an eyebrow. They'd been to Boggy Bottom, Droop and Giggleswick in the last year alone, when most of her mates were saving hard for weekends in London, or summer breaks in Ayia Napa or Ibiza. Not Anna though, give her Boggy Bottom with her mum and dad any day.

'Ugley Green!'

'And what inspired that choice?' Maggie was already laughing before she reached the punchline. 'The lime green tie you're wearing for your daughter's graduation!'

'Cheeky! Come here and say that.' Colin pulled his wife into his arms and twirled her around in a circle, making her laugh all the more. It was a family joke that he seemed to think he was some kind of fashion expert when it came to commenting on

PROLOGUE

'Look at my beautiful girls.' Colin Jones beamed at the reflection in the full-length mirror, as he stood with his arms around his wife and daughter. 'And our Anna, all grown up and ready to go out and change the world.'

'We're so proud of you, darling.' Anna's mother, Maggie, reached up and planted a kiss on her daughter's cheek, almost dislodging the floppy-brimmed hat she was wearing for her daughter's graduation.

'Thanks, Mum. I'm not sure I'll change the world, Dad, but I can't wait to get started.'

'My daughter the midwife.' Colin shook his head, letting his arms drop to his sides as if he still couldn't quite believe it. 'A university graduate in the family. You're definitely the brightest of the three musketeers!'

'Maybe we'll have to let Anna break up the trio, she's got to make her own life now, Col.' Maggie looked from her daughter to her husband and back again as they stepped away from the mirror. Anna was shaking her head so hard she was almost in

To Anna and Harry, who made my greatest dream come true, and to Ellie and Jake who taught me that families are made in more than one way.

xxxx

Dan had already owned a half share in a boat with his brother-in-law when he and Ella met, but when his sister had demanded that her husband spend a bit more time with the family, they'd decided to sell it. At the beginning of the summer, Brae and Dan had bought a small and fairly ancient fishing boat with a view to doing it up, and the four of them had great fun taking it out to the coves around Port Agnes, staying fairly close to the coastline for safety's sake. They'd drop the kayaks into the water in sheltered spots, to get a closer look at the hidden caves and rocky outcrops that defined the coastline around Port Agnes. It had been blissful in the summer, and Ella had thanked her good fortune time and time again that she got to spend her free time with a man she adored – and the best friends who meant so much to both of them – in such a beautiful place, just a stone's throw away from where she'd been born, and where her parents still lived.

She hadn't ventured out in the boat since October and neither had Anna. The boys had laughed and called them fair-weather sailors, but as far as Ella was concerned it was just sensible. She had no desire to be on board in January whilst the boat plunged through swirling waves that rose and fell, taking your stomach with them. Brae and Dan weren't as easily put off and now it looked like they might have paid the ultimate price. She wouldn't believe that, though. It had taken far too long to reconnect with Dan, her childhood sweetheart, and to realise the seaside town where they'd grown up was the only place in the world she wanted to live. Not even a violent storm could take that away from her; she refused to consider it.

'Do you think we should go down to the lifeboat station and wait for news?' Anna asked the question for the third time in as many minutes, as steam filled the room from where Ella's mother,

Ruth, had hung their soaking wet clothes on a wooden clothes horse in front of the fire.

'They told us they'd call as soon as there was news.' Ella pulled down the sleeves of the fleece her mother had found for her to put on. They could have gone straight back to her and Dan's place when they'd left the bridal shop, but she'd managed to leave her key behind when she'd left home in a hurry that morning, and she wouldn't be able to get in again until Dan got home. Assuming he ever did...

Anna and Brae's house was on the other side of town and she didn't have to check with Anna to know that she wouldn't want to be that far away from the harbour when the lifeboat crew finally called. Instead, she and Anna were wearing a motley collection of old clothes that Ella hadn't considered worth taking with her when she'd moved out.

They'd been soaked to the skin, in the true sense of the words, by the time they'd made it to the bakery. It was almost unheard of for her parents' shop to be empty of customers, but the storm had everyone battening down the hatches and her mother had given them her undivided attention from the moment they'd shown up.

'Are you sure I can't get you girls something to eat?' Ruth put another mug of sweet, hot, cure-all tea in front of them both, even though they'd barely touched the first. It was hard enough swallowing a mouthful of tea as the rain continued to lash at the windows and the wind made an eerie wailing noise that barely seemed to let up. The prospect of eating anything was impossible.

'No thanks, Mum.' Ella warmed her hands on the mug, but the cold seemed to have got into her bones, even as the fire continued to roar in the grate.

'What about you, Anna? You look as white as a sheet, have you eaten at all today?' Ruth Mehenick's voice was filled with concern.

'I felt too nauseous to eat this morning before we went to try and find a dress. I think it must have been nerves. It seems ridiculous now, so unimportant.' Anna sniffed, trying and failing to hold back the tears that kept rolling silently down her cheeks.

'It'll be okay, I promise.' Ella crossed her fingers behind her back. She was powerless to keep the promise, but if she believed it enough that had to help Anna get through the wait, which might just help her get through it too.

'Your father's walked down to the lifeboat station to see if there's anything he can do to help.' Ruth raised her eyebrows. Jago Mehenick was renowned for his strong opinions and all Ella could do was hope that her father's interference didn't end up hindering the rescue efforts. She knew him well enough to realise he wouldn't just be able to sit around and wait; it was killing her and Anna as it was.

'That's your mobile!' Anna's shout almost drowned out the ringtone as Ella snatched up the phone.

'Oh Ella, thank God. It's Toni.' It wasn't the voice Ella had so desperately wanted to hear, although judging by her tone, Brae and Dan's disappearance wasn't the only Port Agnes emergency in progress. Toni was another of the midwives at the unit and she was usually pretty unflappable, but there was more than a hint of panic in her voice.

'What's wrong?' Ella looked at Anna and shook her head, sending a message that the call wasn't about the boys.

'I got a call out to Beth Jenson, who thought she might be in the early stages of labour.' Toni's voice was tight. 'It turns out she's a lot further on than she thought and the baby must have turned into the breech position since her last examination. I've called an ambulance, but with the storm and a pile-up on the A39, they don't know how long it'll be before they get here. Even when they do, the paramedics aren't going to be able to help if the baby decides to put in an appearance before they can get Beth to the hospital for a C-section. Her husband's out on call with the lifeboat crew and I can't get hold of any of the other midwives. I know you're not on call but—'

'I'll be there as soon as I can. What's Beth's address?' Ella wasn't sure whether agreeing to help out with the delivery was a good idea, but Toni needed her and so did Beth. It was also clear that Toni had no idea who it was the lifeboat crew were searching for, so at least the news hadn't spread that far yet. For a few minutes Ella could pretend to herself that it wasn't happening too. There was nothing she could do to help Dan; he had experts out looking for him, and just waiting around was unbearable. Beth's husband was one of the people out trying to save Dan and Brae, so the least she could do was support his wife. It was a tiny way of paying back an immeasurable debt.

'Thanks. It's Blackthorn Lodge on Miller's Lane, straight down past Miller's Farm and it's the second property on the left.'

'Do you need me to bring anything?' Ella would fill Anna in as soon as the call ended and give her the option of coming along too. She wasn't sure if Anna would be up to it and she wouldn't judge either way. They had to do what was best for Beth. It was the only thing in their power.

'Just bring yourself, and please be as quick as you can!' Toni disconnected the call before Ella could answer, and she looked across at Anna.

'Toni's with Beth Jenson, out at Miller's Lane. She's in advanced labour and the baby's breech. Toni's called an ambulance but they can't guarantee when they will get there. She needs my help.' Ella unhooked her dad's car keys from the spot where he'd always hung them by the back door, for as long as she could remember.

'I'm coming too. I've got to do something; I can't stand just waiting.' Anna was already up on her feet and it was pointless arguing with her. She was the most capable midwife Ella had ever worked with and, despite the turmoil they were both going through, she was certain Anna wouldn't let Beth down. Somehow they'd have to push away the thoughts of the lives that might be hanging in the balance out in the storm, and help bring a new one into the world.

* * *

If Anna had thought about it, she might have questioned how she was functioning at all, let alone taking charge of Beth Jenson's delivery. It was as if being a midwife was imprinted on her soul and, even if she couldn't keep thoughts of Brae being missing out of her head, muscle memory seemed to have taken over.

'What type of breech do you think we're dealing with?' Anna asked the question as soon as Toni answered the door to Beth's house, her face flooding with relief at the sight of Anna and Ella standing on the doorstep.

'Judging by the position of the heartbeat and what I can tell by examining Beth, I'd say we're dealing with a frank breech.' Toni stepped back to let them into the house.

'Well that's some good news.' Anna caught Ella's eye. They'd agreed on the way over not to mention Brae and Dan's disappearance to either Beth or Toni. It would be better for all of them if they concentrated on the delivery. A frank breech meant the baby was bottom first with its legs bent upwards towards its head. It was the next best thing to being head down, and far less dangerous than if the baby's feet or knees emerged first. Anna just hoped Toni was right.

'How's Beth doing?' Ella shrugged off her coat and took Anna's from her. The rain hadn't eased off and just the short run to and from the car at either end of the journey had been like stepping into a shower on full jet mode.

'She's okay. At the moment she seems more worried that Andy isn't going to make it back in time for the birth than she is about the baby being breech.' Toni pulled a face. 'And she seems pretty stoical through the contractions. She was already in the kneeling position they advised at her antenatal classes when I got here, and she said that was helping a lot.'

'Is she close to the second stage?' Anna followed Toni down the corridor to the kitchen, so they could scrub up for a delivery that didn't sound as if it was going to wait for the ambulance to arrive, or for the storm to pass.

'She went from six centimetres to eight in less than half an hour, so by my reckoning we've got twenty minutes at the most.' Toni looked from Anna to Ella and back again. 'I'm so glad the two of you are here. I was terrified you weren't going to make it, or that the electricity would go off again and I'd be left here alone, in the dark, in both senses of the word. I've never done a home breech birth before, let alone solo.'

'It'll be fine.' The words sounded robotic, even to Anna's own ears. It was what Susie and Janis had said in the shop, after she'd taken the call from the lifeboat crew, and what Ella and Ruth had repeated over and over back at the Mehenicks' place. She needed to convince Beth that it would be fine, though, just as much as she needed to believe what everyone else was saying about Brae and Dan would turn out to be true, and not just a meaningless platitude. 'Let's go and take a look at Beth then, shall we, and see if we can get this baby to put in an appearance?'

Toni nodded and the three of them trooped up the stairs, pausing halfway up as the lights flickered off again for a split second, before lighting up the way again, thank God. This was difficult enough as it was.

'Hi Beth. I'm Anna Jones, one of the midwives from the unit. I don't know if you remember me or Ella from any of your check-ups, but I think you've met us both, haven't you?' Anna crouched down by the end of the bed where Beth was positioned with her elbows pressed into the mattress and her bottom sticking up in the air, like a sort of downward dog yoga move. Beth turned her head to one side and nodded.

'Uh-huh, I've met most of the midwives I think but frankly I couldn't care less right now who delivers this baby, just as long as he gets here safely.' Beth grimaced, grabbing a fistful of the fitted sheet as another contraction took hold.

'So we've got a little boy on the way then?'

'Yes, Andy was desperate for a boy and he got his wish. I'm sure you'll think it's an old wives' tale, but he had me down at the fishmongers twice a week while we were trying for the baby. And he's convinced it's down to the sardines and oysters that we're having a little boy, although I'd much rather have stuck to the cod and chips from Penrose Plaice. Even in the middle of labour I wouldn't say no.' Beth spoke through gritted teeth and Anna forced herself to focus back on the delivery, even as thoughts of Brae threatened to overwhelm her. Everyone seemed to know him and loads of people would be devastated if anything happened to him, but Anna would be broken beyond repair. It scared the hell out of her that she loved him so much because there was so much to lose, but it was way too late to change that now.

'I think you'll have earned a fish supper at the very least after this.' Anna fought to keep her tone light. 'Are you okay for me to examine you?'

'Go for it. Like I said, I don't care who does what, as long as I can get the baby out, and I'm past trying to hang on for Andy's sake. I just want it over now.'

'You're doing brilliantly, sweetheart. Ella, can you take Beth's blood pressure please, while I examine her? Toni, if you can get everything we might need, we'll be ready to go as soon as the baby decides it's time.' There was a good chance Anna might have to intervene to help the baby out if he got stuck in the second stage of labour for too long, but she'd cross that bridge if they came to it. Right now, there was a bit more good news to share. 'You're very nearly at ten centimetres, Beth, and you should feel the urge to start pushing before much longer.'

'Am I going to be able to get him out the wrong way round? My sister said it was like passing a bowling ball when she gave birth to my niece, and she was the right way up.' For the first time Beth sounded panicked and Anna nodded at Ella who moved to the side of the bed, crouching down to speak to their patient.

'You can do this. Lots of women give birth naturally with the baby in the breech position and midwives like us have the privilege of seeing just how amazing women in labour can be. We're right here with you.'

'Toni said she'd never delivered a breech baby at home before.' Beth groaned as another contraction took hold and Anna couldn't stop her eyebrows from shooting up. Sometimes Toni was too honest with the patients for her own good. It was strange when she guarded her personal life with the same level of secrecy as James Bond on a mission for MI5. Anna was going to have to redress the balance to put Beth's mind at rest.

'Ella specialised in difficult deliveries when she was working in London. Lots of women with a breech presentation chose to give birth naturally, didn't they?'

'That's right and Anna has delivered a few breech babies at home, haven't you?'

'Absolutely and they were all fine.' Now wasn't the time to mention the baby who'd had to be resuscitated and another who was hospitalised with hip problems. The truth was that everything had turned out well in the end, and running through a list of things that could go wrong wasn't going to help anyone. It wasn't like they had a choice. The baby was coming and he was coming in the breech position, whether they liked it or not.

'That's good, I didn't fancy being your first too. Ohhhhh!' Beth groaned again and her whole body seemed to go rigid for a moment or two before relaxing again. 'That was a strong one and I can still feel a lot of pressure down below.'

'That's just your body getting ready to push.' Anna examined Beth again. 'You're fully dilated and as soon as that pressure builds up again, you need to go with it.' With the baby in the position he was, there was more chance of the cord being compressed and depriving the baby of blood flow and oxygen as a result. Once Beth started pushing, the countdown on the second stage of labour would begin. They only had an hour to get the baby out before the risk of oxygen deprivation could lead to his blood becoming dangerously acidic, which could prove fatal. So they had to give Beth the best chance of delivering as quickly as she could.

'Can't I start pushing now?' She sounded exhausted, but if she started pushing too early, she was just going to use up energy she didn't have.

'You can, but if you wait until you feel the urge it'll be a lot more effective and the breaks in between will give you a little rest.' Anna had barely got the words out before Beth hauled herself up onto all fours again.

'So much for a rest! I can feel the urge to push already.'

'Being on all fours is absolutely the best position, just go with it.' Ella's tone was positive and Beth started to push.

'Your waters have gone and I can see the baby. He's definitely coming bottom first.' Anna let go of the breath she'd been holding. Seeing a foot or knee emerging first would have been much more dangerous for Beth and the baby. Even Anna hadn't delivered a baby like that at home before and she hoped she'd never have to.

'I want Andy!' Beth screamed as another contraction took hold and as she fell silent again, Anna heard a door crashing open and footsteps running along the corridor below and up the stairs. If Andy was back, that meant they had to have found Brae and Dan...

'Oh thank God, I'm not too late.' Andy flung his coat onto a chair in the corner of the room, rain dripping off his hair, as Beth turned her head to look at her husband.

'They said you were out on a shout and they couldn't get hold of you.'

'Have you found the missing fisherman?' Anna couldn't stop herself asking, before Andy even had a chance to answer his wife. Her heart seemed to physically contract when Andy shook his head.

'They managed to get a message through on the radio that Beth was in labour and they brought me back to the lifeboat station. The rest of the team have gone back out to keep searching and they've met up with a crew from Port Kara too. If they don't find those lads soon, they won't be coming home.'

'Oh God.' The words slipped out before Anna could stop them and she dug her fingernails into the palms of her hand, not daring to look up at Ella, who was clearing her throat. She'd thought for a moment that Ella was going to tell the others it was Brae and Dan who were missing, but she didn't. It was as if an unspoken agreement had passed between them; if either of them acknowledged Dan and Brae's disappearance out loud, it would make it all the more real and they might have to admit Andy was right. Brae and Dan wouldn't be home for the wedding. They wouldn't be coming home at all.

'I know it's horrific, isn't it? It's one of the worst storms I've ever been out in.' Andy moved next to Beth, at the head of the bed. 'But I'm guessing you've had it even worse, haven't you, angel? The message said the baby was breech.'

'He is and I'm really frightened.' Beth pressed her head up against her husband's and he stroked her hair.

'I know, darling, but I'm here now, and if anyone can do this it's you.'

'Beth's doing brilliantly, isn't she?' Toni looked at Anna, who was still struggling to pull herself together, but eventually she managed to nod.

'Absolutely and if a baby's going to be breech, yours is in the best position for a safe delivery. You're just in time to see your son make his entrance into the world.' Anna forced a smile, fighting the urge to ask Andy if Brae and Dan had any chance of surviving out at sea in this weather if they weren't found. She had to focus on the baby, for her own sake, as much as Beth's and her unborn son's.

'I've got another contraction coming, give me your hand!' Beth reached out and grabbed Andy's hand, pushing it into the mattress under her own. Judging by the grimace on his face, she was applying a lot of downward pressure.

'Okay, just go with it. Once we've got the baby's bottom out, the rest of him should follow relatively easily.' Anna wasn't sure she'd have done anywhere near as well in Beth's position, but sometimes too much knowledge wasn't a good thing. 'Are you sure you don't want some gas and air?'

'I've come this far without it, I'm not giving in now.'

'She's the most stubborn woman I've ever met and she won't back down once she decides to do something. She was determined to give birth without pain relief, even when everyone was telling her she'd change her mind once labour started.' Andy grinned, obviously proud of his wife's determination, even if it was presenting a risk that he'd get a bone-crush injury as a result.

'That was before you realised the baby was going to be breech.' Ella paused. 'No one would have any right to judge you if you changed your mind now. In fact, no one should judge anyone for the decisions they make in labour.'

'Some of the women in my antenatal group would.' Beth grimaced again, as another contraction took hold.

'That's it, one more good push like that and I think we'll get his bottom out.' Anna checked her watch. They were ten minutes into the second stage now and there was still plenty of time to get the baby out safely, but there was no doubting how tiring this was for Beth and they needed to keep monitoring her too.

'I can't believe how preachy some woman are when they're supposed to be in a support group like that.' Toni tutted. 'Although, when I ran my first ever antenatal group as a newly qualified midwife working in the community, one of the women admitted she didn't want to breastfeed and I thought the rest of them were going to lynch her. We had to sit through a half-hour lecture from one of the other women about how breasts weren't just playthings. I wanted the ground to open up and swallow me, but I've toughened up at lot since then and I wouldn't stand for it now. I might even be tempted to get out my tassels.'

Poor Andy's eyes nearly popped out of his head at the thought of Toni demonstrating just how versatile her breasts could be, and even Anna couldn't help laughing. It was a fragment of normality in the midst of all the drama. And Toni wouldn't be Toni if she wasn't saying something on the edge of inappropriateness.

'Some of the women in my group are just bloody b—' Whatever expletive Beth had been about to use was cut off as another contraction took hold.

'That's it, you're doing brilliantly, Beth, keep going.' Anna was sure the next push would do it. 'Do you want to come and look, Andy?'

'God, no! I had to sit with my head between my knees for fifteen minutes after I watched Mindy, our cat, having one of her kittens in the summer. If Beth hadn't already been pregnant, I'd have tried to talk her out of it. It might be natural, but it's also pretty damn disturbing.'

'Thank God the human race isn't relying on men to keep topping up the numbers.' Toni pursed her lips. 'I take it you won't be wanting to cut the cord when it's time?'

'Jesus Christ!' Beth screamed the words again, as she finally pushed her baby into the world. Just as predicted, once his bottom was out, the next stage was fairly easy.

'He's here!' Anna's words were redundant as the baby gave a hearty cry, and Beth turned over so her son could be lifted onto her chest. Andy's eyes never left the little boy's face, but thankfully he wasn't giving any indication he was about to pass out.

'Is the baby okay?' Beth looked up at Anna, and she nodded.

'He looks perfect. I'll check him over properly in a minute, but all the signs look good. He's a great colour and he's got a very healthy sounding pair of lungs!'

'I think that calls for a cup of tea, don't you?' Toni was already edging towards the bedroom door. In the end, there were more midwives than there needed to be. Beth could probably have given birth all on her own if she'd had to. To go through a breech birth without any pain relief was incredibly impressive by anyone's standards. She'd even refused medication to help deliver the placenta; she was determined the experience would be as natural as possible.

'Tea would be good.' Anna shivered as the window rattled, battered by the storm still raging outside. As soon as she was sure Beth and the baby were okay, she'd leave Toni to it. Coming to help had been the right thing to do, but the more the hands of the clock slid round with no sign of Brae and Dan, the more difficult she was finding it to imagine a good outcome. Whether it was the right thing to do or not, she had to go down to the lifeboat station so she'd be there as soon as the news came in. She was certain Ella would want to do the same.

The two of them had found a rhythm of working together; they could anticipate what the other one was going to do without having to talk it all through, and today was no different. As they waited for the third stage of labour to complete, Anna checked the baby – who as yet still had no name – and Ella ran through some checks with Beth.

'Your heart rate has shot up a bit. It might be down to the adrenaline high of the delivery, but I'd like to monitor it, just to make sure.' Ella's voice wouldn't have given anything away, but Anna saw the flicker of concern in her eyes. This was more than just a mild fluctuation.

'Here's your little boy, all ready for another cuddle.' Anna handed the baby back to Beth; he was wrapped in a blanket now, his little rosebud lips already pursing and relaxing in anticipation of his first feed.

'He's beautiful.' Beth looked down at the baby, but as she looked up again all the colour seemed to drain from her face. 'I feel really dizzy.'

'Ella, can you take Beth's blood pressure, please?' Even as Anna gave the instruction, Ella was already repeating the check, the flicker of concern in her eyes growing by the second.

'It's really low.'

'She's bleeding.' Anna spoke in a low register trying not to make Beth panic and Ella nodded. 'I think you might be having a bit of difficulty delivering the placenta, Beth. I know you didn't want the oxytocin, but I really think we need it now and it should help stop the bleeding until the ambulance gets here. Then they can take a proper look at the hospital.'

'I don't mind having the injection, but I don't want to go in.' Despite her protests, Beth slumped against the pillow and Andy lifted his son into his arms.

'Is she going to be okay?'

'We just need to get the placenta out, so we can stop the bleeding.' Anna's voice was only slightly steadier than her hands as she loaded the syringe. This was nothing she hadn't done before, but if she'd been distracted and Beth paid the price for that – because of what was going on with Dan and Brae – she wouldn't be able to live with herself.

'Tea's up!' As Toni opened the bedroom door, Anna cut her off. 'Can you check on what's happened with the ambulance, please? Beth's having some problems with the placenta.' She didn't have to spell out to Toni what they were dealing with. The last thing Beth or Andy needed was to panic.

'Of course. Do you want me to do anything else?' Toni's eyes widened. They'd all been nervous about the position of the baby, but that had turned out to be the easy bit.

'No, I'm going to give Beth some oxytocin, then I'll try CCT. Hopefully the placenta will deliver before the ambulance arrives and they'll just need to check at the hospital that it's complete.' CCT involved putting controlled traction on the cord, to help deliver the placenta. It might be a bit uncomfortable for Beth, but it was the best way to stop the bleeding. If that didn't work, they had one more option – to remove the placenta manually. But that was risky, and Anna was already praying like hell that the ambulance would arrive before she had to do it.

Beth's eyelids were flickering now and if her long dark hair hadn't been fanned out across the white pillowcase, she might have blended into it completely, given the pallor of her skin.

'I'm going to give you some fluids that contain electrolytes and minerals, because of how much this is taking out of you. Then Ella's going to clamp and cut the cord. I know you wanted to wait, but with the bleeding we can't afford to delay it as planned.' Anna gestured towards Ella, who nodded. It was the best they could do until the ambulance got there.

Anna administered the oxytocin, before hooking up the bag of fluids. If they could stop the bleeding and keep Beth stable until they got her to hospital, then she'd be okay. If she saved Beth, then surely karma would reward her with having Brae back in one piece too? Either way, she'd do everything she could.

'Okay, Beth, I'm going to apply some pressure on the cord with your next contraction and counter pressure on your uterus at the same time. It might feel a bit uncomfortable and I'm really sorry if I hurt you.' Anna talked herself through the process in her head. It was something she'd done plenty of times before with planned management of the third stage, but it was different doing it because of an emergency. The worst thing she could do was apply too much pressure and make the situation even more dangerous. 'When the contraction comes I want you to push just like you did to get baby out.'

'Let me know if you need me to take over.' Ella understood better than anyone the tension that seemed to be gripping Anna's spine. One mistake could be catastrophic, but having her there to share the burden made all the difference.

'Thanks, I'll let you know, but the oxytocin seems to be kicking in. I can feel her uterus contracting. Okay, come on, Beth, one last push.' Anna held her breath as she applied the pressure again and thirty seconds later the third stage of labour was finally complete. 'Well done, sweetheart, you've done it.'

'Is she going to be okay?' Andy, who hadn't said a word since he'd been passed his newborn son, was almost as pale as his wife. Somehow he'd managed to stay upright throughout all the drama, though.

'She should be fine now, we just need to monitor her until the ambulance gets here. She must be exhausted, though, so try not to worry if she's quiet.' Anna kept her tone as gentle as she could, but he still looked as if he might burst into tears at any moment.

'Her heart rate and blood pressure have stabilised a bit.' Ella managed a smile, as she looked up at Anna, just as Toni came back into the room.

'The ambulance is only five minutes away now.' Toni was breathless, having obviously run back up the stairs. 'It took me ages to find out what was going on. There were two dispatched, but the first one was diverted to attend to some fishermen who were picked up by the lifeboat crew.'

'It must be the job the lads were out on.' Andy was still rocking his son in his arms, his eyes darting towards his wife every few seconds, checking she was okay.

'If they've sent an ambulance, that has to mean they're alive, doesn't it?' Anna turned to Ella, who'd given up on trying to stop the tears.

'God, I hope so.'

'What's going on?' Toni looked from Anna to Ella and back again.

'Brae and Dan were out in their boat when the storm hit and they got into trouble. But when the lifeboat got there, there was no sign of them.'

'It's your husbands who are missing?' Andy looked mortified.

'I'm so sorry! I'd never have said that stuff about how much danger they were in if I'd known.'

'It's okay, we're just so grateful that the crew kept looking for them. That's why we had to come here and help Beth.' Anna wasn't about to waste time explaining that she and Ella weren't actually married to Dan and Brae. She'd had to grab the rail of the bed just to stay on her feet as it was. 'I just want to know if they're okay, or whether... I'm sorry, I shouldn't be burdening you with all of this, while you're waiting for an ambulance for Beth.'

'She's definitely going to be okay, isn't she?' Andy paused as Anna nodded. With Beth's heart rate and blood pressure moving in the right direction, she was as sure as she could be that they'd done enough to get her safely to the hospital. 'That means I owe you everything and I'll do whatever I can to repay the favour. If you take the baby, I'll ring one of the crew. They should be able to tell me what's going on.'

Andy was gone for two minutes at most, but it seemed to last forever. No one spoke, as if they were all holding their breath for the verdict when he returned.

'It's good news. They're being transferred to Truro by ambulance. It looks like they're suffering from exposure and they need to get checked over, but they're okay.' Andy had hardly got the words out, before the sound of a wailing siren filled the air. Anna's whole body seemed to slump with relief and if Ella hadn't pulled her into a hug, she might not have managed to stay on her feet.

'They're okay, it's going to be okay.' Ella repeated Andy's words as she held Anna up.

'Thank God.' She still felt as if her heart could burst through her chest at any minute and, until she saw Brae, she couldn't quite let herself believe it.

A flurry of thank yous – that would never be enough – were

exchanged as Toni let the paramedics in, and Beth, the baby and Andy were loaded into the ambulance.

'I'll go with them, in case the crew need a hand with anything.' Toni wasn't going to get any argument from Anna or Ella; they had their own hospital dash to make. 'I still can't believe what a day it's been. There was me thinking that finding a grey hair in my eyebrow was going to be the biggest drama of my day.'

'In your eyebrow? Just pull it out.' Anna was still feeling giddy with relief, as she peered at Toni.

'Well, maybe not my eyebrow.' Toni gestured downwards and started to laugh. When Ella joined in, Anna couldn't help following suit. It might have been bordering on hysteria, but they could so easily have found themselves unable to imagine ever laughing again.

3

As Ella screeched to a halt in the outpatients' car park, she'd have done a stunt woman in a TV cop show proud. The adrenaline surge from feeling like she couldn't possibly get there soon enough, no matter how fast she went, was still coursing through her veins, but Anna seemed rooted to the spot.

'Are you okay?' Even as Ella asked the question, the answer was obvious. Anna was far from okay. Her face had even less colour than the white knuckles on her left hand, which were gripping the roof handle as if her life depended upon it. Surely Ella's driving hadn't been that bad?

'I can't believe I was standing there laughing with Toni when we don't know for sure if the boys are okay. What if Andy has it wrong and one of them is seriously injured? Once I go inside the hospital and they say the words, things won't ever be the same again. I've been there before.' Anna turned towards her.

'I know what happened with your dad was a terrible shock, but it won't happen again.' Ella shook her head, not truly able to comprehend what her friend had been through. Shock was an understatement. Anna had told her the story the year before; her father had died late in the evening on the day before Valentine's Day, and all Anna could remember about the doctor who'd told her was that she was wearing a pair of flashing love heart earrings. A group of drunks, who'd got bored of waiting to be patched up in A & E, had barged into the relatives' room singing an X-rated version of 'All You Need is Love', just as the doctor had broken the news. Now the prospect that Brae might be taken away from her too, was paralysing Anna with fear.

'I know I'm being ridiculous, but I've just got this sense of foreboding that something is going to go wrong and I'm not going to end up marrying Brae. I can't explain it, but it feels like a physical lump is lodged in my throat.'

'It's the anniversary of losing your mum tomorrow, isn't it?'

'I can't believe you remembered.' Anna squeezed her hand and Ella nodded. She'd already ordered flowers to be delivered the next day, to mark the occasion. In three weeks' time it would be the anniversary of Anna losing her dad and she'd do the same thing then too. Ella hadn't always appreciated having her own parents slap bang in the middle of her life, even when she didn't want them to be, but the more Anna revealed about losing her mum and dad, the more Ella realised how lucky she was.

'Of course I remembered.'

'Seventeen years.' Anna sighed. 'It won't be long before I've lived half my life without them around.'

'I can't even imagine what that's like.'

'I feel almost guilty for how happy I've been lately with Brae and you, and the rest of the team at the unit feeling like a surrogate family of sorts these days.' Anna smiled though her tears. 'But I know that's what Mum and Dad would have wanted for me and they'd have loved Brae.'

'Everyone loves Brae, but especially you.' Ella let go of her friend's hand and opened the car door. 'We need to go and find him, so you can tell him and I'm going to tell Dan just how much I love him too.'

'I will.' Anna looked at her across the roof of the car as they both climbed out. 'Right after I've killed him for taking that bloody boat out in January and taking such a stupid risk.'

'I can already see who's going to be the disciplinarian when you two have kids!' Ella caught herself a second too late and the words were already out. Anna had confided her fears that she and Brae might never conceive and they'd already been trying for over a year.

'Brae couldn't tell anyone off if he tried, he's too nice for his own good and it's just one of the reasons why I love him.' Anna bit her lip. 'But the more time goes past the more I'm worried that it might never happen for us and that I'll never be part of a family again.'

'I'm sure it will happen.' Ella offered up a silent prayer that she wouldn't be proved a liar. 'But even if it doesn't, you've got Brae and what you have is more than most people ever get.'

'I know that, I really do, and I'm trying so hard to be as grateful as I should be for all of that.' Anna tried and failed to paint on a smile. 'I just want that sense of belonging that I had with Mum and Dad, reliving those traditions that were unique to our family. The idea that I might get that back one day was the only thing that got me through when I lost them and I don't know how to come to terms with the fact that I might have lost that too, before I even got it. I'm just hoping I won't have to...'

'There are lots of ways to make a family—' Ella had been about to say that not all of those included having children, but Anna cut her off and this time her smile actually looked like it was meant to be there.

'I know, but I'm not thinking about that for now. All that matters is that Brae and Dan are okay. As long as I've got Brae, I'll get through it, whatever happens.' She linked an arm through Ella's and they ran across the car park, as it started to spatter with rain again. However much Anna might be worrying about falling pregnant, she was right. All that mattered for now was finding Brae and Dan, and Anna wouldn't be the only one who had a few choice words to say when they did.

* * *

Brae had the same sort of hangdog look on his face that he wore every time Anna caught him cheating on their pre-wedding diet pact. Not that she cared if he lost a stone or put on five, she loved every inch of him. But it had been his idea to try and get trim for the wedding, after gaining a pound for every month they'd been together. So finding paper bags, with the Mehenicks' bakery logo stamped on the front, crumpled up in the footwell of his car on a regular basis, had resulted in plenty of *those looks*.

'I'm sorry.' He barely had the chance to get the words out before Anna flung herself at him. She'd fully intended to give him a hard time and tell him just how stupid he'd been. But seeing him sitting there on the bed in the hospital cubicle, the living and breathing embodiment of everything that was most important in her world, all she wanted to do was hold on to him and never let go.

'You're an idiot.' The words were muffled as he folded her into his arms.

'I know. The only thing I could think about was that I might never see you again. It took me all these years to find someone who could put up with me, and who actually seemed to want to, and I almost blew it.' Brae was holding her so close, she could hardly breathe and she couldn't tell if it was his heart she could hear, or her own heartbeat pulsating in her ears again.

'I'd never have forgiven you if you'd died.' She pulled away slightly. 'Why didn't you wait for someone to come and get you?'

'We did, but then the water started coming on so fast and it looked like there was a break in the storm. We could see the cliffs at Titan's Head and we were debating whether to head there and try and hole up in one of the coves, if we couldn't make it to the far end of the beach. We knew we didn't have long to decide, with the black sky rolling in from further up the coast. So we tossed a coin.'

'That's how you decided?' Anna might have laughed if she'd heard the story from someone else, but for Brae and Dan to take such a huge risk on the basis of a coin flip was crazy.

'Heads we went for it and tails we just put the life jackets on and hoped the lifeboat crew got to us before the boat sank.' Brae gave her another apologetic look. 'I lost something on the way back.'

'What?' Whatever it was, it didn't matter.

'Mum sent me some pearl earrings that she wanted you to wear for the wedding as your something borrowed and I realised I still had them with me. I didn't want to leave them on the boat, so I zipped them in the inside pocket of my coat. But then the kayak capsized just as we reached Titan's Head and the coat was weighing me down when we started to swim, so I had to take it off. I tried to keep hold of it, but it slipped out of my hand and the waves carried it back out to sea before I could grab it again. I just couldn't risk going after it.'

'Too bloody right you couldn't!' Anna loved Brae because of how good-hearted he was, but sometimes he definitely took it too far. 'I'm sorry your mum lost her earrings, but I know she'd much rather have you. And it goes without saying that I would too.'

'She wore the earrings when she married Dad, and it meant a lot to her that we'd share something they had on our wedding day. But you're right, we'll just need to find you something else borrowed for the wedding, we don't want to risk any bad luck.'

'I think the less risks we take from now on the better, especially you!' Anna brushed her lips against his, which looked bruised and cracked from exposure to the weather.

'I wouldn't want to risk missing out on all of this. Even getting told off by you is exciting.' He grinned and pulled her closer to him again.

'And we just get the fish course from the Red Cliff Hotel's usual supplier, right? From a professional who knows not to sail straight into the eye of a storm.'

'Whatever you want.' He didn't sound as if he wanted to put up a fight. 'And given that I don't think I've even got a boat now, I guess fishing trips are off the agenda for a while.'

'Thank God for that.'

'Knock, knock.' Ella pulled back the cubicle curtain as she spoke. 'Sorry, we're not interrupting anything are we?'

'Just my fiancée laying down the law about any future fishing trips.' Brae winked.

'As long as you know from the start who's boss,' Ella laughed as she came into the cubicle, holding Dan's hand.

'How are you doing, Dan? Apart from the obvious black eye that is.' Anna winced as she looked at him. He could barely open his right eye it was so swollen.

'The oar hit me in the face when we capsized. They thought I might have fractured my cheekbone, but I got lucky and it's just bruising, so hopefully they'll be discharging me in a bit.'

'I think we all got very lucky.' Ella shot him a pointed look and turned to Brae. 'What about you, are you being let out early for bad behaviour as well?'

'I've broken a couple of bones in my hand, but they said they'd try a splint first, rather than a cast.'

'Why didn't you say anything?' Anna hadn't even stopped to ask him if he was in pain, she'd been too relieved that he'd still been in one piece. When he'd held on to her as tightly as he had, she'd never have guessed he'd hurt his hand.

'I forgot about the pain as soon as I saw you.' His ruddy cheeks coloured to a deeper shade of red.

'So now you realise what you could have lost, I hope you haven't got anything too exciting planned for the stag night when it comes around?' Ella narrowed her eyes, looking from Brae to Dan.

'After today, I think a quiet drink or a meal in Casa Cantare will be more than enough. I'm not sure I could carry off missing eyebrows in the wedding photos anyway!' Brae laughed again and Anna shook her head.

'I love you, but definitely not.'

'I'm glad to hear it too.' Ella turned to her friend. 'Did Brae tell you that if this had happened in a year's time, the lifeboat crew might have had to come down from Port Kara? If that had happened and they'd already been on another job, it might have been too late by the time they got to Titan's Head.'

'No, I haven't really given him the chance to fill me in.' Anna looked at Brae.

'We were swimming towards the cove at Titan's Head when they found us. I don't know if we'd have made it all the way in if they hadn't, but they told us on the way back that the Port Agnes lifeboat station has been shortlisted for closure, because of the cost of repairs needed and the number of other lifeboat stations nearby.'

'We can't let it happen!' Ella's voice had gone up at least an octave. 'If we start spreading the word and set up a fundraiser, I'm sure we'd be capable of saving it between us. It's got to be worth a shot after what they've done for us today.'

'When we send out the wedding invites we were planning to ask people to make a donation to a charity of their choice, if they want to, instead of buying us presents. So maybe we could point them in that direction too?' Anna was just as determined as Ella to help out the lifeboat crew who'd risked everything to save Dan and Brae.

'Brilliant, and I think I might have an idea for an Easter-themed fundraiser. If you can cope with that on top of organising a wedding!' Ella laughed and Anna smiled, despite the sudden sense of foreboding that had washed over her at the mention of the wedding. It was just the stress of the day they'd had, that was all. So why couldn't she shake the feeling that, when it came to bad luck and the wedding, the worst might still be to come?

Anna and Brae were sitting at the end of a row of plastic chairs, waiting for the hospital pharmacy to make up the prescription for painkillers that the A & E doctor had written for Brae. Ella had gone down to the ultrasound department with Dan, to wait for him while he had a second X-ray to double-check that there was no damage to his jaw, since the whole area from his cheekbone to his chin was badly bruised.

'Are you okay? You look a bit pale.' Brae took Anna's hand. 'I'm so sorry if I gave you a fright.'

'I'm fine. We redheads are always pale in January, you should know that as well as I do!' Anna forced herself to smile, even as another twinge of pain tightened in her stomach and fear gripped her spine. She told Ella that she hoped she wouldn't have to come to terms with not having a family with Brae and there'd been a reason for that, which she'd been hugging to herself until she was sure. But now she had a horrible feeling that her little secret would never be any more than that. 'I'm just going to nip to the loo.'

'Okay, sweetheart, I'll see you in a minute.' He looked up at her again as she stood up. 'Are you sure you're all right?'

'I'm fine, I promise.' Even as she turned away from him, her eyes filled with tears as the pain stabbed again – she was almost a hundred per cent sure now what it meant. Her period was nearly two weeks late and she'd resisted testing until now because she'd had this weird idea about tempting fate. Even telling Brae that she might finally be pregnant had felt like she'd be jinxing things and she hadn't been able to bear the thought of it not being true. So she'd kept the secret hope to herself, waiting until her mum's anniversary to do the test. If the test had shown she was pregnant, it would have given her a positive memory of the day that had signalled the start of the worst time in her life. If it had been negative, it couldn't have made the anniversary of that day any more painful than it already was. She didn't need to bother now though.

As much as she'd expected it, the obvious sign that she wasn't pregnant had made her throat close and she couldn't stop sobbing as she sat in the cubicle. Brae would be waiting and worrying by now, but she had to get control of her emotions before she went back out to him.

'Anna, are you still in here, I'm really worried about you.' When Brae called out, more than ten minutes later, she'd finally managed to stop sobbing, but every time she wiped away the tears that were still falling, they just filled her eyes all over again.

'Just go back outside. I'll be there in a minute, I promise.'

'Just tell me what's wrong.'

'There's nothing wrong.' The crack in Anna's voice gave the lie away; it was no good trying to protect Brae, he was going to see right through her.

'You've got one minute and then I'm coming in and this time I'll break the door down if I have to.'

'Okay, just go, *please!*' Waiting until she heard him leave, Anna finally opened the cubicle door and caught sight of herself in the mirror. Her face was blotchy and her red-rimmed eyes weren't going to let her get away with giving Brae a brush-off answer about why she was so upset. It was time to face the music.

'Oh sweetheart, what's wrong?' He pulled her into his arms as soon as she stepped out into the hospital corridor, not giving a damn about the people going past who were already staring in their direction.

'Let's go outside, I know it's freezing but I need some air.'

'Of course, whatever you need is fine by me.' Brae took hold of her hand with his good one and led her outside, waiting as she took a shuddering breath.

'I'm not pregnant.'

'Did you think you were?' Brae's tone was so gentle, all she could do was nod and he suddenly lost all the colour in his face too. 'Is it a miscarriage? I can go back inside and get a doctor? Oh Anna, I don't know what to do to help, but I need to make sure you're okay. I can't risk anything happening to you.'

'It's probably just a late period, I don't know.' Anna bit her lip, tears still spilling down her cheeks. 'If it's a miscarriage, it's really early.'

'You didn't do a test then?' Brae knew she'd spent a small fortune on tests in the last twelve months, but for once she'd resisted and now she'd never know if she'd actually been pregnant.

'Not this time, I just wanted to wait a bit longer.' Anna rested her head on his shoulder as he stroked her hair. 'I wish I had now, at least then I'd know that I'm actually capable of getting pregnant.'

'As long as you're okay, that's all that matters to me, and it worries me to death how much stress you're putting yourself under with all of this.' Brae stepped back, putting a hand under her chin so she had to look up at him. 'You're all I need to be happy.'

'You say that, but it's only because you don't know what you're missing out on.' Anna's throat was still burning with the effort of talking through the tears. 'My dad was like that. He loved his job and my mum so much and it was the reason they never bothered finding out why Mum couldn't get pregnant, but when I came along that all changed. He loved being a dad so much and he always said that I was the greatest gift my mum ever gave him. That's why he bought her a present every year on my birthday, just to thank her. I can't bear the thought of you missing out on that, I just can't. And I can't stand the thought that I won't ever have a family again. It's been seventeen years since I had one and I always thought that one day I'd be able to make that right again.'

'We'll find a way sweetheart.' Brae held her close as she started to sob again.

'What if we don't?'

'We will, but I want you to remember that you've got a family already. You've got me, and Mum and Dad now. You've got my sister and her family too. I know Morwenna can be as annoying as hell at times, but that's how siblings are supposed to be. You're not on your own any more, Anna, and we all love you so much.'

'I know and I do realise how incredibly lucky I am to have you. It's what I told Ella when we found out that you and Dan were okay and it's greedy to ask for more than that.' Leaning into him again, she desperately wanted to say the words she knew

Brae was longing to hear – that it wouldn't matter to her either as long as they had each other. But despite what she'd said to Ella, she just couldn't do it; not because she'd didn't love Brae so much that it scared her, but because she did love him that much. She wanted to give him everything, just like he'd given her, and she just wasn't ready to accept that she probably never would.

4

Valentine's Day had never been a big deal for Anna, at least not until it had started serving as a reminder of the aftermath of losing her father. She'd certainly never seen it as a reason to celebrate, before she'd met Brae. Greg, the last long-term boyfriend she'd had before Brae, had said it was just a con trick that retailers had come up with to part the foolish and their money even more easily than usual. She hadn't been able to come up with a very convincing argument that he was wrong and it had never held that much meaning for her either before. Brae was the sort of person who would happily celebrate at every given opportunity, though. On their first Valentine's Day together, he'd woken her up really early and insisted they walk down to the lookout point and watch the sun come up beyond the harbour. He'd packed a picnic with hot chocolate and pastries that were still warm to the touch. It beat any fancy meal in a restaurant hands down and it was just the start of a day that Anna would never forget. So it was no surprise to see Brae standing at the foot of the bed clutching a beautifully wrapped parcel, when she opened her eyes on 14 February.

'Watching someone while they sleep could be considered weird, you know!' Anna laughed as Brae shrugged, pushing herself into a sitting position and leaning up against the pillows behind her. If it had been anyone but Brae watching her, she'd have worried that she might have been dribbling or snoring, and that her inability to be perfect, even in sleep, could send him running for the hills. Except, for the first time since her parents had died, he'd convinced her that she was loved unconditionally. For some reason Brae seemed to think she really was perfect, and not even seeing her lying in a pool of dribble would change his mind. He'd seen her at her worst already – ugly-crying over things she couldn't change – and he'd just held her until she'd finally been able to stop.

'I don't care if it's weird, it's my favourite way to start the day.' Brae sat on the edge of the bed. 'I'll make you breakfast after you've opened this.'

'Thank you.' She leant forward and kissed him quickly, keeping her lips clenched together, conscious of the fact that she hadn't cleaned her teeth yet. 'Your present is downstairs.'

'Let's just get yours open first.' He started to peel back the paper at one end for her – so impatient for her to open her gift – but then he pulled his hand away. 'Sorry, I just really want to know if you like it.'

'If you bought it for me, I'll love it.' Anna peeled back the rest of the paper and let go of a long breath. 'Oh Brae, it's gorgeous!' There was a stained-glass artist whose work had been on display in the window of Pottery and Paper, the art gallery in town, since before Christmas. But she'd never seen a piece like this before. It was a colourful scene, with a camper van in the centre and a representation of Port Agnes in the background.

'I got the artist's details from a card in Pottery and Paper, and I emailed to ask her if she'd ever made anything with a camper van on. And, as luck would have it, she'd just made this.' Brae smiled again and it was all Anna could do not to leap on him, teeth cleaned or not. She'd told him about her camper van trips with her parents not long after they'd got together, to explain the reason why she had so many reminders around the house. There were camper van salt and pepper pots, a biscuit tin in the shape of a camper, which her mum had bought on a trip to Wales, and even a set of coat hooks, each set into a tiny wooden camper. If it was kitsch she didn't care and neither, it seemed, did Brae.

'It's so lovely. It's even the same colour as Vanna.' The camper van was picked out in sky blue and cream-coloured glass, the colours that her dad had kept Vanna painted, in homage to her origins as an ice cream van.

'That's what I thought, as soon as she emailed me a picture. I'm really glad you like it.' Brae stroked her cheek, holding her gaze. 'I promise, one day we'll buy a real one.'

'They're so expensive.' Anna had dreamt about owning a camper again one day, ever since her parents had died and she'd been forced to sell theirs because the thought of keeping the old van and going on trips in it without her parents was impossible to contemplate. She'd wanted to replace Vanna for a while now, but some of the campers she'd looked at were more expensive than a terraced cottage in parts of Cornwall. It was silly, but the idea of owning one still went hand in hand with her whole vision of family life.

'Once we've got the wedding out of the way, I'm going to start saving for one.' Brae dropped her a wink and she didn't have to ask if he was joking about getting the wedding *out of the way*, like it was an inconvenience – he'd come up with more ideas than she had. There was something else they might need to use the money for after the wedding, though, and Anna steeled herself to say it.

'Maybe we should save for fertility treatment. You know, if the tests show we need it.'

'You know how I feel about having the tests.' Brae's voice was as gentle as ever, even though they'd had the conversation several times before. 'You saw what happened to Jess and Dom when they found out why they couldn't have kids and I can't bear the thought of losing you.'

'I'd never blame you, whatever the outcome. You must know that?' Anna ran her fingers over the stained glass, the smooth surface of the panes between the leading somehow soothing, but she couldn't look Brae in the eyes; he knew her too well. Jess was another of the Port Agnes midwives and a close friend of Anna's, so they'd both been witness to the relationship with her husband imploding when tests had shown that Jess had no chance of conceiving a baby naturally. They were nothing like Jess and Dom, but the outcome could still be catastrophic when Anna had so much pinned on it and Brae knew that better than anyone.

'I know you wouldn't blame me, but what really scares me is that you might blame yourself.' Brae took hold of her hands. 'If you can't have children, I'm terrified that you'll get the thought into your head that you're doing me some sort of favour by ending things, so I can have kids with someone else. But I don't want kids with someone else. I don't want anyone else full stop. I want you and nothing else matters to me as much as that.'

'You say that now—'

'I'll always say it.'

'I can't carry on like this, Brae, not knowing whether there's still a chance or not.'

'All right, if you promise me that, whatever the outcome, you won't get the idea into your head that I'll be better off without you, because I can promise you I won't.' Brae squeezed her hands.

'I promise. I just want to know what we're dealing with, that's all.' Anna was trying to convince herself as much as him, but she'd worry about coming to terms with the outcome when she knew what it was. For now she just needed to know.

'In that case, you'd better open your card.' Brae passed her the envelope he'd been holding and she opened it as instructed. As she took it out of the envelope, a printed piece of paper dropped out. Picking it up she read the email on it, confirming appointments for herself and Brae with the fertility clinic for a full suite of tests.

'I thought you were dead set against it?' Anna widened her eyes, her heart racing in her chest with a mixture of excitement and terror. *They were going to know at last.* She didn't think Brae could top the Valentine's gift of the stained-glass picture, but he'd just done it.

'All I needed was your promise that it won't change things between us, but I'd do anything to make you happy, Anna, because it's the thing that makes me happiest too.'

'I don't deserve you, Brae Penrose, but I've got another present for you before we go downstairs.' Anna leant towards him, her fingers quickly undoing the buttons on his shirt. Maybe Brae was right to worry about how she'd handle the outcome of the tests, but for now all she wanted to do was show him just how much she loved him.

5

'Are you sure we're not the only people in the world doing this, or at least the only adult couple with no kids?' Anna stood back as Brae reached up to hang a painted egg on the Easter tree, which was standing on the windowsill in the bay window at the front of their house. He'd managed to transform Christmas since they'd first met and had given her so many reasons to feel like celebrating again. Now it was Good Friday and, as much as she might laugh at how all out he was going, Brae was managing to make her feel that same childlike joy at Easter too.

'I don't care if we are. After the storm, it feels like we've got more to celebrate than ever, so I'll be taking every chance that comes along to do it.' Brae wrapped his arms around her, but she still couldn't think about the day of the storm without experiencing a physical reaction. 'Hey, what's up? You're shaking.'

'Nothing, I'm just a bit cold.' Anna pushed the unwanted thoughts away. 'Easter with all your family here is going to be brilliant, I can't wait to get married and officially become part of the Penrose family!'

'You might not be saying that after tonight; you don't know

how lucky you got that we were away for this last year. My sister's fancy dress parties are actually categorised as a cruel and unusual punishment under UN conventions.'

'I'm sure it'll be great fun, although I'm still not sure the outfit I've made will pass muster. It's a shame we weren't just allowed to buy them.' Anna glanced across at the costumes laid out on the table in front of her. They still weren't finished and they had less than two hours until Morwenna's party.

'Those are Morwenna's rules and you know what a stickler she is for all of that. I think it's so she can more or less guarantee she looks better than anyone else.' Brae grinned. 'Although she can't award herself the winning prize she always gives out, I think it's enough to know she's got the best outfit, bless her. She still hasn't forgiven us for missing it last year, though, so I didn't dare try to come up with an excuse.'

'There's a prize? Not that I think I'm in any danger of winning.'

'Usually she makes quite a big thing of it, but this year all the losers are going to be penalised and asked to make a donation to the lifeboat station rescue fund.'

'That's a great idea. I wish I could do more to help Ella with all of that, but with the wedding coming up and work it's—'

'No one expects you to take all this on as well. Anyway, from what I've heard, Ella has turned into a campaign chief overnight.'

'She's achieved more already than most people could in a year. But I'm at least going to make the effort to create the most ridiculous fancy dress outfit possible.' Anna took Brae's hand, pulling him towards the sofa by the coffee table. 'What won last time you went?'

'I think last year's was someone dressed as a bottle of Heinz ketchup. At least my outfit covers up a multitude of sins and no one will know how far behind I've got with my wedding diet.'

'Your body is perfect as it is, I keep telling you that.' Anna ran her hand across his chest and he met her gaze.

'Maybe if I was aiming for a dad bod.'

'It's perfect to me.' Anna tried not to flinch at the mention of the word 'dad'. They'd agreed not to talk about babies any more until after their fertility tests. One of the things they'd agreed in the meantime was for Anna to take a break from monitoring her temperature and buying expensive ovulation test kits at a rate that was in danger of equalling the national debt.

She'd also agreed not to keeping going through the 'what ifs' until they knew for certain what they were dealing with. It had turned out to be impossible for Anna to stop going through those 'what ifs' in her head, though, even if she couldn't talk to Brae about them. His response was always the same anyway; as long as they had each other they could deal with the rest. So she'd turned to an internet support group for women who, like her, were in the throes of desperately trying to conceive. She'd even arranged to meet up, face to face, with a few of the forum members who lived locally. Jess was going, too, and it was a relief to feel as if she was building a ready-made support group if the worst really did come to the worst.

'As long as you can deal with me having a body like this, that's all that matters. Although I still can't get over someone like you wanting to be with someone like me. A big ginger lumberjack impersonator, who needs three showers at the end of the day just to wash off the smell of fish and chips.'

'Don't be daft, I'm the one who got lucky. You're the nicest guy I've ever met and everyone else says the same.'

'Nice guys come last, at least until now.' Brae put his arms around her again and suddenly putting the finishing touches to their fancy dress costumes was the last thing on her mind.

'Have we got time to, you know...' She'd never been the sort to manage a come-hither look without feeling like a complete idiot.

'I've always got time for that, but we did it yesterday.'

'Are you complaining?' If Brae was thinking of turning her down in favour of blowing up the balloons that were an essential part of her costume, then perhaps she'd better start working on that come-hither look sooner rather than later.

'Never! But I thought you said we could only do it every other night to maximise the chances of conceiving.'

'And we agreed that we're taking a break from worrying about all of that. I just want to do it when we want to, not because my temperature's spiking on some chart, just like we said.'

'I can't blame you for being unable to resist this body.' Brae grinned again, pretending to pull a muscleman pose.

'I'm only human.' Grabbing his hand, Anna pulled him down onto the sofa, shutting out the rest of the world. Brae had told her time and again that having each other was all that mattered and, when she was lying in his arms, for a little while she could actually convince herself it was true.

* * *

'I was starting to wonder if you were going to make it.' Ella hugged Anna as she and Brae arrived at Morwenna's party, a good half an hour after it had been scheduled to start. She'd do anything for her best friends, but even she drew the line at making her fancy-dress costume and then being stood up by the people whose idea it was for her and Dan to tag along.

Dan was an artist and property developer, so normally he'd be the first one up for a creative project. The trouble was, he'd been so busy working on the renovation of an old chapel down in Port Tremellien, that the creation of the fancy dress costumes had been down to Ella, which was why he was now dressed as he was – a flash of lightning cut out from an old cardboard box, painted silver, and safety pinned to his jumper.

For some reason Morwenna's central heating seemed to be on full blast, even though almost all of her guests were wearing extra layers because of their costumes. Ella's own creation was designed to be teamed with Dan's. She had an old umbrella with holes cut in it and a shirt covered in scorch marks, as if she'd just been struck by the bolt of cardboard lightning pinned to Dan's chest. But if she'd felt inadequate about the design, seeing Anna and Brae's creations made her feel a bit better. Poor Brae was encased in plastic, dressed as a human Twister mat, created, it seemed, by just cutting a hole in the centre of the plastic sheeting that was the basis of the game.

'Sorry, we left the finishing off of our costumes a bit late.' Anna gave an apologetic shrug.

'Well, you'd never guess it!' Ella couldn't help laughing and Anna gave a twirl.

'You're just jealous because you didn't think of dressing in a see-through bin bag filled with balloons!'

'It's great. But I've got to ask one question.' Ella laughed again. 'What are you actually supposed to be? I'm thinking haemorrhoids, but I'm desperately hoping I'm wrong!'

'Oh God!' Anna could hardly get the words out for laughing. 'I'm supposed to be a bag of jelly beans and all the balloons were meant to be different colours, but the only ones I could find were the red ones. I couldn't remember where I'd put the others and, as we were running late, I didn't have much choice!'

'Well I think Brae's going to win the prize.' Dan winked as he shook his friend's hand, making the plastic mat he was wearing rustle like crazy. 'I think the glitter in the beard is a particularly nice touch.'

'We just thought it needed a bit more than the plastic mat and it was all we had time to come up with. I don't think Morwenna's going to be very impressed with our efforts!' Anna seized the glass of wine that Dan handed her, like it was a life raft.

'Well I think the glitter works for you. Maybe it's something you should think about for the wedding. Dan could do his eyebrows to match, you know, as best man.' Ella didn't need to look at Dan to know what expression he'd be wearing.

'You're just full of good ideas lately, aren't you?'

'It's not my fault you left the design of our fancy dress outfits to an amateur like me, Dan, when we had an artist in the house.'

'If my sister doesn't turn the heating down soon, I'll be standing here in nothing but my underwear and only the glitter in my beard to make it look like I'm joining in. It's hot enough to toast bread in here.' Brae clawed at the neck of his plastic cape.

'The thermostat's broken.' Morwenna's husband, Ryan, paused on his round of topping up empty glasses. 'But if we don't want guests to start passing out on us, I think we're going to have to move the party outside.'

'Do you want us to light the fire pit for you?' Brae didn't even wait for an answer, disappearing out into the garden, with Dan hot on his heels.

'Man make fire. Funny how it turns even the most modern men into cavemen.' Ella turned to Anna, noticing for the first time just how much glitter her friend had in her hair. 'It looks like you two had a lot of fun making your costumes!'

'The whole day has been perfect.' Anna swirled the wine around in her glass. 'Do you ever wish you could freeze time, to stop anything from changing?'

'Sometimes. Are you worried that something's going to change for the worse?' Ella still hadn't quite managed to shake off the hangover of anxiety from Dan and Brae almost drowning in the storm, even though nearly three months had passed. For the first two or three weeks after the boys had been rescued, she'd woken up with a start every night, caught up in nightmares that had a far from happy ending. So she wouldn't have blamed Anna if that had affected her too.

'It's nothing I can put my finger on. I suppose it's just that I haven't been this happy since before I lost Mum and Dad. I just need to learn to trust the feeling. I feel like I owe the universe for all this good karma and I wish I was doing half as much as you to help save the lifeboat station.'

'You've done more than enough, I just take these things to extremes. Dan calls me the queen of campaigners; I think it's when I'm most like my dad. I get a bee in my bonnet and I just can't let things go!'

'Thank goodness for that. Losing the lifeboat station would be such a tragedy and I still can't bear to think about what might have happened if they weren't around.' Anna looked pale at the prospect.

'I've stopped having nightmares about it every night, but I still reach out in the early hours sometimes to check that Dan's still there.'

'We were so lucky and if that's my share of luck used up for life, I'll always be beyond grateful that it was used for that.'

Anna hesitated for just a second, looking like she might be about to say something else, before Morwenna blustered into the room, wearing a Little Bo Beep outfit that looked like it had been made by a whole team of professionals. She might not be eligible to win her own competition, but that clearly hadn't stopped her going all out.

'Okay, let's move this party outside!' Morwenna gestured towards the bifold doors at the back of the room. 'My brother and his friend have got the fire pit roaring and the pergola will make the perfect platform for everyone to stand up and give us a little twirl before we decide who this year's grand winner of the DIY fancy dress is.'

'I wouldn't be surprised if Brae and Dan's costumes weren't already merrily burning in the fire pit, just so they can avoid that! Although if Brae burns his, Port Agnes will be shrouded in a cloud of toxic smoke.' Anna linked her arm through Ella's as they headed towards the doors that led out to the garden.

'Me neither! You might not want to get too relaxed out there, though. Not with all this plastic so close to an open flame; you're approximately ninety per cent flammable by my reckoning!' Ella shook her head, both of them laughing. Anna was right, they were so lucky, and they had to save the lifeboat centre whatever it took. Dressing up like a haemorrhoid and a lightning scorched bystander might just be the start.

6

The sensation in Anna's stomach felt like a netful of butterflies desperate to escape. It was a bit like a first date in some ways, but she wasn't just meeting one new person, she was meeting four. Thank God she had Jess with her.

The Cookie Jar, a coffee shop on the high street, was the venue for the first meeting of the Port Agnes infertility support group. Anna had considered asking permission from the trust to make the group official, but she knew better than anyone that the midwifery unit could be a difficult place for someone desperately wanting a baby. Bumping into pregnant women and new mums was hard enough in everyday life, without surrounding the women she and Jess were about to meet with those things.

'How are you feeling?' Anna looked at Jess, after the waiter put the tray of pastries they'd ordered onto the centre of the cluster of tables which had been reserved for their meeting. It had been almost six months since Jess's marriage to Dom had collapsed in the wake of discovering her own infertility and she seemed to have bounced back without too many problems. Jess was a bit of chameleon at times though, switching between being the party girl of the unit and closing down into herself. She'd confided early on in her friendship with Anna that she'd been through the foster care system and that it hadn't always been easy, so she'd probably had to learn to be resilient and self-reliant when she needed to. But Anna wanted to make sure that Jess really was as okay as she seemed.

'I'm fine, I'm just really keen to meet everyone and see what options they're looking at. Although I'm guessing I'm in a slightly different position to everyone else, given that it would take a second immaculate conception for me to fall pregnant, even if my insides were capable of doing their job!' Jess's laugh didn't quite ring true and Anna had to fight not to hug her, knowing that might tip Jess over the edge when she was clearly trying to hold it together. Discovering that her fallopian tubes were so badly scarred that she could never get pregnant naturally had been a hammer blow. Her husband leaving in the wake of that would have made most people curl up and hide, but not Jess. She seemed determined to find something positive to take from it all and Anna just wished she had half her friend's strength.

The clinic they'd chosen had an incredible reputation, but it meant the waiting list for the tests there were much longer than most private clinics, so she and Brae still hadn't had them yet, even though he'd booked a date back in February. She'd pushed him hard to agree to do this and now part of her was wishing he'd never said yes. Wanting to know the truth and knowing it for sure weren't the same thing. Hope might be fragile, but if it was taken away altogether she had no idea what would be left behind. She'd need to be just as brave as her lovely friend, but right now she felt like the biggest coward in the world. Not to mention being a total fraud, who'd set up a support group for other women when she had no idea what she'd do if she got the same news as they'd had.

'Oh hi, I'm looking for the infertility group, am I in the right place?' The woman who'd just come into The Cookie Jar, looked like she might make a bolt for it at any moment.

'Yes, that's right.' Anna got up on her feet, this time fighting the urge to hug a total stranger. 'I'm Anna and this is Jess, what would you like to drink?'

'I'm Jacinda and it's okay, thanks, I can get my own drink.'

'Let me get it, please.' Anna was trying desperately hard to be welcoming, without coming on too strong, but Jacinda still looked like she could turn and head for the door at any minute.

'Thank you.' Smiling for the first time, Jacinda slid into one of the seats. 'I'll have a latte please.'

By the time Anna had ordered the latte, two more of the women they'd arranged to meet had turned up. Along with Jacinda, there was Tara and Lucy. They all looked to be at least five to ten years younger than Anna, and Jess seemed to have them all talking by the time Anna got back to the table with everyone's drinks.

'I'm so glad you could all make it. We're just waiting for India, but I'm guessing maybe something has come up or she's just running a bit late.' Anna glanced at her phone. There were no messages on the WhatsApp group she'd set up for them and she wanted to make a start before Jacinda – who still looked a bit like a rabbit in the headlights – finally decided to do a runner.

'Do you think we should get going?' Jess caught Anna's eye as she spoke, giving an almost imperceptible nod towards Jacinda.

'Absolutely. I know I've messaged all of you on the forum and you've probably all chatted to each other, but I thought we could start with saying where we are on our journeys towards trying to get pregnant.' Anna smiled. 'That's if no one minds?'

'I'll go first, because it'll make everyone else feel better!' Jess rolled her eyes, clearly having decided to adopt the bouncy side of her persona that she wore like a suit of armour. 'I started trying for a baby about two years ago. When nothing happened we had some tests and discovered that my fallopian tubes were really badly damaged and that I'll never get pregnant without IVF. Oh and then my husband decided to leave me, so here I am!'

'My God, how awful.' Jacinda clapped a hand over her mouth.

'What an arsehole!' Tara, who had a voice like the low rumble of thunder, looked as if she'd be ready to put Dom in a headlock were he to suddenly walk through the door.

'That kind of sums up how we all feel about him.' Anna gave Jess a gentle nudge. 'Is anyone else thinking about going down the IVF route?'

'Oh, I'm not doing that.' Jess shook her head. 'I've put in an application to do some respite fostering and I'm going to my first pre-assessment course at the end of the month, to see if they'll let me start the process.'

'When did you decide that?' If Anna sounded shocked, she couldn't help it. She'd known for a while that Jess was open to the idea of fostering and adoption, but she'd had no idea things had progressed this far.

'Only last Monday. I read something on a fostering forum and realised it means I'm eligible to apply as a single foster carer, now that I've been on my own for six months. It all happened really quickly and it seemed like it was meant to be. They came out for an initial home visit to the flat on Wednesday and the fact that they had a spare space on their next Skills to Foster course put things in motion.'

'Wow, well I think it's a great thing to do.' Lucy looked from Jess to Anna. 'I'm going to be going through IVF with ICSI, because my husband's got a very low sperm count, so the sperm will need to be injected straight into the egg to give us a shot. But we've already talked about using donor sperm if the first couple of rounds of IVF don't work, because it's more important that we end up with a baby, than whether it's got our DNA. Henry knows being a mother is all I've ever wanted and he's determined to get past how all of that might make him feel, if it comes to it. Although I'm desperately hoping it won't.'

'Henry sounds amazing, like the polar opposite of Dom!' Jess pulled a face.

'He really does.' Anna swallowed hard; it wasn't just Dom who fell short of Henry's standards, because she did too. If she was as selfless as him, she'd have talked to Brae about the possibility of using donor eggs, given her age, but she couldn't let go of the idea of having her own biological child yet. She wanted a child who was a part of her mum and dad, a part of the family she'd been terrified she'd lost forever. But sitting here and hearing how noble Henry was being, she suddenly felt like the worst kind of narcissist.

'I froze my eggs when I was twenty-five, because I was at the height of my athletics career and I knew the time wasn't right to have a baby, mainly because I had almost no time to meet someone.' Tara shrugged. 'But then, just before I retired, I met Franz, who was on the German javelin squad, and it finally felt right. And I'm so glad I did decide to freeze my eggs, because at thirty-four they've told me my egg reserve is like that of someone forty plus. So this is probably our only chance of creating an Olympic javelin champion together. The only thing we've got to decide is whether he or she represents the UK or Germany!'

'UK all the way, we definitely need an Olympian in Port Agnes.' Jess grinned and everyone else was smiling, even Jacinda. But the smile on Anna's face was so forced it was painful. If Tara had been told her only chance was eggs frozen when she was twenty-five, then where did that leave Anna? A woman of almost forty. She wasn't asking for the moon – or even an Olympic champion – just a baby who was half hers and half Brae's. Surely that wasn't too much to ask for. She needed to turn the focus on someone else before she lost control of her emotions and made the first support group memorable for all the wrong reasons.

'What about you, Jacinda? Do you want to tell us a bit about your journey so far?'

'I was born without a womb.' As Jacinda said those six little words, the grief was written all over her face. 'So I'm going to be using a surrogate in Ukraine, but my husband's family don't know about it because they're quite religious and we're not sure if they'll accept the baby if they know.'

'Really? That's terrible!' Tara clearly wasn't the sort to hold back and Jacinda's eyes had filled with tears.

'We just don't want to risk it, but it doesn't help me feel any less ashamed that my body can't do what most women's can. Reyansh knew from the start what we were going to have to go through if we wanted to have a baby, but it doesn't stop me feeling guilty.'

'A baby should be all the more loved when its arrival has been so hard won, regardless of who carries it and whose DNA it has.' Lucy frowned. 'If the baby's grandparents don't realise that, then maybe they don't deserve to get the chance to be grandparents. I know Henry's parents won't love our baby any less, even if we end up using donor sperm.'

'I get what you're saying, believe me.' Jess's voice had taken on a much softer tone. 'After all, I was in foster care myself. But for some people that family heritage is really important, especially if their wider family isn't there any more either. I think most people can come to terms with letting go of biology if they have to, for the sake of having a family, but it's not for everyone. That said, you deserve the support of both families, Jacinda, but only you and Reyansh know what's right for you.'

Jess caught Anna's eye as she spoke and she had to blink to

stop the tears from coming. Jess had been through so much in her life and now Dom had let her down too, but her words had resonated with Anna more than she'd ever have guessed. They might have lost their parents in completely different ways, but Anna still felt cut adrift from that sense of belonging, that intrinsically human desire to be part of a tribe – a loss that was still shockingly raw after all this time. Letting go was easier said than done and it was yet another reason why she admired Jess so much. No one deserved to find her route to motherhood more.

'What about you, Anna? Will you be doing IVF?' Tara turned towards her and she shook her head.

'We've got our tests next week, but being an older mum, I'm not sure if IVF will be an option if my egg quality is low. I've really got no idea of what our plan B might be.' Anna hadn't expected her voice to catch on the words in the way they did, but thankfully she had a friend she could always rely on.

'After that, I think we all deserve a highly calorific pastry.' Jess passed the tray to Lucy and locked eyes with Anna, giving her a reassuring smile as the other women focused on which of the delicious looking pastries to choose. It gave Anna time to regain the composure she needed to support the women sitting around the table with her. Hopefully she could find some way of helping them through their journeys, even if her road was still so uncertain. Either way, surrounding herself with other women who knew just how bumpy that road could be might just give her the strength to find a way forward, even if it was in a direction she'd never wanted to go.

* * *

Easter Sunday dawned bright and warm, as if summer had already arrived in Port Agnes. It was also Brae's birthday, and

Anna had just about managed to persuade him to have breakfast in bed before he'd leapt up and started dashing around the garden hiding chocolate eggs at a pace that would have put the Easter bunny to shame.

'Are you sure you're going to be able to find all of the eggs again, if the kids don't?' Anna kissed him, when he finally came back to the conservatory that overlooked the garden, where Anna had been sitting watching him with the doors open. He'd spent the best part of an hour emptying the huge bag that had been filled with eggs, bunnies and chicks, as well as the toy lambs the children would be able to keep after the chocolate was long gone. Given the fact that Morwenna was quite strict about what her children ate, Anna had a feeling it was going to be Uncle Brae who helped dispose of a lot of the excess chocolate.

'It's all up here.' Brae pointed towards his head. 'And never let it be said that a single piece of chocolate has ever escaped from my tracking skills.'

'Are you going to open your birthday presents before the children get here?' Anna had piled up his gifts by the Easter tree, but Brae was shaking his head.

'They'll be here any minute and we can do the presents after they've gone tonight.' He took hold of her hands. 'Easter might be the next best thing to Christmas as far as I'm concerned and a good excuse for another big celebration, but as it falls on my birthday this year, I want that bit to just be us.'

'I hope you're not banking on me having bought that Agent Provocateur underwear you said would suit me, as a gift to you, are you?' She raised her eyebrows.

'No and as long as you aren't holding out hope of me looking sexy in any underwear you might have bought me, then neither of us will be disappointed. But then you never disappoint me.'

'Uncle Brae, Auntie Banana!' Brae's nephew, Thomas,

suddenly came hurtling through the side gate of the house and into the back garden. Thomas had come up with the nickname Anna Banana on the second or third time they'd met and it had stuck. Even his little sister, Ava, who was only three, used a variant of it.

'Auntie Nana!' Chasing along behind her brother, Ava charged into the conservatory and threw herself at Anna.

'Hello sweet pea.' Holding the little girl in her arms, she was reluctant to let go. For a second or two she could pretend that Brae's niece belonged to them, the maternal pull making her squeeze a little too tightly as Ava squirmed to be set free again, so that the Easter egg hunt could begin.

'Eggs, eggs, eggs!' Ava and Thomas were both jumping up and down and chanting by the time Morwenna and Ryan caught up with their children. Anna couldn't help wondering if they realised how lucky they were, but then people usually didn't when even the greatest of gifts came easily. She'd seen parenthood up close often enough to know it wasn't all sunshine and flowers either, but she'd still give anything to take the rough with the smooth.

'Off you go then, Uncle Brae.' Morwenna winked at her brother, holding up two bottles of red. 'While I open the wine for me, Ryan and Anna.'

Twenty minutes later, Brae was still racing around the garden trying to keep up with the children who weren't showing any sign of running out of steam.

'Do you think I should take over for a bit and give him a break?' Ryan swirled the red wine around his glass as he spoke, making his suggestion sound half-hearted at best.

'No!' Morwenna topped up all three glasses again, ignoring Anna's protests that she didn't want any more. 'He's in his element, he's the biggest kid of the lot of them. It's just as well you're too old to have kids, Anna, because you've got a gigantic one for life!'

'I've just got to check on the lunch.' Anna just about made it to the kitchen before the first tear rolled down her cheek. Brae's sister had twisted the knife without even knowing it. It was an incredibly thoughtless thing to say to anyone, even for someone like Morwenna who had a reputation for overstepping the mark. So Anna was going to have to blame it on her future sister-in-law knocking back too much wine, far too quickly, if she wasn't going to resent her for the rest of their lives for touching the rawest nerve possible.

She and Brae had decided not to tell Morwenna, or any of Brae's family, that they were trying for a baby. As lovely as they were, they could be a bit overbearing. But she'd never expected Morwenna, or any of them, to just assume they wouldn't have a family because of her age. She wouldn't be forty until the end of the year and there were plenty of women her age who fell pregnant; she'd seen the evidence herself. If they hadn't been trying for over a year already, it might not have taken her breath away with quite the force that it had. But if her tears spilt onto the roast potatoes as she pretended to check them, then Morwenna only had herself to blame.

* * *

'Are you sure you're okay? You've been really quiet all afternoon and you hardly ate anything at lunchtime. I wish you'd have a sandwich too.' Brae took the plate from Anna as she came into the lounge. He'd wanted to make her something to eat when he'd said he fancied a sandwich, but she'd insisted on making it, because no one should have to make their own food on their birthday or their anniversary. It was a tradition she'd had with her parents, from ever since she'd been old enough to make cheese on toast. For a good few years after that, until she'd mastered the ability to make anything more exotic, cheese on toast had been the dish of the day on her parents' wedding anniversary.

'I just had a bit too much of that good red wine that Morwenna brought over, that's all.'

'Maybe if you ate something, you'd feel a bit better. I mean look at this!' Brae peeled back the top slice of bread to reveal the thickly sliced turkey and the cranberry stuffing lying on top of it. Easter was like a second Christmas in every way as far as Brae was concerned, and it was a happy accident that it had fallen on his birthday for once.

'I might have something later. I want you to open your presents first, I've been waiting all day!' She'd bought a trip to Rome for a weekend in October as Brae's main present. As the owner of a fish and chip shop, he'd had a somewhat disloyal passion for pizza and he'd mentioned more than once that he'd always wanted to visit the Italian capital. Being able to head off for a weekend was one of the benefits of being child-free and they might as well make the most of it.

'I've got something for you first.' Brae pulled a midnight-blue box out of his pocket and slid it up the arm of the chair towards Anna.

'I know you think Easter should be like a second Christmas, but I didn't think we were going as far as giving gifts?'

'This is my birthday present.'

'So why are you giving it to me?'

'I got the inspiration from your dad.' Brae squeezed her hand. 'It got me thinking, when you said that he bought your mum a present every year on your birthday, to thank her for giving you to him. The best gift I've ever been given is you coming into my life, and so I've decided to mark that every year on my birthday by giving you a present to say thank you.'

'Oh Brae, you really are too good for me.' Anna opened the box to reveal a bangle made from hammered silver, with two linked hearts forming the clasp. 'It's really beautiful.' He really was the kindest, most thoughtful man on earth. He'd filled the hole in her heart that she hadn't ever believed anyone could. There was no way she could ever repay him for that; the only way she could even come close was by giving him the greatest gift of all – if she could.

'When we're together, it just works, like the hearts on the bangle that keep it together. It doesn't need anything else; anything you added to the bangle would just be a bonus and I honestly feel the same way about us.' Brae pulled her towards him. 'Ryan mentioned he thought Morwenna had upset you earlier and he told me what she said.'

'It doesn't matter.'

'It matters to me that she upset you and I told Ryan that if she ever pulls a stunt like that again I'm going to say some things I won't be able to take back, but I think he'd already given her a bit of a talking to. I'm so sorry she upset you.' He stroked her hair. 'But what doesn't matter to me is whether we end up having kids or not. Like I keep saying, and I'll spend my whole life reminding you of this if I have to, in the end, as long as I've got you, I've got everything.'

'I love you so much.' Anna pressed her lips against his and for the first time in hours, some of the tension left her spine. She already had the best person in the world and he was right, she just had to keep reminding herself that anything else really would be a bonus.

7

The good weather from the long Easter weekend continued into the second half of April and, if she wasn't on call or doing home visits, Anna had started walking into Port Agnes when Brae left early for work. His cousin, Pete, was running the shop and its small self-contained dining area most evenings, with the help of a team of young part-time staff. It meant that Brae was able to spend that time with Anna, when she wasn't working, and he did the majority of the day shifts in the fish and chip shop as a result. His day started as early as six a.m. on Fridays and Saturdays, to give him enough time to get the prep for the whole day done and be ready to open up for lunch from eleven.

After leaving Brae at the shop, Anna headed up the coastal path and then onto the footpath that weaved through the farm-land above Port Agnes, eventually leading to a path that opened up by the back of the car park at the midwifery unit. It was defi-nitely preferable to running in Anna's book – there was no pain involved – and it was so lovely to immerse herself in springtime in Port Agnes. The lambs chasing each other across the fields epitomised joy and the footpath even skimmed Honeypot Flower

Farm, where daffodils and tulips swayed in the breeze and their gorgeous scent seemed to cling to Anna's skin. No wonder the Three Ports area, which comprised Port Agnes, Port Kara and Port Tremellien, had come in the top ten happiest places to live in the UK. There'd been some celebrities moving into the Port Kara area, where some of the large seafront properties even had their own beaches. They might just get a celebrity delivery at the unit one of these days.

Anna always felt better for walking to work and it was really helping her keep a positive mindset and her determination to follow Brae's lead and count her blessings. Living and working in Port Agnes, with a close team who she also considered to be good friends, was just one of those blessings.

'Morning!' Anna greeted Jess as she came into the staffroom. 'From the look of the board we're not going to have a chance to have a morning briefing today!'

'It doesn't look like it, does it? Gwen and Frankie have been in with one of the mums for hours, but she panics every time they leave apparently. Ella's lady is at eight centimetres and with Toni and Bobby away, that leaves me to cover the home visits since you've got all the clinics this morning.'

'Thank goodness I've got Bev and Louisa on call for home births, otherwise we'd definitely need to clone ourselves! What time is Bobby's graduation ceremony? I can't wait to see the photos.' Anna had organised the rosters so that Toni and Bobby could both be off together. Bobby had been a midwifery assistant initially and had then trained to be a midwife. The story was that Toni was attending his graduation ceremony in her role as his mentor, but it was obvious she was there because they were in a relationship. Albeit a secret one.

'I think Anna said it was two o'clock.' Jess turned towards her. 'While I've got you to myself, I need to ask you a big favour.'

'Go on.'

'Can I put you down as a reference for my fostering assessment? Presuming I even get that far.'

'Of course, you know I'll do anything I can to help. Are you nervous about the course tomorrow?'

'Petrified! I don't know what I'm going to do if I they turn me down. Once I decided to foster it felt like it was meant to be and the reason why I had to go through all that crap with Dom. But if I don't end up fostering, then what was the point of all of that?'

'You'll be fine, Jess. Just be you and they'll sign you up in a flash, I'm sure of it. And, trust me, the reference I write you is going to be incredible!'

'Thanks Anna.' Jess blew her a kiss. 'Are we still meeting the others in The Jolly Sailor on Monday night?'

'Yes, well Tara and Lucy are going to be there, but Jacinda wasn't sure if she'd make an evening meet up. I just hope it isn't because we chose a pub.'

'I take it you still haven't heard from India?' Jess furrowed her brow. They'd both been worried about the fact that India hadn't turned up to the first support group meeting, after she'd seemed so desperate to meet up when they were chatting online.

'I messaged her after she didn't turn up to The Cookie Jar and she never replied. She seems to have left the online forum too, so I'm hoping it's because she's found out she doesn't need it any more, but there's not much more I can do.'

'Definitely not. And what about you? When do you get your results?'

'Next week.' Anna's attempt to keep her tone casual made it turn into a squeak. They'd finally had their tests the week after Brae's birthday and it had been Anna who'd almost backed out in the end, when the reality of knowing the outcome had hit her in a way that he'd understood all along.

'It'll be okay, whatever happens. You and Brae will work it out together; he couldn't be more different to Dom.'

'I'm so sorry for the way he's treated you.'

'I'm going to be fine and so are you.' Jess gave her a hug and, at a good ten inches shorter than Anna, it could have felt awkward if they hadn't been such good friends. 'Right, I'll have to get on the road to Port Kara, or I'll be late for my first home visit.'

'If I don't see you before, good luck for tomorrow and remember they'll be lucky to have you!'

Anna just about had time for a quick cup of tea before her first clinic. She was seeing both her own patients and some of Toni's. By the time it got to half past twelve, her stomach was rumbling and she was starting to wish she'd made time for breakfast before heading into Port Agnes with Brae.

'Hi Jade, come in.' Anna looked up and smiled as her last patient before lunch came into the room. Toni was her assigned midwife, but it was the unit's policy for all of their patients to meet as many of the midwifery team as possible during their pregnancy; this gave them the best chance of knowing the midwife at the delivery, if they chose to give birth at the unit or at home. Anna had already met Jade once before, earlier in her pregnancy, but she was now at thirty-eight weeks and could potentially deliver any day.

'You might need a crane to get me back up from the chair. I got indigestion just doing up my trainers before I came out today!'

'Bless you! That's just baby taking up all the room and pressing against your stomach.' Anna gave her a sympathetic smile. 'Are you feeling okay other than that?'

'Apart from being worn out because I have to get up three times a night to have a wee, because a certain little mister presses against my bladder even more than my stomach!'

'Hopefully it won't be for much longer now and it'll all be worth it when he arrives, although I don't have to tell you that the sleepless nights won't ease off any time soon!' Anna laughed. 'Have you thought about your options if he doesn't put in an appearance by the time you get to forty-one weeks.'

'Whatever it takes to get him out!'

'There are a few things to think about if you're induced. It's a bit more likely to lead to an assisted birth, like a forceps delivery, than if you go into labour naturally. So it means you wouldn't be able to give birth in the unit or at home.'

'I was never planning to give birth at home anyway!' Jade pulled a face. 'And you don't do epidurals here, do you?'

'Unfortunately not. Is that something you think you'll go for?'

'I'm rubbish with pain. I stubbed my toe last night and cried for about an hour afterwards, so I'm not the sort to try and convince myself that I'll grit my teeth through labour.'

'I think you're being really realistic about what's right for you.' Anna had seen lot of ladies in labour transfer to hospital when they couldn't cope with the pain relief on offer at the unit and the realities of how it would affect any individual woman could never be guaranteed. There was never any judgement from the Port Agnes midwives about the choices their patients made, though.

'The only thing that worries me is how many people I'll be allowed to have in the labour room with me.'

'Every hospital has its own policy on that, but most restrict it to a maximum of three and they're not keen on birthing partners swapping in and out, because of the risk of infection.'

'I obviously want Alfie there, but I'd also like my mum to be there and it's really important that my nana can come too.'

'That's lovely, three generations of the family seeing its newest member arrive.' Anna had got better over the years at not experiencing a twinge of envy every time someone mentioned having their mother at the birth. She'd also heard it all in her time as a midwife. Quite a few of her ladies had wanted their fathers at the birth, along with their mothers, and one woman had even wanted her brother there. It had taken all of Anna's composure not to pull a face that gave away her true feelings on hearing that particular request.

'My granddad died just before I found out I was pregnant, and it's been the thing getting Nana through her grief.' Jade sniffed, wiping away the tears that had sprung up in her eyes with the end of her sleeve. 'They were together for sixty years and she said she wouldn't have been able to face the future without him, if she hadn't had the baby to look forward to. She doesn't drive and she finally sold his car this week, but she's insisting on spending the money to buy me the most expensive pram she can find. We're going out shopping straight after this, but I can't help feeling guilty that she's spending all that money.'

'Don't feel guilty, it's so lovely that you having the baby has given her something to look forward to.' Anna gestured towards the examination table. 'You could record the sound of the baby's heartbeat on your phone when I use the Doppler, if you like, and you could play it to your nana when you meet her later.'

'She'll love that, she's out in the waiting room already.'

'Really? Why don't you bring her in then?'

'Is that okay?' Jade was already on her feet and she'd gone from tears to smiling in an instant. 'I didn't know if she'd be allowed in for the checks.'

'Of course she is, as long as you're happy with that?'

'I'll be back in two secs!' Jade shot out of the door and less than a minute later, she was back with her very sprightly looking grandmother in tow.

'Hi, I'm Anna, one of the midwives looking after Jade.'

'I'm Lilian, Jade's nana.' The older woman couldn't seem to

stop smiling. 'I'm eighty-three next birthday and I've never heard a baby's heartbeat in real life before. They didn't let us listen in back when I had Jade's mum and auntie. I can't believe I'm about to start with my first great-grandson!'

'Let's get Jade settled then and see if we can get the baby to give you his big performance.' Anna was already silently praying that the baby's heartbeat would be really easy to find. It wouldn't only be a disappointment if he was tucked in a position where it was difficult to hear, it would probably send Jade and her nana into meltdown.

Within five seconds of Anna putting the Doppler on Jade's stomach, the sound of the baby's heartbeat came through loud and clear.

'Oh Jade, can you hear that?' Lilian bent over and kissed her granddaughter's forehead. 'Your grandpa would be so proud of you. He so wanted one of you girls to have a son. He loved having two daughters and three granddaughters, but he kept saying that your generation would have to even up the balance a bit.'

'I hope he can see what's happening.' Tears were sliding out of the corners of Jade's eyes again, as she turned to look at her nana. 'I wasn't going to tell you this, until he arrived, but me and Alfie have decided to call the baby Arthur, after Grandpa.'

'Really?' It was barely more than a croak, as the word caught in Lilian's throat.

'Yes, really, there was never any other choice. And if he turns out to be half as lovely as Grandpa, I'll be a really lucky mum.' Jade held out a hand to her grandmother. 'Oh don't cry, or I'll never stop.'

'These are happy tears!'

'You two are getting me going now and I won't be able to get through the rest of Jade's checks at this rate!' Anna took the box of tissues off her desk, taking one and passing the rest on to Lilian and Jade. Days like this reminded her that she had the most privileged job in the world and it made her blessings all the easier to count.

* * *

Ella wouldn't tell Anna why they so desperately needed to get down to the harbour by half-past five; she just kept giggling to herself at the prospect of whatever it was they were going down there to see.

'If it wasn't way too early to be sorting out my hen night, I'd be worried that I'm going be ambushed by the Dreamboys or something.' Anna screwed up her face. 'Which, just for future reference, would probably be my definition of hell!'

'If your idea of hell is perfectly toned men parading around in their underpants, then you are going to love this!'

'Can't you just tell me what it is?'

'No, it'll spoil the surprise and you'll find out in about three minutes anyway!' Ella pulled into a space in one of the side roads that led off from the harbour. 'We need to head up to the slope behind the bakery. That's where they're doing it.'

'Doing what?'

'Just come with me and you'll find out.' Ella almost broke into a run as she took the alleyway that bordered her parents' bakery on one side. It opened up onto a stretch of common land where the most exciting thing Anna would normally expect to see would be a family flying kites, whilst trying to avoid dog walkers and the occasional group of kids playing football. Except today there was a spotlight set up on a tripod and very professional-looking photographer with the sort of long lens Anna assumed was only used by the paparazzi – not to mention the small crowd of onlookers.

'What on earth is going on?' Anna turned to her friend, still none the wiser about what they were looking at.

'Look up there, at the top of the slope!' Ella pointed to what looked like an old fashioned butcher's bike with a load of blankets piled up in the crate on the front. 'Have you worked out who it is yet?'

'Oh my God, is it Brae?' Anna peered harder as the bike came further down the hill. It was definitely Brae, wearing a bright red hoodie, and it wasn't a pile of blankets in the crate, there was someone wrapped in a cream-coloured sheet.

'Yep and that's Dan wedged into the crate on the front, with his legs hanging over the side. They're supposed to be Elliott and E.T.!'

'I could ask why, but my biggest concern right now is how on earth Dan's ever going to get out again and whether they've got any chance of stopping before they plough into the crowd!'

'It's for the lifeboat station fundraiser.' Ella didn't take her eyes off the bike as she spoke. 'Port Kara has been getting loads of publicity because a couple of the beach houses have been bought by celebrities recently. So the boys decided to re-enact a few classic Hollywood movie scenes to get some traction on social media, off the back of our famous neighbours, to see if it helps with the fundraising.'

'Who's the photographer? Oh God!' Anna screamed as Brae attempted to stop the bike, tipping both him and Dan onto the grass, but thankfully they got straight back onto their feet.

'He's one of the artists who sells his photographs in Pottery and Paper, so Dan managed to rope him in to help out.' Ella shook her head as the sound of Dan and Brae laughing carried on the air. 'I think we better take out a couple of insurance policies on them, though, because next on the list is attempting to recreate the balloon lift from *Up*!'

'I'd assume you were joking, but nothing would surprise me with those two.' As Anna looked up again, Brae and Dan were heading across the grass towards them, the crowd who'd turned out for their *E.T.* re-enactment still watching their every move.

'What did you make of our Hollywood debut then?' Brae grinned, pulling Anna in for a kiss before she even had the chance to answer.

'I'd be happier if you had stunt doubles!' Anna couldn't help laughing, as Brae let her go. Dan still had the sheet – which was now covered in grass stains – draped around his head and neck.

'We're working our way up to doing the ending of *Titanic* in the harbour; we've just got to work out if it's going to be me or Brae who gets to play Rose and lie on the piece of wood, while the other one slips beneath the waves like poor old Jack.'

'In that get up, I think it's pretty obvious which one of us should play Rose!' Brae patted his friend on the back and another wave of happiness washed over Anna. It was going to be so much fun seeing what else Brae and Dan came up with, all because they wanted to try and save the lifeboat that had given all four of them so much to be grateful for. Anna and Brae might be too old to ever quite manage the sixty years that Jade's grandparents had spent together, but still having him around at all was by far the easiest blessing to count. She had so much more than most people – a job she loved, community spirit that made every corner of Port Agnes feel like home and friends she was closer to than some people were to their own families, not to mention a fiancé who would do anything to make her happy. Even if the test results did their worst, maybe that really could be all she needed.

8

Jess took a deep breath as the last still of the video faded away to nothing. Watching the little boy's story unfold on screen made her chest tight, memories she wasn't even sure were real flooding her body with adrenaline. Fight or flight they called it. The trainers running the fostering skills course had warned all of the participants that it would kick in at some point and that no one would judge them for walking away at the end of the training, having decided that fostering wasn't for them. Jess wouldn't be one of them, though. She was determined to fight, even if she had to sit and get control of her emotions for at least two minutes after the video had ended.

The rest of the participants were already gathered around the table at the back of the room, drinking coffee and eating biscuits. None of them looked as if the video they'd just watched had rocked them to the core. Maybe it was because none of the others were on their own. The most forthright of the group were Sally and Ian, a middle-aged couple whose own three children had grown up and flown the nest. All three of them had done 'terribly well for themselves' according to Sally when they'd been introduced to one another at the start of the day, and now they wanted to give something back and let another child have the same wonderful opportunities that their own children had been given. The next couple were Richard and David, who'd been married for two years and were doing the course to decide whether fostering was for them, or whether they should consider another route to parenthood. Glancing over at Richard, who looked at least ten years older than his husband, it was obvious that he wasn't quite at ease as he'd seemed at the beginning of the day. It was reassuring to think he might have been affected in some way by watching the video too. The last of the group were Mohammed and Fatima, who'd both worked in children's residential homes for several years and didn't look like there was anything that could faze them.

'You look like you need a coffee.' Richard was already pouring it as Jess approached the table. She'd kept her own introduction short and sweet – when it had finally come to her turn – wondering if the other participants could hear her heart hammering as they turned to look at her.

'Hi, I'm Jess and I'm a midwife. I'll be applying as a single foster carer, just to carry out some respite initially, and I can't wait to get started.' She hadn't missed the way that Sally's eyebrows had shot up behind her fringe when Jess had dared to utter the word *single*, and for a moment she'd been tempted to elaborate on the story. But if she'd gone down that road, she might still have been in the middle of her introduction now, four hours later, instead of taking the cup of coffee Richard was holding out.

'I found that video a really difficult watch.' Jess met his gaze and there was just the slightest flicker of recognition in Richard's eyes. The trouble with pre-approval training was that it didn't just provide the participants with information; the trainers were also making an assessment to see if the participants had what it took to be foster carers. Jess couldn't fail, not again. And it didn't look like Richard wanted to risk it either by being too honest about any doubts he might have, and David was watching him like a hawk. That was one of the downsides of being in a couple, it wasn't just yourself you'd be messing things up for if you put a foot wrong. At least that was one thing Jess didn't have to worry about any more.

'I think it's supposed to give us a realistic idea of what to expect, but it was heartbreaking hearing some of the stories about what the children have been through.' Richard picked up a small wicker basket from the table. 'Shortbread?'

'No thanks. I just hope I'd know how to help a child like that last little boy. The responsibility of getting things right is terrifying.'

'I wouldn't worry, Dexter and Helen said the course will help weed out the people who aren't up to the job.' Sally cut into their conversation without waiting for an invitation, giving Jess a pointed look. 'And, let's face it, this is going to be really tough for you. For a start you've never had any children of your own, not to mention the fact that you're *single*. It's going to make it all that much tougher.'

'Actually lots of our friends are foster carers and some of the best are doing it on their own.' Fatima waved a half-eaten short-bread biscuit in the air. 'Carers working one-on-one with a foster child can create an even closer bond with them sometimes.'

'Ah, but are your friends childless too?' Sally wasn't backing down and she couldn't have known the effect her words were having. It was such a small word – *childless* – but when you spent your day surrounded by pregnant women and babies, and when being childless had ended your marriage, it suddenly took on a whole new significance. Jess had lost count of the times that women she was caring for had asked whether she had any children of her own and, when she told them she hadn't, the doubt in their eyes was obvious. How could a midwife who'd never given birth herself possibly be as good as one who had? There were even other midwives who'd openly expressed the same opinion – thankfully not since she'd joined the team in Port Agnes – but it had happened from time to time back when she'd been based in a maternity unit in the hospital. Now she was about to embark on a whole new adventure and there were already people suggesting that she was somehow inadequate, just because she'd never managed to have a baby of her own.

'I think you've got to accept that this is going to be difficult for *all* of you.' Helen, the foster carer who was running the course alongside a social worker from the local authority, squeezed Jess's shoulder. 'Having a stranger in your home 24/7, not to mention the behaviours you're likely to see, is going to be really hard to deal with regardless of your marital status. Me and my husband, John, felt like our whole world had been turned upside down when Shay first arrived in our lives. I'm sure working as a midwife has some really challenging moments too and you'll have developed loads of transferable skills you can use when you're fostering.'

'I hope so.' Jess's voice sounded weirdly detached, but then she hadn't felt like her normal self in ages, so she couldn't expect to sound like it either. Once upon a time she might have had to tone herself down for something like this and stop trying to be the life and soul of the party, making everyone laugh. But just lately life seemed to have toned her down all by itself.

'You don't *look* like a midwife.' Ian gave her an appraising stare. 'Although there is a touch of Barbara Windsor in her *Carry On Doctor* days about you.'

'Ian!' Sally gave him a sharp jab in the ribs with her elbow, making his cup and saucer wobble.

'What about you and David?' Jess turned back to Richard. It was easier to ignore Sally and Ian than respond to their comments in a way that Helen wouldn't count against her. 'Do you know yet if fostering's the right choice for you, after today?'

'It's certainly not going to be a walk in the park if we go down that route, but then we didn't really expect it to be, did we, Davy?'

'No! We watched loads of documentaries on YouTube and I think I must have read all the Cathy Glass books.' David smiled with the sort of confidence someone only had when they knew they'd revised every possible question on the test before they even turned over the paper. 'Did you do a lot of research?'

'A bit.' Jess shifted uncomfortably from foot to foot, wondering if David was going to ask her to elaborate. The last thing she wanted to do was tell a room full of strangers exactly how in-depth her research had been, but they seemed determined to make her the centre of attention for some reason. At least it was good practice for the panel who'd be making a recommendation about whether they thought she'd be a good foster carer.

'I wouldn't worry about how much research you've done; not everything out there is true anyway. The whole purpose of these Skills to Foster courses is to give you an accurate picture of what fostering is all about, to make sure it's a good fit for you.' Helen had a kind face, her apple-shaped cheeks making it look as though smiling was her go-to expression. It must have made it so much easier for the children who turned up on her doorstep with their possessions in a bag for life, and a social worker stopping them from running in the opposite direction. Jess was going to have to work on smiling more again. She was getting there, but it didn't come as naturally as it used to.

'Sorry about dashing off before the end of the video, but I needed to take a phone call.' Dexter, the social worker who was leading the session with Helen, came back into the room like a whirlwind. He was tall, with dark hair that looked like he'd missed at least one appointment with his barber and a grazing of stubble, all of which somehow really suited him rather than making him look scruffy. He probably spent his whole life running from one crisis to another, trying to sort things out, but when he smiled the weight of the world seemed to lift off his shoulders.

'No problem, Dexter.' Helen smiled again too, handing him a cup of coffee. 'We were just talking about how difficult some of the videos we've shown are to watch, and how it's not always a good idea to take everything you read about fostering as gospel, unless you hear it from someone who has experienced it first-hand.'

'Exactly, that's why I always ask Helen to do these courses with me. I might see some of it from the point of view of a social worker, but I don't know what it's like to have that responsibility every minute of the day.' Dexter ran a hand through his hair, making his thick silver wedding band catch the light. Jess curled her left hand into a fist as a reflex, suddenly aware of the lighter strip of skin on the ring finger of her left hand where her own wedding band had been until recently, when she'd finally decided to take it off. The last thing she wanted was to invite any more unwanted questions.

'Are things always as difficult as they were in the last video?' Even as she opened her mouth, Jess hadn't intended to ask the sort of question that might make Dexter and Helen put a giant cross against her name. But she had to ask, she had to know what she was getting into and whether there was a snowball's chance in hell she could actually do it. She hated the thought of wasting anyone's time, but even worse was the thought of letting a child down the way she'd been let down. She'd never forgive herself for that.

'We do try to show you the worst-case scenario, but the likelihood is there will be some tough times ahead for those of you who go on to become foster carers.' Dexter looked at her levelly; he had bright blue eyes and an apparent ability not to blink for an unnerving length of time. 'But there are some cases where we've matched young people with their carers and it's all just fallen into place, as if the children have always been there. It's important that you all understand that's not the norm, though, and that there'll more than likely be a lot of bumps along the road, but your supervising social worker will be there to help you through that.'

'You're only doing respite anyway, aren't you, Jess?' Sally manoeuvred herself into the space between Jess and Dexter. 'So it's not like *real* fostering.'

'You won't be saying that when you're desperate for a respite carer to give you a break.' Dexter's face was deadpan, but as he turned away from Sally he dropped Jess the perfect wink. 'Okay, five more minutes and we'll move on to everyone's favourite activity of the day – role play!' He laughed at the groans that went up in response and Jess crossed her fingers behind her back, silently praying that she wouldn't be asked to play the role of a foster child. She wasn't sure she could pull off a game of 'let's pretend' without the past she'd fought so hard to bury suddenly rushing back to the surface when she least wanted it to.

* * *

'At last, I've been dying to know how it all went!' Anna had snatched up the phone on the first ring, so it didn't sound like an exaggeration.

'It was fine.'

'Hmm, I know that tone. Only you can say "fine" like that and make it sound about as appealing as root canal surgery.' There was no fooling Anna. Jess had hoped she might be able to keep things non-committal over the phone, when her friend couldn't all-too-easily read the expression on her face, but clearly not. When you worked side by side as community midwives, navigating life-and-death emergencies, there was a tendency to form bonds quickly.

The last six months had really set the seal on Jess's friendships with all the other midwives, but especially with Anna and Ella. They'd been so supportive since Dom had left. They'd barely got past their third anniversary before their relationship had fallen apart, and she'd felt ashamed of failing so spectacularly and so quickly too. She'd even thought about sending back the wedding gifts they'd never actually got round to using – the bread maker that had seemed essential to becoming the kind of domestic goddess all good wives were supposed to be, not to mention the champagne glasses for all the celebrations they were supposed to have together for the next fifty-odd years. One thing that had got far more use than anticipated in their last year together was the cotton bedding meant for the spare room, where Dom had taken up almost permanent residence when things had started to go wrong.

Jess hadn't wanted to tell anyone about that. The rejection she'd experienced all through her life was something she'd kept to herself, but she'd found herself opening up to Anna, who lost her parents when she was so young, and to Ella, who wouldn't judge her for just about managing to limp through three years as a married woman. After all, Ella had been jilted on the steps of the registry office, half an hour after her wedding was supposed to start. In comparison Jess had to admit she'd had it relatively easy.

'The training day was pretty good, but a bit of reality check about what I might be getting into. It was just some of the other people there...' Jess sighed. 'They all seem to have it so much more together than me and none of them were on their own. What if I can't do this by myself?'

'Of course you can! Jess Kennedy can do anything she puts her mind to!' Anna had got into the habit of talking about Jess in the third person when she was having a wobble and it always made her laugh because of how ridiculous it sounded. Although it would be even more worrying if she ever reached the stage where she started talking about herself like that.

'I just don't want to let anyone down.'

'You never do.' There was a pause as Jess desperately tried to think of something to say in response, but she was still rubbish at knowing how to accept anything that might pass as a compliment. 'Are you still there, Jess?'

'Yes, sorry, the line went a bit funny.'

'Okay, well I won't keep you hanging on too long. I know Ella wants to hear how you've got on too, but we didn't want to bombard you with calls. So we wondered if you've got time for breakfast tomorrow, as none of us are working. You could tell us all about it then.'

'I could meet you at The Cookie Jar?' The little café served traditional Cornish fayre, from Mehenick's famous pasties through to home-made clotted cream ice cream. They also did a delicious breakfast, called 'the fisherman's feast', which probably contained more calories than one person was supposed to consume in a day, but thankfully nothing fishy unless you were the sort of weirdo who'd be tempted to order a side of kippers.

'That sounds perfect. Nine o'clock okay for you?'

'Absolutely, I'll see you then. And thanks, Anna.'

'For what?'

'For your support and checking in on me, it means a lot.' Jess laughed. 'But if you tell anyone I said that, I'll flat out deny it!'

'I won't say a word, I promise! See you tomorrow.'

'See you then.' Ending the call, Jess was so busy thinking about everything that had gone on in the training, she didn't notice the man lurking in the shadows at the edge of the car park, until he stepped out.

'Jesus, you made me jump!' Jess clapped her hand over her mouth. Would blasphemy count against her when she was being weighed up as a foster carer? It could have been a lot worse, though; she'd been very close to saying something that would definitely have counted as a swear word.

'Sorry! I didn't want to interrupt your phone call, but I wanted to talk to you before you left.' Dexter gave her an apologetic smile, the shadows under his eyes hinting at the long day he'd had. The Skills to Foster course was usually run over two days, but the local authority were experimenting with compressing it into a single day this time. It had made for a very long session and it was almost eight o'clock, daylight already beginning to lose its battle with the dark despite the lengthening days of spring.

'It's fine, I was miles away, thinking about work.' Jess was already trying to figure out just how much of the phone call he might have overheard. If he'd been lurking there when she'd been telling Anna that she didn't think she was up to being a foster carer, that would definitely mean she had another big cross against her name. It couldn't be a good sign that he wanted to catch her before she left either. Maybe he wanted to break it to her that they didn't think she had what it took, so she didn't waste any more of their time.

'I just wanted to check that nothing that happened today put you off the idea of fostering?'

'I found some of the videos difficult to watch, but as much as the responsibility terrifies me, it just makes me want to help kids like that even more.' There was something about Dexter; something that made her blurt out the truth, the whole truth, and nothing but the truth when she looked into his eyes – even though she'd rather have pretended that none of it scared her quite as much as it did.

'I'd be more worried if you weren't terrified of the responsibility. That means you'll try all the harder to get things right. The applicants who worry me the most are the ones who think they've got all the answers.' He grinned and she had a feeling she knew exactly who he meant. 'I'm really glad the training hasn't put you off, because Helen and I both thought you had at least as much to offer as everyone else who was there today.'

'Thank you.' For a second Jess was tempted to ask if he'd got her mixed up with someone else, but for once she managed not to say more than she needed to.

'I'll see you at the next pre-approval training, then, when we start to look at the sort of children who might be a good match for you.'

'Great, see you then.' Somehow Jess had managed to pull off sounding casual, as if this sort of praise was what she'd expected all along. It was just a good job Dexter hadn't noticed how much her legs were shaking.

Opening the door of her car and sinking into her seat, she looked around, checking Dexter wasn't still standing close by before she allowed herself a little whoop of celebration. Maybe there really was a chance she could do this after all and take her life full circle. For the first time in a long time there just might be something to look forward to.

9

Anna looked at the clock in the staffroom for the hundredth time, as a wave of nausea threatened to take hold of her. She had the afternoon off to go to the private clinic where she and Brae had chosen to have their fertility tests, to get the results. Going to the GP in Port Agnes had felt strangely invasive. She didn't want anyone who knew her personally to find out the test results before she and Brae did, and over the years of heading up the midwifery unit she'd got to know most of the GPs in the area. Even having them refer her and Brae for tests would have felt like a hotline to the Port Agnes grapevine, Hippocratic Oath or not.

The last half an hour at work had passed achingly slowly, because all she wanted was to be with Brae; he was the only one who really understood just how much was going on inside her head. There was a flip side though; every time the second hand on the clock made its way back up to twelve, she was closer to being told something she might wish she'd never heard. She just wanted a chance, that was all. Surely it wasn't asking too much?

'Are you all right, my love? You look a bit peaky.' Gwen bustled into the staffroom, setting down her handbag on the desk, a waft of the perfume she was wearing making Anna cough. 'Sorry, I've just given myself a couple of squirts of my new perfume and I think I was a bit overenthusiastic!'

'What is it?' Anna could taste the bitterness on her tongue, almost as if Gwen had sprayed the perfume straight on it.

'It's Aphrodisiac from Ann Summers. I bought it when I was in there getting some new underwear.' Gwen grinned and Anna couldn't help laughing. She'd been dreading how Gwen might finish that sentence and frankly nothing would have surprised her.

'It's very distinctive.' Anna glanced at the clock again, the smile slipping off her face. It was almost time.

'Are you going to tell me what's up? Or I should I just mind my own bloody business, like my Barry's always saying?'

'I'm going for the results of some tests this afternoon.' The words were out before Anna could stop them. Gwen wasn't exactly known for her discretion, but there was something about her physically that reminded Anna so much of her mother. If the other woman had offered her a cuddle she wouldn't have hesitated, even if there was a distinct possibility of being suffocated by a cloud of Ann Summers perfume.

'Oh darling, it's not... You know, *the big C*, is it?'

'Oh God no, nothing like that!' Guilt pricked Anna's skin. There were people out there right now, far too many of them, waiting to get the results of tests far more terrifying that she was about to get. In an instant, and without even knowing it, Gwen had somehow given her more perspective than she'd had in months. 'It's fertility tests, to see why we aren't having any luck.'

'I'll be keeping everything crossed you get the results you want, even my legs, and I usually only cross those when I laugh or sneeze!' Gwen winked. 'And if the worst happens, and you need a reason to look on the bright side, losing control of your bladder is a lot less likely to happen if you haven't had kids! And there are other benefits too.'

'Such as?' Anna was genuinely curious, knowing how much Gwen adored her children and grandchildren.

'You can go wherever you want to at the drop of a hat, without having to pack a million bags or organise a babysitter. You'll be much better off financially and you can take up wild hobbies or extreme sports without worrying about your kids, plus you'll get to lie-in. But best of all you get to keep that lovely fiancé of yours all to yourself and, let me tell you, I'd douse myself in Aphrodisiac if I had the chance of a few hours on my own with someone like Brae, never mind a lifetime!' Gwen laughed and Anna had to agree – there would definitely be some upsides to having Brae all to herself, if it had to come to that.

'Oh and then there's the sex.' Gwen was deadpan as she looked in Anna's direction again. 'When my Andrew was born he had the biggest head I've ever seen on a baby; he looked like a lollipop bless him and I was worried the weight of it might mean he'd never stand up! Thank God he grew into it pretty quickly, but for the first year after I had him, Barry said it was like chucking a chipolata down the lifeboat station slipway whenever we had some alone time. And, to be honest, I couldn't disagree.'

Anna was still laughing to herself when Brae picked her up from the car park outside the unit. She wouldn't tell him the story yet, just in case they needed something to cheer them up later.

* * *

Anna was frantically trying to read the doctor's expression as he sat in front of them with the file that contained their destiny. He was a fertility specialist, though, who probably gave out good and bad news on a daily basis, so he'd no doubt become an expert at wearing a mask of impassivity.

'Well the good news is that neither of you have chlamydia.' For a moment Anna thought it was the doctor's idea of a joke, but he was nodding reassuringly. 'That means there's unlikely to be any damage to the fallopian tubes, which I know you were worried about, and the scans and X-rays bear that out.'

It had been a particular concern of Anna's, given that it was the reason for Jess's infertility and meant there was zero chance of her falling pregnant without IVF. Brae had only needed two tests, one for chlamydia and one for his sperm count. Anna's list had been far longer, involving the scans and X-rays the doctor had mentioned, injecting dyes and taking blood. If they could rule out Brae's only other test, if there was a problem, it was definitely down to her.

'What about the sperm count?' Anna looked at the doctor as she spoke, knowing what he was going to say before he even said it.

'It's excellent.' He turned towards Brae. 'Well above average for a man of your age. In fact the number, shape and motility are all excellent.'

Brae just nodded, but for a second or two Anna wondered if the doctor was going to hand him a certificate. Something he could hang on the wall to prove he was a so-called 'real man', and an above-average one at that. Anna already knew that, though. Brae was way above average in every way. Swallowing hard, she cleared her throat.

'And the rest of my tests?'

'As I said, there are no issues with the fallopian tubes, the lining of the womb, or the womb itself, all of that is functioning exactly as it should.' The doctor pressed his lips together as he paused. 'The issue really comes down to what your FSH levels tell us about your ovarian reserve.'

'What does that mean?' Brae asked the question that Anna already knew the answer to. She'd spent far more hours reading it all online than she wanted to admit.

'Women are born with all the eggs they're ever going to have and, naturally, as a woman gets older, her egg reserves diminish. The tests show that Anna's are lower than we'd expect, even for a woman of her age.' The doctor turned back towards Anna again. 'I'm afraid they're closer to the levels we'd expect in a woman in at least her mid-forties.'

'So I won't be able to get pregnant?' Anna held her breath. She needed to hear him say it out loud, before she had any chance of moving on, and she gripped Brae's hand all the tighter.

'It's highly unlikely. I'm sorry.' To his credit, the doctor genuinely looked like he meant it. 'You could try a drug like Clomid to stimulate release of your remaining eggs. It's far from a guarantee of success, but it'll give you the best chance there is of a pregnancy, although I'm afraid it's still pretty slim. It's an option we could talk about once you've had the chance to process everything I've told you, to see if you think it's worth trying. I can give you some information on all your options to read through together.'

'What about IVF?' Brae suddenly sounded like the desperate one, clutching on to the last bit of hope there might be.

'Using your own eggs?' The doctor sighed. 'I could sit here and encourage you to give it a go, tell you that it happens. But the truth is, you'd almost certainly be throwing your money away and putting immense stress on yourselves for a tiny chance of success. If you want to go down the IVF route, then the best shot you've got, which has pretty good odds, would be to use donor eggs.'

'From a much younger woman.' Anna said the words, not

needing anyone to acknowledge them. So that was it, she was obsolete on the baby-making front. Like an old iPhone that no longer ran the apps everyone wanted to use. It might be kept on the bedside table and used as an alarm clock, but it was no good any more for the purpose it was designed for and neither was she.

* * *

Brae handed the menus back to the waiter after he'd taken their orders. He'd insisted on coming out for a meal to celebrate the fact that their tests had suggested there was still a chance of Anna getting pregnant, even if she didn't see it that way. The doctor had said '*highly unlikely*', but in her head it had translated as '*never going to happen*' and she had to be the realist if she was going to be able to come to terms with it and consider their other options, instead of holding on to what she saw as false hope. She could have assumed it was easy for Brae to celebrate – after all, he was probably capable of repopulating an entire country, should the need ever arise – but it wasn't. She could see in his face that he'd much rather have been the one 'at fault'. She had to keep those words in, though. For the first time ever, she was having to run through in her head what she said to Brae, before the words came out. She couldn't give even a hint that she regarded herself to be to blame, or he'd be hurting even more than he already was. It was brave faces all round.

'There are loads of articles online about women in their late forties getting pregnant.' Brae held up his phone. 'I found some when you were on the phone to Ella.'

'You know why those pregnancies made it into news articles, don't you? Because it isn't the norm. There's about a three per cent chance of me falling pregnant with the FSH levels I've got without any treatment and it's still a real long shot even with the fertility drugs.' Anna squeezed his hand. She didn't want him holding on to hope that was no longer there. When Ella had rung to ask for some advice about a patient, Anna hadn't wanted to tell her the results over the phone. She needed to work out in her own head, and with Brae, where they went from here. 'The worst thing about this is that there won't be another you running around.'

'One of me is more than enough.'

'There could never be too many for me.' Looking across at him she meant every word. Her journey to having a family had started off from a desire to replicate what she'd had with her parents, but now it was about Brae more than anything else. 'I bet you were the cutest kid.'

'You've seen some of the photos. Morwenna especially loves getting the ones out where I had to have a frosted lens on one side of my glasses, until my eyes corrected themselves. I'm not sure even a mother could call that cute!'

'You were, though, like a red-headed version of the Milky Bar Kid.' Anna smiled at the thought.

'I always wanted to be a policeman rather than a cowboy. I had the uniform with a little high-vis jacket and everything. My absolute favourite thing was arresting Morwenna, although I have to say she always put up a really good fight, being a good bit older than me.'

'Did you have a lot of holidays, or was the squabbling too much for your mum and dad to bear?'

'Not really. Mum and Dad worked long hours in the shop, and Morwenna wouldn't be seen dead with me in public once she got into her teens, so I spent a lot of time on my own, until Jasper came along.' Brae still had photographs of his beloved dog up in the house. Jasper had been a black Labrador, with one dark brown eye and the other one bright blue. Apparently the breeders had offered him to Brae's dad for half price and Jasper had found himself a home.

'Have you ever thought about getting another dog?' Anna knew better than anyone that you couldn't just replace what you'd lost, but she could imagine how big a hole Jasper had left in Brae's life when he'd finally had to say goodbye to his best friend.

'We lost him just before I joined the Navy and there hasn't been a right time since, but I still expect to see him whenever I go up to the flat above the shop.' Brae's cousin, Peter, lived there now, but it was where he'd grown up, with Jasper apparently sleeping on his bed for the entire ten years of the dog's life. 'I was eight when we first got him and we used to go off together on adventures that seemed huge to me back then. We'd head to the beach and I'd lift up the biggest rocks I could from the rock pools, and Jasper would stick his nose straight in. There was more than one occasion when he came off worst from a run-in with a crab, but he never let it put him off.'

'I wish I could give you the chance to relive all those adventures through a little boy or girl of your own.' Anna could picture it now, Brae like an excited kid himself, loving every minute of the chance to relive his childhood the way that only parents of young children could. She was trying desperately not to break her promise to Brae and blame herself, but it was really hard.

'Let's not rule anything out for now, but let's not rule anything in either.' Brae looked straight at her. 'Whatever happens we've got each other and, okay, so we might not choose to go rock pooling, but we can make a million memories that are just for us. It's going to be okay, Anna, I promise. In fact, it's going to be bloody brilliant.'

'I know, and you're not the first person to point out that there could be some upsides to staying child-free. In fact, Gwen had her usual unique take on it.' It was the perfect moment to pass on

Gwen's pearls of wisdom to Brae. He was right, rushing into any definite decisions would be stupid and she could finally begin to see a road ahead for just the two of them, if that's what they eventually decided. Trusting one person to be her everything, with the risk of losing that, was almost as terrifying as being relied upon to be another person's everything. But Brae made her believe it was possible and she wouldn't swap what she had with him for an alternative life with anyone else. It was finally time to start looking forward and one thing she knew for certain was that she couldn't wait to be his wife.

10

'Welcome to the first annual bumps and buggies May Day treasure hunt, in aid of the fund to save Port Agnes Lifeboat Station.' Public speaking always made the butterflies in Ella's stomach take flight, and usually the groups she addressed were no bigger than an antenatal class of around ten or twelve. But the turnout for the treasure hunt had exceeded her wildest expectations. She'd already dispatched Dan and Brae to buy some more sweets and little gifts to fill the woven paper May Day baskets that would be given out to the children by the Green Man at the end of the treasure hunt. Even though there was a grand prize for one lucky winner to discover, none of the children would be going away empty-handed. Every family taking part was paying an entrance fee, and the May Day baskets and most of their contents, as well as the grand prize, had been donated by local businesses.

'Thank you all so much for supporting this event and it's brilliant to see just how many people value the work of the lifeboat station enough to try and save it. A special thanks to my colleagues at the midwifery unit for helping organise the event and spread the word. Lastly, thanks to all the local businesses who have supported us. There's a list of all the contributors on the back of your entry pack.' Ella was aware that her words were coming out faster and faster. She was as anxious to get on with the treasure hunt as her audience, and there were already a few children pulling hard on their parents' hands to get going.

'You'll also find the first clue in your pack, which you can collect from the stand.' Ella smiled at her friends standing behind the trestle tables ready to hand out the information. Anna had been only too keen to volunteer, despite how busy she was with plans for the wedding. Ella had also roped in Toni and Jess. Most of the others had been involved in pulling the event together in less than a week. Frankie, one of the midwifery assistants, had been particularly tenacious at persuading businesses to donate, but she'd headed off to New Zealand the day before, to spend the next month with her daughter and her family. Frankie would have been more than happy to stand in front of the crowd, but it was up to Ella now.

'Okay, I'm going to read out the first clue, but you'll find some extra hints in your pack. Here we go... *Get to the Green Man clue by clue, how fast you go is up to you. Where the beach huts stand – row by row – is now the place you need to go. Find the spring wreath on the door and for the second clue you'll search no more.*'

As soon as she'd finished, there was a flurry of activity and a surge towards the trestle tables. The event had initially been aimed at the antenatal and postnatal patients of the unit – hence the 'bumps and buggies' treasure hunt – but word had obviously got out, and there were children up to the age of at least eight excitedly ripping open the entry packs in anticipation of winning a prize. Some of the families had made a great effort to get into the spirit of Beltane too, with outfits ranging from toddlers dressed as fairies, to one very heavily pregnant lady in a full morris dancer's outfit.

'I can't believe how many people are here.' Anna squeezed her waist, as she came over with Toni and Jess once all the treasure hunters had set off towards the beach huts.

'Neither can I.' Ella grinned. 'I had a horrible feeling no one was going to show up. But if we can keep this momentum going and get everyone to sign the petition and spread the word to family and friends, it might just make a difference.'

'Of course it will.' Toni was wearing a sunflower headband and long-sleeved T-shirt emblazoned with the words '*You Are My Sunshine*'. She was usually the most no-nonsense of all the midwives, but there was definitely a twinkle in her eye today. 'I'm sorry I can't stay for the whole thing, but I've got a—'

'Date?' Jess cut her off before she could finish.

'No, a prior engagement. I'm meeting a friend, that's all, but I'll come down to the beach huts before I head off.' Toni shot her a look which suggested that any further discussion would not go down well. But they all knew she was meeting Bobby. Ever since Ella had joined the midwifery unit, Toni and Bobby's relationship had been obvious to everyone who worked there, but it was something the two of them weren't willing to make public. If Ella had been forced to guess the reason her friends were so determined to deny their relationship, she'd have taken a punt on it being something to do with their families. But after Ella getting jilted on the steps of a London registry office had inadvertently been caught on camera and gone viral, she knew exactly what unwanted attention felt like. So she was the last person to poke her nose in other people's relationships.

'What about you, Jess, are you coming down to the beach huts to follow the rest of the treasure hunt trail?'

'Absolutely, I didn't wear this outfit for nothing!' Jess did a twirl. She was dressed as the May queen, complete with a headdress that looked like it weighed almost as much as she did.

'Come on, last one to the beach huts is the designated driver on Anna's hen night.' Jess turned and winked, before somehow managing to sprint off in the direction of the second clue, despite her cumbersome costume – clearly determined not to be the only one drinking lemonade on Anna's hen night.

* * *

By the time they reached the beach huts, most of the treasure hunters had found and read the second clue. Anna had pinned a copy of it to the outside of the beach hut that Brae had bought her on the first anniversary of them getting together, and which – for one day only – had a spring wreath hanging on its door, so that the treasure hunters would know exactly where to stop. There were a few stragglers, though, and someone had unpinned the clue, so Ella decided to put them out of their misery.

'Okay, if you're looking for the second clue, here it is. *Above the giant's shoulders sits his head, with a house of light that's white and red, like the dancers' ribbons you might see, you'll find the clue for number three!*'

'There's a maypole by the lighthouse at Titan's Head, that must be it!' The woman dressed as a morris dancer grabbed her partner by the hand, and the remaining treasure hunters followed after her. All except one.

'You couldn't take the baby for a bit, could you?' Dan's sister, Lissy, gave Ella an apologetic look. 'I know this is your event, but a certain someone is getting very impatient to claim his prize from the Green Man. I might skip the rest of the treasure hunt and just do the meet and greet before it all gets too much for Noah and Tegen and they have a meltdown!'

'That's where insider info about the Green Man's where-abouts can come in really handy.' Ella smiled. Lissy had her hands full as it was. Her husband had finally been able to give up his job to help run their small farm full-time, but almost as soon as he'd come home from working away, she'd fallen pregnant again. It had been a shock at first and Lissy had been very tearful, but she'd risen to the occasion the way she always did. Raising a four-year-old, a two-year-old and a baby, as well as running a farm was enough to make anyone exhausted. When Ella had reconnected with Dan, more than ten years since their romance had fizzled out, she'd soon realised that his sister relied on his help to get by, and it was one of the reasons she'd fallen for him again so quickly. She was more than happy to help out where she could too, and looking after Dan's gorgeous baby nephew was never a chore. 'You can leave Bailey with me whilst you go and see the Green Man, and I'll meet you in half an hour. I think the first of the treasure hunters should be arriving by then.'

'Brilliant, you're a star! There's a bottle in his bag and a pouch of organic sweet potato if he wakes up. Are you sure you don't mind?'

'Yum, cold sweet potato!' Ella grinned. 'Of course I don't mind. Any excuse I get for a cuddle with Bailey is fine by me. If he doesn't wake up, I might have to give him a little prod.'

'Feel free! I'll see you later then.' Lissy gave a quick wave, before running after her older son and daughter, who needed no encouragement at all to leave their baby brother behind.

'Are we going up to the lighthouse, or have we got time for a cup of tea?' Anna looked into Bailey's pram. If anyone was willing the baby to wake up even more than Ella, it was Anna.

'There's always time for tea and I'm not going to any more of the clue sites. Dad is up at the lighthouse, ready to give out banana bread and cookies to all of the kids. Mum is at the harbour with a couple of her friends, and Dan and Brae are already at the end of the trail, which is why Lissy wants to get

Noah and Tegen there before the mad rush. We might as well hang back here for twenty minutes and go straight to the end too.'

'It's just a shame there's none of your dad's cookies to go with the tea.' Toni looked around the beach hut. 'Have you got any biscuits, Anna? Tea's not really tea without them, is it?'

'I think Brae might have eaten the last of them when we came down for a walk on Sunday. We always sit in here for a bit whenever we come down, with a cup of tea, looking out at the sea and making plans.' Anna shrugged. 'It probably sounds boring, but it's the best part of my week.'

'I think it sounds sweet.' Jess squeezed her arm. 'When I was with Dom, I spent most of my free weekends freezing my butt off on the side of a rugby pitch, watching him and his mates half killing each other in the name of sport. Then I got to watch him down several pints, in the clubhouse. Thank God I don't have to do that any more.'

'Let's just hope you don't get matched with a rugby-mad foster child.' Toni laughed, making Bailey stir in his pram.

'Can I get him out?' Anna turned to Ella, who nodded.

'Of course, he's really cuddly, especially when he first wakes up. I'll stick the kettle on.' Ella passed a bag to Toni. 'And if you look in there you should find a box of Dad's cookies that he made especially for us.'

'Now you're talking.'

'He's perfect.' Anna held Bailey close to her, gently rocking the still sleepy baby in her arms.

'You're a natural, Anna. I bet you and Brae can't want to start making babies.' Toni laughed again, making the baby's eyes shoot open, but he still didn't cry.

'Sadly I don't think it's going to be that easy.' Anna's voice was quiet and, as Ella looked over, her friend's eyes had filled with tears.

'Oh God, Anna, I'm sorry I didn't mean to put my size seven feet in it.' Toni frowned, but Anna shrugged.

'You haven't, honestly.' Somehow she managed a smile. 'I'd mentioned to Jess and Ella that I was having some tests to see why we hadn't managed to fall pregnant after a year of trying, but I didn't want to say too much to anyone until we got the results.'

'You don't have to tell us anything, unless you want to.' Ella looked at Anna, but she was already nodding.

'Because of our age, well my age really, I suppose I should have suspected it might not be completely straightforward.' Anna stroked the back of Bailey's head. 'But because Mum didn't have me until she was about my age, I just thought it would be okay, but then I got the results.'

'What did they say?' Jess held out a cookie as she spoke, but Anna shook her head.

'I've got a very low egg reserve. Even for someone of my age it's well below average.'

'So does that mean you definitely can't get pregnant?' Toni asked. Ella seemed to have lost the ability to say anything at all, grateful that she could busy herself with making tea. Anna and Brae were made for each other, and they'd make the most wonderful parents too; she couldn't bear the thought of that being taken away from them.

'No, but it means that my chances of falling pregnant naturally are much lower than they would be for an average woman who's almost forty and that's already dropped significantly to start with.'

'What did Brae say?' Ella finally found her voice, as she put the teapot on the little table in the centre of the beach hut.

'Exactly the same thing as he's been saying every month since we stopped taking precautions and he had to scoop me up from the bathroom floor every time I discovered we still weren't pregnant – that he's marrying me to be with me and if we have children that will just be a bonus.' Anna hesitated. 'You know Brae, he always says the right thing. When we first got the news, we talked about just stopping altogether. But after I'd read through the information the doctor gave me, I wanted to try one last thing before we give up and Brae said he'd do whatever it takes. The doctors have agreed to put me on Clomid to stimulate release of whatever eggs I've got left, but they've told me the odds are stacked against me. They warned me that there's a higher risk of twins, but even having one baby doesn't feel like it's ever going to happen. I never wanted to be a midwife who doesn't ever experience giving birth, but we're starting to talk about other options, thanks to the infertility group that Jess helped me set up. Corny as it sounds, when I'm with Brae, I feel as if there's nothing we couldn't work out together.'

'It's not corny, it's what we all want. It just seems so unfair that you and Jess have brought so many other people's babies into the world, but you might never be able to give birth to your own.' It was the closest Toni had ever come to expressing that sort of emotion.

'What about you, are babies on the agenda?' Jess gave Toni a quizzical look, but she played her cards much closer to her chest than the rest of them.

'It'd have to be an immaculate conception, unless I find myself a man.' Toni didn't miss a beat and Ella nearly choked on the cookie she was eating. She'd caught Toni and Bobby kissing in the staffroom at the midwifery unit only the week before, and they'd come out with some convoluted story about a lost contact lens. Ella didn't want to embarrass them by asking why they needed to have their lips locked together and their hands in one another's hair to search for a missing contact lens. It was hard to believe they thought they were doing a good job of keeping their relationship secret, but if that's what they wanted, everyone seemed willing to play along with it.

'What about you, Ella?' Jess turned towards her.

'One day, but for now Dan and I are enjoying being Auntie and Uncle to Noah, Tegen and Bailey. Well, honorary auntie at least.'

'I'm surprised he hasn't asked you to marry him yet.' Toni was straight in with the killer question again, seemingly forgetting that she'd put her size sevens in it once already.

'I don't know if I could go through all that again, not after last time. The whole wedding thing just brings me out in a cold sweat.' Even though being jilted had turned out to be the best thing that could have happened to Ella, it didn't stop a wave of heat rising up her neck every time the subject came up. Weller, her ex-fiancé, had been in love with his best man and thankfully he'd found the courage to call off the wedding, even if he had left it until the last minute. They were friends now – and not getting married had brought Ella home to Port Agnes. But it had definitely put her off the idea of a big wedding too.

'You didn't mention that when I asked you to be my maid of honour,' Anna laughed.

'Weddings for other people are great, just not for me, and I cannot wait for your big day.' Ella glanced at her watch. 'But if we aren't at the end of the trail by the time the first treasure hunters show up, we might both end up single.'

'I wouldn't miss seeing Brae dressed as the Green Man for the world. He's been practising a Brian Blessed-style voice for days, bless him.' Anna really did light up every time she spoke about her fiancé, and it made Ella smile too. Whatever happened with her friends on the baby front, they'd be okay because they had each other. Her own wedding day might have been a complete disaster, but she'd do everything she could to make sure Brae and

Anna's day was perfect; she couldn't imagine anything standing in their way.

* * *

'Do you think this make-up is ever going to come off?' Brae turned to look at Anna and the green tinge to his face might have made him look queasy if his beard hadn't still been stained with face paint too.

'You've got nine weeks until the wedding, so as long as it's gone by then I think I can live with it!' Anna slid her hand into his as they walked along the sea wall towards their beach hut. There wasn't anything about Brae she wanted to change. The fact that he'd been prepared to dress up as the Green Man to entertain the children at the end of the treasure hunt – even if his costume wasn't exactly flattering – summed him up perfectly.

'I hope it doesn't take that long. Ella looked mortified when the make-up remover she tried didn't work, but I'm sure it'll be fine when I get home and get in the shower. I might need you to get in with me, though, you know, just to make sure I get it all off.'

'And there was me thinking you wanted to have your wicked way with me!'

'I always want that.' Brae pulled her towards him as they reached the door of the beach hut. 'I'd even forgo the promised cuppa and the last of Jago's cookies for that.'

'I promise you'll get your back scrub in the shower later, but there's something I want to talk to you about first.'

'That sounds ominous.'

'It's nothing to worry about, it's just we always seem to find our best solutions when we're down here.' Anna opened the door of the beach hut and put the kettle on straight away, while Brae set up the table and chairs, so they could look out at the sea.

Setting two mugs of tea onto the table and handing Brae the promised cookie, she sank onto the chair next to him.

'Come on then, what is it you want to talk about?' Brae's tone was gentle, but it probably wouldn't have taken him many guesses to work it out. All of their serious conversations seemed to be about one thing these days.

'I told the girls about the results of my fertility tests today.'

'Did it help, telling them?'

'It did and I was chatting to Jess on the way up to meet you at the end of the trail.' Anna let go of a long breath. 'She seems definite now that she wants to foster after she had a bit of a wobble, wondering if she could do it.'

'Is that what you want to talk about, us fostering? You know I don't mind what we do if the Clomid doesn't work; fostering, surrogacy, adoption, or whatever else it is that leads to us becoming parents, if that's what you really want. But I'm going to keep saying it until you believe it, however long that takes – as long as I've got you that's all I need.'

Anna reached out to touch him, the warmth of his leg under her hand mirroring her feelings. To be told again and again that she was all someone else needed was amazing, but to actually believe it was something else altogether and she really did. Nothing could hurt them now, at least not enough to break what they had, and it was making her brave enough to take another risk trying something else if the Clomid came to nothing. 'I don't want to foster.'

'Okay.'

'But I think I could come around to the idea of adoption. I just need to let go of the idea of getting a part of Mum and Dad back by having family of my own.' Anna sighed. 'And the scariest thought of all is that any child we adopt might end up wishing that someone else had become their mum.'

'Can I ask you a question?' Brae put his cookie down, which was about as serious as things ever got with him. 'If you discovered tomorrow that there'd been a mistake at the hospital when you were born and that you were sent home with the wrong people, would it change how you felt about your mum and dad?'

'Of course not, but—'

Brae cut her off before she could finish.

'No buts. Just tell me why not?'

'Because they were brilliant parents, I couldn't have asked for anyone better.'

'Any child we adopted would say the same about you and what you've just said proves it's got nothing to do with genetics.' Brae stroked the side of her face, making her shiver despite the warmth of the afternoon sun. 'As for letting go of getting a part of your mum and dad back, you don't have to do that either. The way you bring a child up will mirror all the bits you loved about your own upbringing, and that will make your parents a part of the child's life much more than biology.'

'What did I do to deserve you?'

'You just got lucky I guess!' Brae laughed and the tears prickling Anna's eyes were definitely the good kind. Jess had said she'd ask for some advice on first steps towards adoption once she'd been assigned a social worker and there was nothing more precious than hope. It was another option, another avenue for them to explore. Maybe there would be children one day, and they could all pile into a camper van to head off on an adventure somewhere with a crazy place name, with a dog the kids loved every bit as much as Brae had loved Jasper. If they got that dream, it wouldn't matter how those children got there. Even if they didn't, there'd be other roads to travel and with Brae by her side, she'd never have to do that alone again.

11

Jess dropped two Berocca energy tablets into a glass of water, watching them fizz and spin around as she stood in the kitchen area of the staffroom making a cup of coffee. Once upon a time a breakfast consisting of double the stated dose of energy tablets, followed by a chaser of generously sugared black coffee, would have been the result of a heavy night out. Now all it signified was another sleepless night, trying to work out if she might be about to make the biggest mistake of her life. If she didn't count her short-lived marriage to Dom.

It had been less than a week since the Skills to Foster course and, when she'd spoken to Dexter straight afterwards, Jess had felt certain she was doing the right thing. So much so that she'd fired off an email to the assessment team, asking if she could start the process as soon as possible. When she'd spoken to Anna and the others about it, she'd felt even more confident that fostering was what she was meant to do. But then she'd made the mistake of googling what to expect during the assessment.

Diving into the depths of the internet was a bit like following Alice down the rabbit hole. She'd found plenty of sites that enthused about the joys of being a foster carer and others that painted a far less rosy picture, but nothing she'd read had worried her all that much. At least not until she'd happened upon a blog called *Things I Never Knew About Fostering*, written by an anonymous woman whose bio said she'd been a foster carer for ten years. Jess had scrolled back through the posts until she'd got to the first one, which was titled:

The Inside Inquisition

The first thing I discovered I didn't know about fostering, was the depth my assessing social worker would go into about my past life. Every detail of the people I've loved and lost, every hurt, failure and mistake, was laid bare for her to pick over. I had to sit with a virtual stranger and discuss how I felt about things I'd promised myself I'd never think about again, knowing it was her job to judge me, with no guarantee that going through all that would result in me becoming a foster carer. Even ten years down the line, I'm still not sure I'd have done it if I'd known.

Jess had forced herself to read the rest of the post, fight or flight kicking in all over again, but this time she wanted to run. The thought of revisiting things she'd spent twenty years trying to forget was something she just wasn't sure she could do – even if she wanted to. Losing her mother and then being abandoned by her father were bad enough, but a second rejection, from the people she'd seen as her rescuers, and who'd abandoned her all over again, had broken something inside her she wasn't sure could ever be fixed.

Apparently Dom would be asked for a reference too, and invited to give his opinion about whether he thought she had the skills it took to be a foster carer. It didn't matter that he had walked out on her not long after the party at Anna and Brae's the previous Halloween, when they'd had yet another row about her failure to produce a baby of their own. As far as Jess was concerned, his opinion had stopped counting for anything when she'd seen him ten days later, draped around one of the girls from his office, when he and Jess were supposedly still trying to work things out.

If the assessment team had contacted her the day after she'd read the blog post, she'd have told them she was pulling out. But twenty-four hours later, she was back to having no idea what to do for the best. Maybe it would do her good to confront the past. She was always telling her patients that their fears about childbirth were almost certainly going to be worse than the reality. Once you were in labour, you just had to get on with it. And, once it was finished, the prize at the end meant most women would willingly go through the pain ten times over. She'd almost convinced herself that worrying about going through the assessment would be worse than actually doing it, when her phone had pinged with a text alert.

✉ From Dom
Hey J-J. Hope u r ok? Let's meet 2 talk. Miss u xx

She didn't want to meet Dom. There was nothing to talk about, no explanation he could belatedly come up with that would even begin to justify his behaviour. It seemed horribly unfair that he might hold her future in his hands, when he'd already stolen the one she'd thought they had all mapped out.

Thank God for the distraction of work. She might not have slept well, but Jess was determined to make sure she was still on top of her game. After tucking into yet another one of the fisherman's feast breakfasts with Anna at The Cookie Jar the day after the treasure hunt, she'd made a promise to herself that she'd start every day for the rest of the week on a healthy note, with a kale smoothie and a handful of pomegranate seeds. But she'd already resorted to vitamin drinks and coffee instead, and her stomach was growling in protest, making her fingers itch to reach out for the tin that was almost certain to contain some of Gwen's home-made biscuits. Role modelling a healthy lifestyle was one of the many things a foster carer was supposed to do, but when one of Jess's fellow midwives was as handy with a food processor as Gwen was, it didn't exactly make it easy to settle for a carrot stick.

'Morning, Jess.' Anna's smile almost instantly turned into a frown. 'Are you okay, you look really pale?'

'Just another sleepless night, I know I said I was certain I was meant to foster, but the more I read about it, the more all the old doubts start creeping in.'

'Oh no, you seemed so ready the other day, has something happened?'

'I'm just weighing up whether I can face going through the assessment process. It's pretty invasive by all accounts and things with Dom are still a bit raw, not to mention... well, you know.' Jess didn't need to elaborate. Anna had been the first person at the midwifery unit she'd told about growing up in foster care herself. There'd been a problem with getting clearance when Jess had first joined the unit, because of a gap in her address history when she'd turned eighteen, and the only way to explain it had been to tell the truth. Jess had spent three months sofa surfing with friends and acquaintances after her foster parents had turfed her out a week after her eighteenth birthday. Back then eighteen had been the cut-off point for the higher rate of fostering payments and Jess was no longer financially viable. Realising that she came down to a monetary value for the people who'd claimed to love her had been one of the most painful things ever to happen to her – far worse than finding out that

Dom had been playing hide the sausage with his boss's personal assistant.

Thankfully, when her foster carers had sat her down and told her she needed to find somewhere else to live, she'd already had a place at uni to study midwifery and a student loan all lined up. She'd only had to spend three months on friends' sofas before she'd moved into halls of residence, working shifts in the local Pizza Hut in between lectures and work placements, and somehow she'd got through the first year. Moving into a shared student house with three of the girls from her course in the second year had felt like another major milestone. She was a survivor; nothing and no one would ever hurt her like that again. The only thing that had been worse than that was losing her parents in the first place.

'What happened to you is all the more reason for you to go for this, Jess.'

'Anyone would think you were looking forward to me cutting down my hours, so you can get rid of me for good at some point!'

'You know that isn't true, and you weren't even supposed to be here until ten this morning, were you?'

'No, but one of my ladies who's a bit anxious about her birth plan asked me if I could fit her in again this week and I said I'd squeeze her in before my other appointments.'

'In that case, you deserve one of Gwen's chocolate chip shortbreads and I'll feel a lot less guilty if I'm not the only one sneaking in an early raid on the biscuit tin before the others arrive. Last week Toni actually started keeping track of how many of Gwen's biscuits everyone had eaten. She said it was to make sure she didn't eat too many, but I'm not so sure!'

'I bet she didn't count Bobby's quota!' Jess could almost guarantee it.

'Come to mention it, I don't think she mentioned Bobby's

name, although I have to admit I think I'd already eaten his share before he even did a shift last week.' Anna laughed. 'It's that whole wedding diet thing. As soon as you start trying to cut stuff out, it just makes you want to eat it all the more!'

'I'll slip a couple of biscuits into the top drawer of my desk for us to have later, before Toni starts dusting for fingerprints! But you'd better have one to tide you over until then; this wedding planning lark can take it out of you.' Jess handed Anna one of the shortbreads, but it would be a few hours before she'd have time to have the biscuit she'd saved for herself. She'd have to get moving if she was going to make sure she didn't keep her first patient waiting. It might not always seem like it, but some things were even more important than where your next biscuit was coming from.

* * *

The Red Cliff Hotel was perched so close to the edge of its name-sake, there were warning signs all along the road that led up to it about not veering off the designated pathways. The views were spectacular, right across Port Agnes to Titan's Head and out to the Sisters of Agnes Island, where the old convent was now a five-star hotel. If Anna could have got married anywhere, it would have been on the Sisters of Agnes Island, where Brae had proposed in the hotel's conservatory. But the truth was she didn't really care where they got married, as long as they did.

'Are you sure you don't mind spending your afternoon off at a wedding fair?' Anna slipped her hand inside Brae's as they walked up towards the hotel from the car park.

'I'm only here because I'm on a promise.' Brae laughed.

'Oh really and what promise is that exactly?'

'The promise of food. I seem to recall you saying that we'd be sampling some food and drink, so we can finalise the menu now that the sea bass caught by my own fair hand isn't an option.'

'I know food will always be your first love, but I'm very glad that I'm your second.' Anna leant into him, breathing in the familiar scent of his aftershave.

'Nothing comes ahead of you, not even the salted caramel brownies that are apparently the chef's speciality.' Laughing again, he turned her to face him. 'I keep thinking that the next time we're in the hotel together it'll be because we're getting married.'

'Not getting cold feet, are you?' Looking up at him, she already knew the answer.

'I'm more worried about you suddenly realising how much better you can do. Even Morwenna keeps telling me that I'm punching above my weight.'

'That's what siblings are for, to keep you grounded!' It was Anna's turn to laugh and, for once, the longing she'd always felt for a sibling of her own was way below the surface. Brae's family had welcomed her in, and seeing how he interacted with his sister and her family just did more to convince her that he was everything she wanted in a partner. His niece and nephew adored him, but then she was yet to meet someone who had a bad word to say about Brae. If anyone was punching above their weight, it was her.

The grandly-named ballroom at the Red Cliff Hotel was probably host to weddings and conferences more often than it was to actual balls, but it had been transformed into a wedding wonderland of pink, champagne and silver, with fabric hung in swathes from the ceiling and confetti seemingly covering every surface. Anna didn't envy whoever was going to be clearing up afterwards.

'How are we doing with buying clothes for the honeymoon?' Brae raised an eyebrow and Anna nudged him in the ribs.

'We? You've actually got the cheek to say, *we*?' She shook her head. If it was down to Brae, the packing would happen the night before and probably consist of a couple of pairs of shorts, his three favourite T-shirts and a pair of flip-flops stuffed into a bag for life. He had a million good points, but organisation wasn't one of them.

'You're so much better at all that than me, though.' Brae grinned. 'Morwenna did warn you that you're getting yourself hitched to a big kid.'

'She also warned me that you might suggest fish finger sandwiches for the wedding breakfast after the sea bass idea fell through, so I suppose I should count myself lucky that you're even willing to try a taster menu.'

'I'm not ruling out the fish fingers! But did you see those grilled cheese sandwiches on that stall as we came in? They're made with Wild Garlic Yarg and if they taste as good as they look, we might need to rethink the menu.'

'I want to believe you're joking!' She really couldn't be certain, though. Brae was a foodie through and through, and he was also Cornish born and bred, so any opportunity he had to bring his beloved county into the wedding plans was not to be passed up. Much as Anna loved Cornwall, and particularly Port Agnes, she drew the line at having Yarg cheese toasties on the menu at their wedding.

'How about a compromise and we ditch the diet for the day and have one of their sandwiches for lunch, before we finalise the menu for the wedding?'

'It's a deal.' Linking her arm through his, she pulled him in the direction of a stall covered in bouquets and buttonholes. After the wedding at the hotel, they'd be having a couple of nights back at the cottage before heading off for a honeymoon in the States a few days later. Brae had promised her they'd find time in between to take her bouquet over to the churchyard where her parents were buried, even though it meant a three-hour round trip. Yellow roses had been her mother's favourite flowers and she was really keen to include them in her bouquet.

'I hope you're going to buy some of that fisherman's cord?' Brae pointed towards some rope that looked out of place on the stall and much heavier than the twine that was wrapped around the stems for some of the bouquets.

'What's it for?'

'The bride and groom each have a cord and when they're fastened together they represent the beginning of two lives becoming one.'

'That's right.' The woman behind the stall stood up, although it looked like it was a big effort. Her face was grey and almost waxy looking, and the smile she seemed to be forcing definitely hadn't reached her eyes. 'It's also where the expression *tying the knot* comes from and a fisherman's knot is supposed to be the most secure of all, so it's a Cornish tradition.'

'That's lovely.' Anna made a mental note to ask the hotel's event planner if they could include the knot tying into their plans. It would be a really nice way to bring Brae's love of Cornwall into the ceremony.

'I can also make knots from the same rope to go on your bouquet or even as buttonholes.' The woman swayed as she spoke, grabbing onto the edge of the stall to stop herself from falling forward.

'Are you okay?' Anna moved to the other side of the trestle table, catching hold of the woman's elbow and helping her to sit down again.

'I don't know.' The woman lowered her voice. 'I'm pregnant and I haven't been able to keep anything down for a few days.'

'How far along are you?' Anna caught the look of surprise that crossed the other woman's face. 'It's okay, I'm not just being nosy. My name's Anna. I'm a midwife at the unit in town. If you're local, you probably get your antenatal care with us?'

'I haven't got that far yet, I'm only six weeks. I've lost two babies before, one at seven weeks and one at nine. I didn't want to jinx things by booking in or telling anyone other than my husband. I thought it might be a bug when the sickness first started. All the books I've been reading say morning sickness doesn't start until about five or six weeks at the earliest, and I've had it for three weeks already. I can't help thinking something might be wrong.'

'Okay, sweetheart, I know how hard this is when you've been through so much in the past, but I want to try and put your mind at rest if I can.' Anna put a hand on her arm. She understood the desire to have a baby all too well, the feeling that you'd do anything, even keep it hidden from the rest of the world, if it meant the baby stuck around. She still had no idea if she'd miscarried back in January, or whether she'd never been pregnant at all, but either way it had hurt like hell. The same tortured look was reflected in this stranger's eyes. 'What's your name?'

'Miranda.' The woman gave her a watery smile. 'I'm so sorry. You're off work today, you shouldn't have to be dealing with this.'

'Don't worry, she's never really off duty and she likes it that way.' Brae's voice was warm. He didn't need to tell Anna how proud he was of her for her to know it. 'Do you want me to leave you to it? I'm sure the hotel can find you and Anna somewhere private to talk. I could go and ask them.'

'Actually, would you mind phoning my husband instead? If I do it, I might start crying and then he'll panic.' Miranda slid her phone across the stall. 'He's the top number in my contacts and the code's one, two, three, four. I know, I know, it's terrible! Tom's always telling me I've got to change it.'

'What do you want me to say?' Brae looked at the phone as if it was a hand grenade with the pin pulled out.

'Just that I'm with a midwife but I'm fine, and maybe ask him if he can come up a bit sooner than planned. He was going to take over from me on the stall after lunch, when it usually gets really busy. But I think I might need him now.'

'Okay, I'll go outside and call him, it's a bit too noisy in here.' Brae headed towards the door. 'I'll be back in a bit.'

'Your fiancé's lovely, when's the wedding?' Miranda turned back to Anna as she spoke.

'He is and not until July; we're having the wedding here.'

'It's a lovely venue. I go to a lot of places for these fairs and this is definitely one of my favourites.' Miranda managed a wobbly smile, but she was still far too pale for Anna's liking.

'Thank you, but I'm more worried about sorting you out right now. When you say you haven't managed to keep anything down for days, do you really mean *anything*?'

'As first I just went off food. But for the last twenty-four hours or so, I haven't even been able to keep water down.'

'We need to get you on some IV fluids as soon as possible in that case, something with electrolytes so we can get you back on an even keel.'

'I'm losing the baby, aren't I?' Miranda's eyes filled with tears again and this time they slid down her face. A few people had approached the stall, but luckily they seemed to have thought better of it and realised that now wasn't a good time to shop for bouquets and buttonholes.

'I can't say for certain without a scan, but it sounds to me like you've got hyperemesis gravidarum.' Anna squeezed her hand again. 'Don't look so worried, it's just the medical term for severe morning sickness. Unlike normal morning sickness, it tends to come on earlier in the pregnancy and it's not uncommon for it to start at three weeks, like it did for you.'

'Will it hurt the baby?'

'It's you we need to look after. There's some good news though. As horrible as it is, hyperemesis gravidarum is caused by higher than normal levels of the pregnancy hormone hCG. If you were losing the baby, those hormones would drop.'

'Oh my God, really?' Miranda leant forward in her seat, a tiny bit of colour coming back into her cheeks as she did. 'Tom and I want this baby so much and after losing the first two, I was convinced it was going to happen all over again. If my body couldn't even hold on to water, how could it hold on to the baby? I felt useless, when it's what a woman's body is supposed to be designed for. Does that make any sense at all, or am I as all over the place as I feel?'

'It makes perfect sense.' Anna stopped herself saying any more. It was her job to comfort her patients, not offload her problems on to them, but she understood exactly what Miranda meant; she knew how intoxicating hope could be. If things didn't work out, she needed Miranda to know that she wasn't to blame for that either. 'And losing the babies wasn't your fault.'

'It's just so hard to accept that there's no reason for it. In a way it'd be easier if there was something I could do differently this time around.' Miranda sighed. 'Do they know what causes the extreme sickness, is it something I've done? Something I'm eating that I shouldn't be?'

'No one really knows for sure what causes it, but it's definitely not something you can control. Sometimes it can have genetic links, and it's more common in multiple pregnancies, but mostly it seems to just be bad luck.'

'Would a scan this early be able to show if everything was okay?'

'They should be able to see the sac and there's quite a good chance they could see a heartbeat, even as early as this.'

'I've never even got that far before. By the time I went for scans, it was already too late.' Miranda wiped her eyes with the back of her hands. 'If they pick up a heartbeat, does that mean I'm less likely to miscarry?'

'It drops to about ten per cent if a heartbeat's picked up at this stage.' Anna didn't have to ask Miranda if she wanted a scan. 'I think the best thing we can do is get you admitted to the hospital for some IV fluids and see if we can arrange a scan at the early pregnancy unit at the same time.'

'I can't go without Tom. If the worst happens and he's not there... I just can't go through it again without him.'

'Of course not. Hopefully Brae will have managed to talk to him and we might even be able to get him to meet us there, to save time.' Anna looked up to see Brae crossing the ballroom. 'Talk of the devil.'

'Did you manage to speak to Tom? Was he okay?' Miranda attempted to get to her feet for a second time, but she started swaying again and Anna helped her back into the chair.

'He's fine and he's on his way.' Brae handed her the phone. 'More importantly, how are you doing?'

'Thanks to Anna, I'm not quite as panicky as I was.'

'We can drive you to the hospital and get Tom to meet us there?' The last thing Anna expected was for Miranda to shake her head.

'If I leave the stall now, I'll never get another pitch. It's taken me three years on the waiting list to get a slot at this fair and, like I said, it's probably the best one around.'

'I'll look after the stall while Anna takes you to the hospital.' Brae smiled. 'I'm not saying I know anything about floristry, but I'm used to dealing with customers and, if I know the prices of everything, I can at least take the money and write down the contact details of anyone who wants to place an order.'

'Are you sure?' Miranda widened her eyes as he nodded. 'If I had the energy, I'd give you a hug.'

'No thanks necessary. I can wait here until Tom gets back after the scan, or until the wedding fair finishes, if it takes that long.' Brae caught Anna's eye again. 'I'd want someone to do the same if Anna was in your situation.'

'You really are fantastic and the least I can do is make your wedding bouquet.' Miranda gestured towards the table. 'As well as the ones on display, there's a book with lots of other styles I can do.'

'Thank you so much, but I just want to get you to the hospital as soon as possible, so we can worry about everything else later.' Anna helped Miranda to her feet, putting an arm around her waist.

'I'll ask the people next door to watch your stall for five minutes, so I can help Anna get you out to the car.' Brae disappeared to speak to the couple running the neighbouring stall, who were selling personalised wedding favours. 'Right, they're going to watch it until I get back.'

Brae all but carried Miranda out to the lobby of the hotel and ran down to get the car, pulling it up right outside the front door and helping Anna to get her in.

'I really love you.' Anna kissed him briefly as he opened the driver's door for her.

'You too.' He tucked a stray strand of hair behind her ear as he spoke. 'I hope it all works out okay, you know, with the baby.'

'So do I.' As Anna slipped into the driver's seat, she couldn't help wondering if Brae was talking about more than just Miranda's baby. They hadn't done anything about the prospect of adoption yet, but every time she spoke to Brae about it, or showed him some of the research she'd done, she was more at peace with the idea of letting go of her original dream. Creating a family so purposefully took someone really special; Brae fitted the bill perfectly and he'd balance out any inadequacies she had. After the wedding they could start making plans to take things forward and start the assessment process. She just hoped she wouldn't experience the same doubts as Jess was having about fostering when the time came.

* * *

The sonographer ran the scanner across Miranda's stomach, as her husband Tom held on to her left hand. She was gripping the drip stand that was finally getting some fluid into her body with the other hand. Miranda had begged Anna to stay with them until after the scan and, positioned at the end of the bed, she saw what was on the screen before the sonographer even spoke.

'Okay, well the good news is I can see a heartbeat.' The sonographer turned the screen slightly, so Miranda and Tom could see the flickering heartbeat of their unborn baby. 'There's the first sac, with the heartbeat in it.'

'The first sac?' Miranda flashed Anna a look and she nodded, but the sonographer wasn't finished.

'Yes, there are two, but there's no heartbeat visible in the second sac yet.'

'Does that mean that one of the babies has died?' Miranda's voice caught on the last word. The poor woman had been through this twice before, and the pain of her previous losses was written all over her face.

'It might just be because it's too early to pick up the heartbeat yet.' Anna didn't want to give Miranda and Tom false hope, but she'd seen enough early pregnancy scans to know it was a strong possibility.

'Your midwife's right.' The sonographer nodded. 'It can mean that the embryo isn't viable, but it's more common at this stage for it to be because it's just too early. You could definitely still be looking at a twin pregnancy.'

'Twins!' Tom's face lit up with a mixture of excitement and terror, but Miranda shook her head.

'Let's not get too excited yet, it'll just make it worse.' She seemed to be gripping his hand all the harder. 'If the second baby doesn't turn out to have a heartbeat, does that mean I'm going to lose the other one, too?'

'Try not to worry about that.' Anna spoke softly. 'Like I said before, seeing a heartbeat cuts the risk of miscarriage down to ten per cent. It's all really positive so far, so just try to hold on to that.'

'That's right.' The sonographer smiled as Tom stood up and shook her hand. Anna could almost feel the love between him and Miranda filling the room, and their sheer joy at finally getting a step closer to the baby they'd been longing for was obvious. Miranda was probably ten years younger than her, and Anna couldn't help wishing for the thousandth time that she'd found Brae earlier. There was nothing more pointless than wishing she could change the past, though. She had so much to be happy about and they had so many exciting plans for the future. The wedding was just around the corner and sharing his surname might seem like an old-fashioned gesture to a lot of people, but it would be another sign they belonged together. The Penroses, whether that was two, three, four, or a menagerie of ten – with dogs, cats and a tortoise – it would be *their family name*. And the only thing Anna would have changed was to have the wedding even sooner.

12

Anna set down the tray of hot drinks on the desk. Toni was in one of the delivery suites, assisted by Bobby, supporting a second-time mum-to-be whose labour appeared to be going perfectly to plan. Gwen was out doing home visits, which left Anna, Ella and Jess in the staffroom. Anna was running a clinic that was due to start in less than twenty minutes. It meant she had just enough time to grab a drink with the others, assuming no one came into the unit with an emergency, or because they'd gone into labour.

'What's on the menu for the wedding breakfast, then?' Ella took the tea that Anna passed her.

'We're going for pan-fried hake, smoked hock of ham, or wild garlic mushrooms for the first course, then topside of beef, slow-roast pork belly, or spinach ravioli for the main course, and there are three or four dessert courses, all served with either Cornish ice cream or clotted cream, of course!' Anna's stomach grumbled as she reeled off the list. She'd burned the porridge she'd made for breakfast, too distracted by an email from the hotel to even notice the smell of scorched oats and milk until it was too late. She'd never have pictured herself as the sort of person who got so fixated by the small details, but planning the wedding was definitely taking over of late and it was just one more reminder of how much she missed her mum.

'Were the choices all down to Brae, or did you get back to the hotel in time in the end?' Ella broke a chocolate digestive in half, dunking it into her tea.

'Once the sonographer at the Early Pregnancy Unit told Miranda everything looked okay, I dropped her home with her husband and went back to the hotel. Poor old Brae had been manning the stall all afternoon, and he'd almost filled the order book by the time I got there. So he's got a backup plan if the fish and chip shop ever goes belly up!'

'You know when someone says: "*so and so is the salt of the earth, they'd do anything for anyone*", they really are talking about you and Brae.' Jess smiled. 'Dom probably wouldn't have given up his Saturday afternoon rugby, even if I'd been the one having a pregnancy scan, let alone him doing it for a total stranger.'

'Is he still messaging you?' Jess had confided in Anna that there'd been a lot more messages from Dom since she'd decided to foster and she had a horrible feeling it was contributing to Jess's wobbles about the whole thing.

'I think he must have split up with that girl from work and he seems to think there's still a chance for us.'

'And is there?' Ella took the words out of Anna's mouth.

'No...' Jess hesitated for a moment. 'I miss him sometimes, but I don't know if that's because I actually miss him, or whether it's the whole package of his family that I miss. His mum and dad were always so lovely to me and I sometimes find myself driving in the direction of their house for a cup of tea after work, and for his mum to tell me it will all be okay however bad my day has been.'

'You can come over to mine any time you have one of those

days.' Anna might have been less than a decade older than Jess, but she suddenly felt strangely maternal towards her.

'You know I'm going to take you up on that, don't you?'

'The same offer goes for me.' Ella smiled. 'And sometimes I have leftover cakes from the bakery!'

'Hey, that's not fair, how am I supposed to compete with that?' Anna rolled her eyes. 'I'll just have to come to yours for tea and cake with Jess, and we can all put the world to rights together.'

'Now there's an offer I can't refuse.' Jess looked resolute. 'You can start by helping me find a good solicitor. I think the only way Dom and I are both going to move on, is if we make things official and I think it'll help with the foster panel's decision too.'

'No more doubts about going through the assessment process then?' Anna couldn't help smiling at how vigorously Jess was shaking her head.

'No, I'm definitely doing it. I know it's going to be hard, reliving a lot of the stuff I went through, but nothing worth doing ever comes easy, does it?'

'It really doesn't and you're going to make so much difference, Jess.' Anna gave her a hug. 'And we're here for you whenever you need us, aren't we, Ella?'

'Absolutely and with as many cakes from Mehenicks' bakery as you can face!' The fact that Jess could make two such life-changing decisions all by herself couldn't help but inspire Anna. The wedding plans might be in danger of taking over her life, but there was no excuse for her not to email a few adoption agencies, just to get some more information. The next meeting of the infertility support group, which was coming up soon, would be a chance to talk more about the option with Jess and other women who really understood. Suddenly she didn't want to wait until the wedding was over to take the next step in her life with Brae.

* * *

Tamara Scott's cheekbones would have put a supermodel to shame. Even with her neat little baby bump, which looked nothing like the average full-term pregnancy, there wasn't an ounce of spare flesh on her. Her hip bones might have all-but disappeared as she lay down on the examination table, but her ribs were still clearly visible and when she sat up again after Anna had run all the checks, even Tamara's backbone pressed against the skin of her back.

'Everything looks okay with the baby, although she might be a bit on the small side, but nothing you need to worry about.' Anna gave Tamara what she hoped was a reassuring smile, but it didn't stop the younger woman's eyes looking so sad.

'I've been trying to eat, I really have. I just find it so hard.'

'You're doing great. You've gained twenty-six pounds so far, that's only two pounds off the target we set and you've still got two weeks to go.' Anna had gone back through the notes before Tamara's appointment. She'd spent the last twenty years, since turning thirteen, battling eating disorders of one type or another. She'd been hospitalised several times due to anorexia and it had left her with a number of problems, including a stark warning from her doctor that she'd never be able to have a baby unless she gained weight. As a result she'd put all her efforts into trying to get healthy to have a baby with her husband, Luke. The struggle with her body image had continued, though, and she'd been bulimic right up until the pregnancy was confirmed. The demons she was fighting didn't disappear overnight just because she was pregnant.

'My consultant said I should aim for closer to forty pounds, because I was so underweight to start with.' Tamara wrung her hands in her lap. Sometimes Anna could happily swing for consultants who gave out such prescriptive advice, without really seeing the woman sitting in front of them. For Tamara, gaining twenty-six pounds was the equivalent of climbing Mount Everest. She'd had cognitive behavioural therapy for the body dysmorphia she'd suffered as a teenager, but she still battled with obsessive behaviours and there was a risk that being pregnant could trigger a relapse.

'Pushing yourself too hard, too fast, is only likely to have a negative effect in the end. You're doing exactly the right thing, taking it slowly and trying to gradually increase the amount you're eating.'

'I'll never forgive myself if the baby has any problems because of me. I want it all to be perfect for her, and for her childhood to be everything mine wasn't.'

Tamara's anxiety seemed to stem from her problematic start in life. She'd told Anna enough about it for her to feel almost guilty that her childhood had been so idyllic. Jess was better placed to understand how much impact this could have. Even now Tamara's past was blighting her present and Anna's was pretty much perfect in comparison. She just wished she could do more to help her come to terms with it all, but sometimes it was a challenge to even get her to open up.

'How are you finding being off your medication?' Tamara had been taking anti-anxiety medication prior to falling pregnant and had stopped overnight when she'd got the positive test. It wasn't what her doctors or Anna would have recommended, and there were other medications she could safely take during the pregnancy, but Tamara wouldn't hear of it. She was working as hard as anyone Anna had ever met to turn her life around for the sake of her unborn baby, but she still seemed desperately fragile.

'Some days are more difficult than others, I'm not going to lie.' Tamara swallowed so hard it was audible. 'But I don't want to risk

Belle's health by pumping her body full of second-hand medication.'

'It doesn't have to be like that, there are—' Anna barely got the chance to start the sentence before Tamara cut her off.

'I know what you're going to say; that there are some medications I could take. The thing is, I've always used them because they take the edge off life, you know? They dull things and blur it all, not just the tough bits. But when Belle comes, I don't want that. I don't want the edges to be blurred, or not to remember the details of those first few weeks and months. Some people can take medication and function perfectly normally, but it's never been that way for me. Up until now, I didn't want it to be.'

'I can understand that.' Anna wanted to give Tamara a hug, but she looked as if an overly enthusiastic embrace could snap her in two. Not to mention the fact that it might have made it harder to stay professional. 'Are you still having therapy sessions?'

'Twice a week. I don't know where I'd have been without that,' Tamara looked across at her, 'and without your support. I just wish I could have the baby here at the unit, with you.'

'I know. I wish I could be there with you, too. But the consultant has recommended a hospital delivery and I think it's probably the safest option to make sure you get everything you need. I'll be straight in to see you and Belle as soon as I hear she's arrived, though!'

'You'll be really welcome, but I won't be saying the same for everyone.' Tamara wrapped her arms around her bump, as if offering the baby an extra layer of protection. 'I'm going to tell them on the ward that if my parents show up, they're to be sent away.'

'It's up to you who you allow onto the ward and who you involve in Belle's life, so you've got every right to make that decision.' Anna couldn't see any winners in the situation. Tamara had burst into tears during their very first consultation and it had all come out. She'd never forgiven her parents for sending her to boarding school at the age of seven, when her brother had come along. According to Tamara, he'd been the golden child, the son her parents had always wanted, and he'd never been sent away to school.

Tamara had described spending most of her first year at boarding school crying, making her an easy a target for bullies as a result. She blamed the years of relentless bullying that ensued, and what she saw as her parents' rejection, for causing her eating disorders. When Tamara had first told Anna about her childhood, she'd said that food was the only thing she was in control of and so she'd used it bury her emotions.

Maybe there was more to her parents' decision than Tamara's interpretation, but it was something she'd decided she could never get past, and their regular attempts to try and build bridges just seemed to make things worse. Anna would have given anything to sit down and have one last conversation with her parents, and a big part of her was willing Tamara to change her mind and give her mum and dad another chance. But that wasn't her job. It wasn't even her therapist's job to tell Tamara what to do. All they could do was be there to listen, and support her and the baby. Only time would tell if Belle's maternal grandparents would ever get a chance to meet her. Tamara might be right, they might not even deserve the chance to get to know their grandchild. Not everyone experienced the unconditional love from their parents that Anna had never once doubted, but that's what family was all about. It was more than DNA; she'd seen enough evidence of that in her job. Families came in all shapes and sizes, and they all looked different, but the happy ones all had one thing in common – they had love. And thankfully it looked like Tamara had finally found it too.

'Luke's parents are going to do a great job of being grandparents. They raised a man patient enough to put up with someone as crazy as me! So we can't go wrong if we follow their example.'

'You're not crazy and you've got to stop giving yourself such a hard time. You've made loads of changes so you can give Belle the best possible start, and you should be really proud of everything you've done.'

'Now you sound like Luke! But it means a lot hearing that.' Tamara paused for a moment. 'Just in case this is the last time I see you before Belle arrives, would it be really inappropriate to ask for a hug?'

'I thought you'd never ask.' Anna held out her arms as the younger woman stepped forward. It was moments like these that made her fall in love with midwifery all over again. Being there to share the most amazing journey another woman would have, even if she never got to experience the whole of that journey for herself, still made her a million times luckier than most. Giving birth was such a small part of being a mother. God knows there were enough women, maybe even Tamara's mother, who'd done that but who didn't deserve to be parents at all. And that's where she and Brae could step in. They just needed the chance.

13

Brae carried another box down from the loft, where he'd put them all at Anna's instruction when she'd first moved in.

'What's in this one?' He smiled that easy smile of his and Anna's heart immediately lifted. The prospect of going through the boxes filled with possessions from her parents' house, which she hadn't been able to bear to throw away, would have been so much harder without him. There'd been some things that she'd kept out on display in every house she'd lived in since – everything from the camper van biscuit tin to the pair of silver lovebirds that her father had bought for her mother on their twenty-fifth wedding anniversary. A lot of the other stuff was just shoved into boxes and it was finally time to decide if she could let some of it go.

'It's probably just more of Mum's books. She could never throw any away, it was one of the millions of things she thought was unlucky. She'd never put new shoes or her house keys on the table, and if she saw a single magpie she had to keep her fingers crossed until she saw a four-legged animal.' Anna shook her head. 'Not that it did her any good in the end. Bad luck, in the shape of cancer, found her anyway. I took loads of her books down to the charity shop after Dad died too, but I couldn't bear to part with her favourites, the ones she kept on the bookcase in her bedroom.'

'I can easily put some more bookshelves up in the office.' Brae moved behind her and put his arms around her waist. 'It might make me look a bit more intellectual. Instead of just filling them with the single shelf of books I've got, amongst the stacks of flyers for the fish and chip shop.'

'You're perfect as you are and I never want you to change.' Anna spun around in the circle of his arms to face him. 'I'm so lucky that I get to spend the rest of my life with you.'

'I'm the lucky one.' Brae kissed her and it would have taken absolutely no persuasion for her to forget about unpacking the boxes, but he pulled away and groaned. 'Anna Jones, if you only knew the things you do to me! It's a good job you're not around all the time, or I'd never get anything done, but you've got to be at work in an hour and I don't want to end up giving Ella anything you want to keep.'

'Maybe we should save ourselves for the honeymoon now, anyway?' Anna laughed at the look of horror that crossed Brae's face. He was right, though. It wouldn't be fair of her to expect him to sort through the boxes and decide what to give Ella when she came over later. She'd asked them if there was anything they could donate as stock for the eBay shop she'd set up as her latest fundraising venture for the lifeboat station. 'Come on then, let's sort through it all.'

Brae slid a knife carefully down the tape that sealed one of the boxes and pulled out the first book. 'It's a Beatrix Potter, *The Tale of Squirrel Nutkin*, and it looks like there's lots more in here.'

'She had the whole collection, she used to read them to me when I was a kid.' Anna felt a warm glow at the memory and smiled. It was amazing to finally be able to think about the good times without being blindsided with a pang of longing that overwhelmed the memory. 'They weren't just bedtime stories, either. I'd climb into bed with her in the mornings on the days when I didn't have school; we'd snuggle up together and she'd read to me. I loved it.'

'It sounds perfect and there's no way we're getting rid of any of these books. They're getting a shelf all of their own and not hidden away in the study either. I'll ask Dan if he can recommend someone to make shelves for the alcove in the living room, so they can take pride of place.' Brae handed her the first book and pulled out another one and she felt another huge surge of affection for the man standing in front of her. For some people, romance meant huge bouquets, or jewellery judged by its price tag. But this was real romance, Brae's gentle thoughtfulness that never needed any prompting.

'Thank you.'

'What for?'

'For everything, for being you.' She squeezed his hand, as he passed her another book, two photographs fluttering out from between the pages.

Picking them up, he handed them to her. 'Is this your mum and dad?'

'Uh-huh.' They were tiny little photographs, much smaller even than the old Polaroids her father had taken of her in the mid-eighties when she'd been a toddler. One picture was of her mum standing by a road sign, and the other one was of her dad.

'Do you recognise where they were taken?' Brae looked over her shoulder, as she turned the first photograph over.

'No, but that's Mum's writing on the back.' It was as familiar to Anna as her own. There, in her mother's distinctive loopy handwriting, were the words *1974 Rest and Be Thankful trip*, and on the other *1972 Once Brewed/Twice Brewed trip.*

'Are those some sort of tours? The second one sounds like a beer festival.'

'No, I'm pretty certain they're village names.' Anna's mind was working overtime. 'You remember I told you about the trips we used to do in Vanna, our camper van? We'd find the weirdest sounding places we could in Dad's road atlas and plan our next trip there. It looks like they were doing it long before I came along.'

'In the camper?'

'No, they didn't get that until I was eleven, but we had an old tent before that, the sort you'd expect to see army cadets use. Mum said they'd had it ever since they were married, but I never thought they'd started the road trips back then too.' Anna looked at the photographs again, trying to work out if her parents' early road trips somehow diminished the times they'd shared together as a family – one of the things that had made them the three musketeers.

'Are you okay, sweetheart?'

'I just always thought that was our tradition, a family thing that no one in the world but the three of us did.'

'It was.' Brae put his arm around her shoulders. 'They just started it when they were a family of two and carried on when they were a family of three, or four if you count Vanna.'

'How did you get to be so brilliant?' Anna looked up at him, loving him even more than she'd done five minutes before. He'd made sense of it all in an instant. Not just the fact that her parents had shared those wonderful times together, even before they'd shared them with her – making precious memories that money couldn't buy – but because it had made her realise something even more important. Her parents had already been a family, before she ever came along. When you found the right person, all you needed to make a family was the two of you, and Anna knew beyond any doubt that she'd already found hers.

* * *

Ella ran her hand down the last page of names. 'Two thousand and thirty-seven, two thousand and thirty-eight, two thousand and thirty-nine. Not bad, but we need to get to 10,000 signatures before the government will respond. So I think we're going to have to take it online.'

'Can the government do anything? I thought the lifeboat station was funded by the RNLI?' Dan's voice drifted across from the other side of the room, but she didn't look up.

'They get a tiny percentage of their funding from government sources, but it's more about raising the profile of the whole campaign and getting MPs to lobby the RNLI to keep the lifeboat station open. It worked in Ceredigion.' Ella had been researching other lifeboat stations under threat and the Ceredigion MP had got involved in lobbying the chief exec of the RNLI when they were going to lose their all-weather lifeboat. So there was no reason it couldn't work for Port Agnes, especially as there was a small chance it could result in more funding from the government too. 'I don't suppose the charity wants to lose the lifeboat station any more than we do, but they have to make tough decisions when they only get so much funding. I want to raise as much as I can to change their minds.'

'God you're sexy when you're campaigning!' Dan came up behind her and wrapped his arms around her waist. 'It's why I fell in love with you in the first place, you're always trying to make the world a better place, and nothing gets me going like a woman with a spreadsheet full of signatures!'

'Carry on talking like that and you'll be sleeping in the spare room until August!' She spun around to face him. If he was going to pretend to give her a hard time, then two could play at that game. 'And there I was, planning to celebrate getting 500 signatures in the last two days alone, by taking off an item of clothing for every hundred signatures.'

'That's an unconventional campaign tactic, but I like it.' Dan slid a hand inside her jumper and she sighed, wishing they had time to carry on what they'd started.

'While I fully intend to fulfil *all* my campaign promises, I haven't got time to deliver on that particular one right now.'

'Disappointing, but I get it.' Dan pulled her closer to him. 'Joking aside, I'm really proud of you for doing all of this. I can't believe how much you've got organised in such a short time.'

'Half term seemed to be a really good time to try and get the kids involved.' Ella leant her head against his shoulder. 'Although a biscuit baking contest with a room full of kids is suddenly feeling like a crazy idea.'

'It'll be great and it was really nice of the school to let you use their food tech classroom.'

'The coxswain's wife is the head of year seven, so she managed to swing it. I just hope I can keep control of the room.'

'Their parents are going to be there, aren't they?'

'Uh-huh, but I've seen how competitive some parents can get about their kids, so it's the parents who worry me more.'

'It'll be brilliant, don't worry. I'll be there and some of the others are going, aren't they?'

'Anna and Brae are coming down to do the judging with Mum and Dad. Toni and Jess are on call, but they're going to come down for a bit if they can, and Bobby's bringing his niece.' Ella glanced at the clock. 'We'd better get going, it's nearly half past.'

'I'm glad your dad's going to be there. I need to have a word with him.' Dan picked up his keys.

'What are you two cooking up now?' Ella couldn't help smiling. When she'd first met Dan, her father had been less than impressed. As an incomer, or an emmet, as Jago liked to call them, Dan represented everything her father railed against. But, when they'd reconnected, Dan had managed to prove himself worthy and it had become obvious to her father that no one worked harder to preserve the heritage of Port Agnes than Dan, and now the two of them were as thick as thieves.

'Never you mind. You'll find out when it's time.' Dan tapped the side of his nose. Whatever it was they were plotting would have to wait. There was a room full of kids waiting to start baking biscuits and Ella wasn't coming home until she had at least another hundred signatures on her petition. It was because of the lifeboat crew that she still had Dan, and she'd do whatever it took to save their station.

* * *

The smell of freshly baked biscuits was making Ella's stomach rumble so loudly that Anna turned to look at her.

'Did you skip lunch again?'

'I was too worried about how this was going to go.' It seemed silly now, looking out at the flushed faces of the children anxiously peering through the doors of their ovens every thirty seconds or so. The prize for the winning batch of biscuits was a family pass – and a chance to meet and feed the rescue donkeys – at Trelawney Farm and Adventure Playground, which was just off the main road between Port Agnes and Port Kara. All of the children taking part would also be given a goody bag.

The prizes had been donated, and the families taking part

had each paid £20 to enter. There was a raffle and donation box too, so Ella was hoping to add at least another £300 to the fundraising pot. There was a chance they could have made more just by auctioning off the prize, but spreading the word and collecting as many signatures as possible was more important. A biscuit baking contest would generate some great pictures for the social media pages she was going to set up too, and that was definitely going to be their best chance of hitting the magic ten thousand signatures.

'The kids are having a brilliant time.' Anna gestured towards a little girl who was dropping Smarties onto the mountain of icing she'd already piled on top of her biscuits.

'Almost as good as my dad!' Ella could see Jago moving between the tables, telling all the children how amazing their biscuits looked, and she'd overheard him telling at least three of them that he'd never tasted anything so delicious. He was Port Agnes' answer to Paul Hollywood, except he was far more generous with his praise.

'Christmas at your house must have been amazing when you were little. I bet you got to make gingerbread houses and all sorts.' Anna turned towards her.

'It was. Dad always made a big thing of Christmas and all the Cornish traditions of course, and as for the food... well, you can imagine! When Dan spent his first Christmas with us, he couldn't get off the sofa for about three hours after we'd finished dinner. Last year it hit him almost as hard. So he reckons he's going into training to prepare for this year. Luckily he's still got six months to go!'

'That sounds like a good plan!'

'Maybe you should have got in training for judging the contest today. A lot of the biscuits seem to have about three times as much topping as biscuit.'

'It'll be fine.' Anna laughed. 'I mean it's a hard job, but some-body's got to do it!'

* * *

Anna had been confident that she had, by far, the best job of all the volunteers, but an hour later, she'd have eaten her words if she could stand the thought of one more morsel passing her lips.

Brae let out a low whistle. 'I can handle a sugar rush with the best of them, but judging those biscuits nearly finished me off!'

'Me too, but you did a great job seeing as I hit breaking point about two-thirds of the way through. It was really sweet of you to make sure all the kids got a prize today.' Anna caught hold of Brae's hand as they headed back towards their cottage. It was typical of him to order a medal for all the children who'd taken part, to go with their goody bags of sweets. He'd also bought a trophy in the shape of a whisk for the overall winner, so that they'd have something to remember the day by once they used their pass to the farm. His reputation as the nicest guy around wasn't going away any time soon.

'They all did so well and it's just a bit of fun, isn't it? Ella's campaign is whipping up a great sense of community spirit, as well as helping save the lifeboat station.'

'She's been amazing, but I feel guilty that I haven't done more to help.' As Anna spoke, Brae pulled her towards him.

'You, my beautiful, brilliant fiancée, are running a midwifery unit, pulling together a wedding and turning up and helping out at every event Ella comes up with. Not to mention making an oaf like me the happiest man in the world. Do you know how often I look at you and can't believe how lucky I am that someone like you would even look in my direction?'

'Don't be ridiculous. I'm the lucky one.' Anna closed the space between them, enjoying the warmth of his lips as they met hers. She didn't want to be anywhere else, with anyone else, but she'd been dying to talk to him ever since she'd opened the email from the adoption agency that morning. They finally had some time on their own, so now was as good a time as any. 'I heard back from the adoption agency today.'

'That was quick.' Brae searched her face and she nodded.

'It was just information giving, but I sent them a list of questions and they answered all of them. Shall we sit down?' She gestured towards the bench that looked out across the water towards the Sisters of Agnes Island.

'Is it a sitting down sort of conversation?'

'I'm just not sure I can walk and tell you all the information on the way home, I'm not as good at getting up the hills as I used to be as it is!'

'You make it sound like you're eighty. If we had a race, you'd be home and back again before I was even halfway there.' Brae took hold of her hand as they sat down. 'Come on then, tell me all about it. Am I going to need to get fit enough to run home to pass the medical to be an adoptive parent?'

'That's one question I didn't ask them.' Anna squeezed his hand. 'The good news is that we seem to meet the eligibility to adopt.'

'What is it?'

'To be honest I was quite surprised about how open they were. I was worried about my age.'

'Well there's a surprise.' Brae shook his head, but his tone was gentle.

'I know, I know, but I thought it might count against us, or mean they'd only let us adopt an older child, but it doesn't make a difference.'

'That's great.'

'Uh-huh.' Anna looked at the floor, still trying to work out how she felt about what she was going to say next.

'What aren't you telling me? This is all great news as far as I can tell.'

'My age doesn't make a difference to our chances of adopting a baby, because they're almost non-existent anyway.' Anna met his gaze and it was her turn to try and read his expression. 'The social worker from the charity said that most of the children they place are quite a bit older and they've usually been through the care system and had a really tough time of things before the court makes an adoption order.'

'They sound like exactly the sort of children who deserve to have a mother like you.'

'Do you think we could really do it?' Anna had reread the second to last paragraph in the social worker's email at least ten times:

Not everyone makes a good adopter; lots of the children have complex needs and carry their earlier traumas with them. As such, you'll need to be resilient, incredibly patient and empathetic, but with the right support most of the children settle into their new families with time.

'You can do anything you put your mind to and I know whatever decision we make about this – going ahead with applying to adopt, or not – it'll be the right one, and for all the right reasons too.'

'I wish I had as much confidence in myself as you do.'

'That, my darling, is just about the only thing I'm better at than you.' Brae kissed her gently and then pulled away again. 'There's no need to rush into any decision, is there? Let's just enjoy the fact that it's another option we've got.'

'I've got to admit it is quite nice not to hear the tick tock of time running out for once.' There had been a real shift in Anna's mindset over the last few weeks, and it was all down to Brae. He'd made her realise that she'd already found her family, even if it was just the two of them. It was his encouragement that had made her take the first step in setting up the infertility support group and sharing her experiences with Jess and the others, which had opened her heart and her mind up to the possibility of adoption. She already owed him more than she could ever repay and she finally felt excited about the wedding and their future together beyond that, without a shadow hanging over her.

'I'm going to make the most of every moment I've got you to myself.' Brae pulled her to her feet. 'I might even be able to motivate myself to start jogging home. That way, I could have a six-pack by the time we decide whether to adopt or not.'

'Let's just stick to walking for now.' Anna leant into him. He was right, there was no need to rush into anything. She just hoped he was right about everything else too, and that she'd know what the best decision was. The only thing worse than the thought of letting Brae down was the prospect of letting a child down too.

14

Anna's last appointment of the day was a booking-in appointment with a patient called Lucille Dench. The first appointment with any new mums-to-be took a lot longer than most of the others and Anna would spend the time finding out about Lucille's medical history, as well as outlining the types of tests she would be offered in the first ten weeks of her pregnancy. One of the most important things Anna would cover was what support Lucille had at home and she'd also try to gently unpick whether there might be any issues. Sadly domestic violence tended to escalate during pregnancy and sometimes the booking-in appointment was the expectant mother's only chance of getting the help she needed to escape from a dangerous situation, before it was too late.

'Lucy! I had no idea it was going to be you!' Anna got to her feet as her friend from the infertility support group came into the room. 'Are you okay with me being the one to book you in, as I can always ask one of the other midwives if not?'

'I know, no one calls me Lucille unless it's something official and I don't think I know anyone's surname from the support group. But I'm okay with it, if you are?' Lucy's voice was quiet and she could barely seem to make eye contact with Anna.

'Of course, I'm so thrilled for you and I couldn't think of a better way to end the day. Come on in and take a seat.' Anna smiled, but Lucy still looked strangely deflated. 'Are you okay?'

'I just feel so bad.'

'What's wrong? Is it nausea?'

'No, I mean I feel bad because I'm coming in here and telling you I'm pregnant, when I know everyone else in our group is still struggling. I feel so guilty, especially because I didn't even have to have the treatment.'

'Oh Lucy, don't feel guilty.' Anna didn't care if it wasn't protocol and she didn't even ask permission before giving Lucy a hug; sometimes it was the only thing that would do. 'I'm so happy for you and the baby clearly has excellent timing! You were due to start treatment last week, weren't you?'

'My periods have never really recovered from so many years of using the contraceptive implant, when I thought falling pregnant would be so easy.' Lucy managed a half-smile at last. 'So the IVF clinic have been tracking my cycle to try and work out when I should start the fertility drugs. They gave me a pregnancy test, just as a precaution, and it came back positive.'

'That's amazing!'

'I don't think it's sunk in yet. They kept telling us there was almost no chance of conceiving naturally with Henry's sperm count the way it was.' Lucy let go of a long breath. 'I just keep thinking it must be a mistake and I can't let myself get excited in case it doesn't stick.'

'Oh sweetheart, I know it's hard when you've wanted this for so long, but these things happen a lot more often than you think.' There was a tiny part of Anna that was aware she was trying to convince herself, almost as much as she was trying to convince

Lucy. Miracles happened all the time. 'I think the research shows that nearly a fifth of women end up falling pregnant naturally in the six years after they stop having IVF treatment. So it stands to reason that there must be quite a few who fall pregnant whilst they're waiting too.'

'But it's not going to happen for Jacinda, is it? She keeps texting me to ask how it's all going and she's going out to Ukraine after our next get-together.' Lucy's mouth turned down at the corners. 'If the surrogate falls pregnant, she's got to pretend to her husband's family that she's carrying the baby herself. How crazy is that? She's the one who could have used a miracle, because I've had nothing but support from my family and Henry's, but she's not suddenly going to grow a new womb, is she?'

'Jacinda would hate the idea of you not being able to feel excited about the baby, because of everything she's going through.' For a split second Anna thought about admitting that Lucy's news had actually given her a tiny bit of hope. It proved that things weren't always black and white when it came to fertility, but confessing to a tiny bit of hope out loud was a risk. Anna had to keep it damped down. She'd come so far in accepting what might never be, with Brae's support; she never wanted to go back to feeling that something she might not ever have was the only way she could be happy.

'Tara said pretty much the same when I rang to say I wouldn't be coming to the support group meeting at her house this week.'

'You're not going to come any more?' It felt as if a weight had settled on Anna's chest as Lucy shook her head. 'I hope you change your mind. Jess is thinking about leaving too, now that she's decided to foster. But we set up the group to be there to support each other and, for me, none of that changes when one of us gets closer to becoming a mother. One way or another.'

'Are you still thinking of adoption?'

'We're talking about it...'

'But?' Lucy raised an eyebrow and Anna shrugged.

'It takes a special kind of person to adopt, so it's not something to rush into without really thinking it through.'

'Well you're definitely up to the job if that's what you decide to do; you've made me feel a hundred times better already.' Lucy's smile finally looked genuine. 'Now the only thing I'm dreading is having to be weighed! I lost three stone so they'd let me start the IVF treatment, but I'm still way off where I really should be.'

'You did brilliantly to lose all of that weight and it might have made all the difference.' Anna opened Lucy's file on the computer. 'Don't stress about anything like that, we can make a plan for what will be a healthy weight gain for you for the pregnancy, but the best thing you can do is relax and enjoy it as much as possible. So we'll start off with the easy bit and check your address and medical history, then I can take your blood pressure and run you through the tests we recommend. If you agree to them all, I'll take some blood too. I'm guessing you're not too worried about needles, after all the preparations for the IVF?'

'I was about to be turned into a pin cushion during treatment, so I think I'm getting off really lightly.' Lucy smiled again. 'I'd like to stay in the group if no one minds and I just hope me and Jess will be the start of a clean sweep, so that we can turn it into a mother and toddler group at some stage!'

'That would be great.' Anna nodded, trying to get the image of a chubby red-haired toddler out of her mind. If she and Brae adopted, they'd almost certainly be bypassing that stage of parenthood. If she couldn't be more like Jess and accept that an alternative route to parenthood meant letting go of some expectations – with rewards that would far outweigh that – then she didn't have what it took to adopt. Whatever Lucy might think.

It was painful to admit that she might not have what it took, but she'd supported mothers-to-be before who were suddenly gripped by the fear that they might not love the baby they were carrying, and worse still that they might not even like it. She always reassured them that the bonding would come, even if it wasn't instant. Caring for a newborn, who relied on you totally, was such an integral part of that, but adoption could mean skipping to the middle. She had to be certain that the perfect family picture she'd spent so long building up wouldn't blind her to the gift of adoption. The children out there waiting for a family deserved the sort her parents had given her, and she wouldn't step forward until she was certain she could deliver.

* * *

'You don't really want me to wear that, do you?' Anna picked up the stretchy black and white body-con dress that Jess had laid out on the table in front of her.

'It's sexy. Anyway, have you seen what the boys are wearing?' Jess raised her eyebrows. 'I could have got us matching inflatable sumo wrestlers' outfits if I'd known you'd prefer that.'

'It's just that I would have worn my Spanx if I'd known.' The packaging on the outfit described it as a *'classy convict costume'*. Was there such a thing as a classy convict? Either way, it came with an accompanying plastic ball and chain, and a matching black-and-white hat. 'Are we all wearing the same thing?'

'No, I thought you should stand out. You are the bride after all!' Jess grinned. 'The rest of us have got orange jumpsuits. I'll open the first bottle of Prosecco to help get us in the mood.'

'Okay.' Anna picked up the dress again as Jess disappeared to pour the drinks. It was going to take more than one glass of Prosecco for her to feel comfortable wearing this.

'Sorry, maybe I shouldn't have delegated organising the hen

night outfits to Jess. I thought it would just be a sparkly L-plate, or a tiara with a veil that you could ditch when you've had enough.' Ella gave her a sympathetic smile.

'It might not be my thing, but it's lovely that she's gone to all this trouble and I know how busy you've been with the fundraising.' Anna was determined to have the best night ever, even if it might take most of the bottle before she felt brave enough to put on the dress. She didn't have sisters, a mum, or even an aunt to invite along to her hen night, but being surrounded by so many good friends who wanted to make the night special, was definitely the next best thing.

'For what it's worth, I think you'll look great. If I was marrying Brae, and had access to unlimited fish and chips, I probably wouldn't be able to leave the house without the help of a forklift truck.'

'The orange jumpsuit would have clashed with my hair anyway.' Anna's wavy red hair meant she'd never have been able to get lost in the crowd, even if she hadn't been wearing skintight black-and-white stripes. 'Although I'm glad you and Dan organised the joint hen and stag do itself. I'm not sure I'd have coped with what Jess might have come up with.'

'So you didn't fancy drinking shots off a male stripper's washboard abs?' Ella laughed. 'There's just no pleasing some people.'

'In that case, I'll make sure you get a hen night to remember. I'm thinking naked waiters, dare cards you have to act out with strangers, and a giant willy-shaped cake, just for starters.'

'You can read me like a book!' Ella looked at Anna, as they both started laughing again. 'But you do know you'll have to fulfil your promise to organise it, if I ever do get married. I'm making you maid of honour, even if you're seventy-three by then.'

'Dan would ask you tomorrow if he thought you'd say yes.'

'I wouldn't count on it.' Ella rolled her eyes. 'I've told him so many times that I don't think I'd ever be able to do it again after what happened last time, I've probably put him off for life.'

'Have you changed your mind? If you have, you could always ask him.'

'I don't think—'

'Prosecco ladies!' Jess came into the room balancing a tray with cocktail glasses filled to the brim, breaking off their conversation.

'Why is it purple?' Anna eyed the glass suspiciously. She couldn't remember what had happened after the end of the New Year's Eve party that Jess had thrown the year before, or even getting to midnight come to that, and it had all started with a similarly colourful-looking cocktail.

'There's sloe gin mixed in with the Prosecco. I made the gin myself.' Jess swirled the drink around the glass. 'I can be quite the domestic goddess, as long as I've got the right motivation.'

'Is this what we had on New Year's Eve?' Anna wanted to remember her hen night, and not just from a series of photos she had an increasingly hazy recollection of even being in.

'No, that was Parma violet gin and champagne. Much more potent than this; you'll be fine. Anyway, I've got to make the most of being the queen of the cocktails, because once I start fostering this will all be a thing of the past.' Jess thrust a glass towards her just as there was a knock at the front door.

'That'll be Toni, I'll get it.' Anna passed her glass to Ella, glad to escape before Jess could suggest they downed it in one.

'Sorry I'm a bit late.' Toni was clutching two bottles in each hand – a potentially risky move – but it was Anna's jaw that hit the floor.

'You look a-maz-ing!' Toni was barely recognisable. Her hair had been transformed from a mid-brown, mid-length bob, to a black and silver graduated cut. Her eyebrows looked like the sort that teenage girls spent hours perfecting before they went out, and she had false lashes that went on for days, not to mention the impractically long nails that matched her hair. If anyone was going to stand out at the hen night, it was going to be Toni. Usually she was understated, rocking a no make-up, up-at-dawn-to-milk-the-cows, country girl-next-door look, which Anna had thought reflected exactly who Toni was. This was like when goody-goody Olivia Newton John suddenly turns up at the end of *Grease* with spray-on trousers and an attitude to match.

'Thanks, I'm still getting used to it.' Toni wrinkled her nose. 'I can't even pull my pants up properly with these nails. Tonight might be a good test of just how close we really all are, because I'm going to need one of you to follow me to the ladies loo every time I go.'

'We're midwives, I think we can handle it.' Anna grinned and stepped back to let Toni in. 'The question is, what's brought on the new look?'

'I was just feeling old before my time.' Toni shrugged. 'Mousey brown hair and a dull complexion. I was basically beige.'

'You always look fantastic to me, but there's no way anyone could describe you as beige tonight.' Anna followed her down the corridor of the cottage. 'You do know that Jess is going to force you to wear an orange jumpsuit, don't you? You'd look far better in the black and white convict's outfit she's bought me, than I will.'

'I doubt that.' Toni scooped up one of the glasses of sloe gin and Prosecco without even pausing for breath, and downed the lot. 'I need a bit of Dutch courage to go out like this. I keep thinking it's too much.'

'I was just about to say how amazing you look.' Ella handed Anna a glass.

'Me too and I think we should all toast your new look, as soon as we've had a drink to toast Anna's big night.' Jess topped up Toni's drink.

'Cheers!' The four of them clinked their glasses together. The other midwives, and the rest of the hen and stag party were meeting them at the first venue.

'Am I allowed to know where we're going?' Anna took a large gulp of the purple cocktail sloe gin, which tasted dangerously good.

'Not until you've got changed into your outfit, although you might need to wear a coat over the top.' Ella dropped just enough of a hint to set Anna's mind racing all over again.

'If I look as lumpy in this dress as I'm expecting to, everyone's going to be grateful I've kept my coat on.' Anna picked up the package containing the fancy dress costume and then took another sip of Jess's cocktail. The more the sloe gin and Prosecco slipped down, the less self-conscious she felt about putting it on. A couple more toasts to the evening ahead and she might even be willing to undo the top button of her coat before the night was out.

Ella and Dan couldn't have chosen a less summery location for the first part of the sten do, which was apparently the proper name for a joint stag and hen do. The ice rink was about eight miles outside Port Agnes, on the road to Port Tremellien. It was a new addition to an activity centre, on a site that had once been a dairy farm, and the old milking shed had been converted to house the rink itself. The centre ran other activities, including paintballing, and its claim to fame, according to the signs on the approach road, was the longest zip wire in the South West. For one night only there was a huge banner strung across the back wall of the rink, bearing Brae and Anna's names. The roof of the old milking shed was strung with twinkly fairy lights and it would have been quite a romantic scene, if one of the stags – wearing his inflatable sumo suit – wasn't lying like a stranded whale in the middle of the ice, with three others trying desperately to help him to his feet. Dan had secured a private booking for the first two hours of the sten do and it turned out Ella was a whizz on the ice. Sadly, the happy couple weren't quite so graceful.

'I'll let go of the side if you promise not to let go of my hand.' Even as he tried to stand slightly more upright to take hold of Anna's hand, Brae's legs almost went out from under him.

'I'll do my best, but I'm only marginally better at this than you.' Anna grinned; they both had the bruises to prove it and she was glad that Ella had the foresight to tell her to bring a pair of jeans to wear under the convict's dress. But she hadn't laughed this much in ages. Brae, bless him, was like a newborn foal when he took to the ice. It was only a few weeks since the splint had been taken off his hand, after breaking a couple of small bones in the boating accident that had taken longer than expected to heal. He'd been told his hand was completely healed now, although Anna doubted Brae's doctor would have been pleased to see him repeatedly landing palms down on the ice.

'I didn't know I could even do the splits until ten minutes ago.' Brae grinned. 'Anything to avoid falling forward onto my hands for the twentieth time!'

'I must admit, I thought your sumo costume was going to split from here until next week when you got up.' Anna laughed again. 'All that's for my eyes only now, you know! Although your last night of freedom isn't quite what it should be, having me tagging along.'

'I've never been happier in my life than since we got together and I don't want another second of freedom, if that's what you want to call it. I wish I'd met you ten years ago, so I could have had ten years longer with you.'

'I wish we had too and then we'd have—'

'Don't.' Brae pressed his mouth against hers, cutting her off before she could finish.

'You don't know what I was going to say.' She murmured the words when he finally pulled away.

'Yes, I do.' Brae suddenly let go of the barrier and shuffled a couple of steps forward. As he looked over his shoulder, he wobbled badly and had to grab hold of the side again.

'What are you doing?'

'Showing you just how much you've got to look forward to, being married to a man with the skating moves and body of Baloo from *The Jungle Book*! Have you got your phone with you?'

'I think so.' Anna slipped a hand into her coat pocket. 'Yes, here, but you using a mobile on the ice is a recipe for disaster. Not to mention that I'll probably end up needing to buy a new phone.'

'Just record me for the next five minutes and I promise it will be worth it.' Brae dropped a wink and seconds later he disappeared into the group. When the others around him cleared, she saw him in the centre of the rink, arms flailing as he fought to stay upright. Then, without warning, he went into a spin, which was really more of a fall, and could only finish in one place; on the floor, in a heap. Thankfully he landed on his bottom, with a thud that couldn't fail to draw everyone's attention, the plastic sumo suit not offering much protection at all when it came down to it. Anna kept filming as Brae tried and failed to get to his feet, laughing so hard that the mobile phone was shaking. It took four of the sumo wrestlers and a couple of convicts to finally get him up on his feet and back to the safety of the side.

'Did you get it all?' Brae looked at her, as she slid slowly across the ice towards him, hoping no one would jostle her even slightly. She'd definitely end up on her backside again if they did.

'I think so and it was hilarious. But it was a big risk, too, given that you've just recovered from a broken hand, and I still don't get why?'

'Because Ella said she needs as much content as she can get for the social media pages she's set up to save the lifeboat station, and the films I've been re-enacting with Dan have been going down really well. I thought me making an idiot of myself on the ice might help keep the momentum going and I wanted a viral video to go in Ella's favour this time.'

Anna propelled herself forward, circling her arms around his waist. 'If I ever sound like I'm anything less than the luckiest girl in the world, then I'm sorry. You do so much for everyone, but I want you to know I'd do anything for you.'

'Anything?' He widened his eyes.

'What have you got in mind?'

'Right now?' He paused. 'I'd like you to drag me back to a non-slippery surface, so I can kiss you without worrying that I'm going to end up on my behind, or worse still, my face. Oh and maybe grab one of those hot chocolates with whipped cream and marshmallows. It might be June, but it's flipping freezing in here when you've landed on the ice as often as I have!'

'Hot chocolate? You're so rock and roll.' She held out her hand. 'But I can't think of anything I'd rather do, or anyone I'd rather do it with.'

'Stick with me baby and you might even end the night with a cup of tea and a chocolate digestive.'

'You know I love it when you talk dirty.' Anna slid towards the exit of the rink, clinging on to Brae's hand as if her life depended on it.

* * *

It was hard trying to run for the loo and keep your legs crossed, but Ella would have to master it if she was going to get there in time.

'I don't think Jess fully thought this through, getting us all jumpsuits when we were heading to a bar famed for the size of its cocktail pitchers.' Ella dashed into the first open cubicle, with Anna taking a more sedate pace behind her.

'Feeling better now?' Anna smiled as Ella emerged a couple of minutes later.

'Much!' Washing her hands, she was just about to ask if Anna was having fun when she heard someone shouting.

'I don't know why the hell you turned up here, anyway. Just go home!' Suddenly the door of the ladies' cloakroom burst open, whacking against the tiled wall with a powerful thud. Jess might be small, but if she'd given it much more force she could have taken the whole thing off its hinges.

'Are you okay?' Almost before Ella had got the words out of her mouth, Jess had dissolved into noisy sobs.

'What's wrong?' Anna was already at her side.

'It's Dom. He saw some pictures on Instagram and he worked out where we were tonight. He keeps asking me to meet up with him to talk and for some reason he thought tonight was the perfect opportunity. There's nothing I want to say to him that I haven't already said, but he just won't take no for an answer.'

'Do you want Dan to have a word with him?' Ella was slightly hesitant. Dan wasn't the sort to make threats to anyone, but, if Jess was this upset, she was sure he'd be willing to step in to help protect her from Dom's unwanted attention.

'Thanks, but I don't want to make things worse.' Jess sniffed. 'I'm terrified that if I don't keep him onside, he'll wreck things when they ask him to write a reference for my fostering assessment.'

'Surely he can't do that? Can't you explain what he's been like?' Anna furrowed her brow as Jess sighed.

'I could, but what if the social worker or the panel think I'm just making excuses and choose to believe whatever Dom writes?'

'They must deal with this sort of stuff all the time.' Ella put an arm around her. 'The best thing you can do is be honest with your social worker about how things are with Dom, from the start. Then, whatever he tries to do to mess things up, he won't get away with it.'

'And if that doesn't work, we'll put him on the ice with Brae and that'll be the end of him!' Anna grinned and, for the first time, Jess managed a smile too.

'You're right and I'm sure it'll all come up in the first session with my social worker. Like Ella said, they'll have dealt with much worse than Dom.' Jess sounded like she was trying to convince herself. 'If I ever risk another relationship again, I need to model it on what you guys have got with Brae and Dan. Maybe if Dom and I had been able to communicate properly in the first place, we'd never have got ourselves into this state.'

'I can't be as upfront with Dan about everything as I should be.' Ella tucked her hair behind her ear. 'He thinks I don't want to get married again because of what happened with Weller and, when he first mentioned it, I really didn't. But the closer we've got to Anna and Brae's wedding, the more I realise I would like to get married eventually. Maybe not right now, but I don't want him to think it's totally off the cards forever.'

'So tell him!' Jess made it sound much easier than it was.

'I'm worried if I mention it, he'll feel like he has to ask me. I couldn't bear the thought of getting engaged to someone who's only done it because they felt pressured. Been there, done that, and got the *"jilted at the altar"* T-shirt. I'll just have to keep dropping subtle hints and hope he gets it.'

'Anna could make sure you catch the bouquet at her wedding.' Jess wiped the mascara from under her eyes as she spoke; at least it was distracting her from worrying about Dom.

'Yes and maybe I could pretend I'm taking Anna's wedding dress to the dry cleaner's afterwards and I could ask him if he thinks it would suit me!' Ella laughed. 'Or I could just sit around the house wearing it like Miss Havisham, until either the cobwebs consume me, or Dan finally realises I wouldn't mind if he popped the question.'

'I'd like to say I've heard worse ideas, but I'm not going to lie.' Jess grinned. 'I'm feeling much better, though. I don't know what I'd do without the two of you.'

'Just as well, because you're stuck with us. And, as your boss, I'm going to have to insist you both get back out there and have a good time.' Anna pulled open the door and ushered them out of the ladies' cloakroom.

'Yes ma'am.' Ella saluted and followed Jess back out into the corridor, a shadow moving up ahead as two figures sprung apart.

'Toni?' Ella stepped back and Toni actually shrieked.

'We were just...' Toni's mouth was still moving, but for an uncomfortable few seconds nothing else came out. 'Bobby just had something in his eye, I was looking to see what it was.'

'In a dark corridor?' As Jess asked the question, Ella nudged her. Toni had used a similar excuse the last time they'd been caught and they were obviously sticking with a theme. If that was what they wanted, Jess would just have to play along with it too.

'You don't owe us any explanations.' Anna's voice was gentle, but Toni was shaking her head so hard she was in danger of losing the dangly earrings that complimented her new look.

'We're not together!' Poor Bobby didn't say anything, but there was a sadness in his eyes and Ella couldn't help wondering what he made of the desperate attempts to keep their relationship secret.

'Okay, whatever you say.' Jess's tone made it obvious she wasn't buying it, and it was hard to believe that an intelligent woman like Toni really thought she was convincing anyone.

'Shall we get back to the party before the others give up on us?' Anna smiled, but Toni was still radiating enough tension to power Port Agnes.

'I'm in! There's a jug of mojito with my name on it. See you later.' Ella was already following Anna down the corridor, and even Jess had picked up the pace. Fascinating as it might have been to be a fly on the wall when Toni and Bobby finally spoke to one another, Toni looked capable of swatting anyone who hung around flat against the wall. Sometimes you just had to know when to walk away.

15

Anna looked down at her phone as it buzzed in her hand, right after she'd turned it on again following her morning clinic. There was a voicemail from an unknown number.

'Hi. It's Luke Scott here. My wife, Tamara, is one of your patients. She's having pains, which she insists are just those practice contraction things. But I don't know, they seem pretty bad. Sorry, I know she's not booked in for a home visit, but I just wondered if you could pop by and check her over. If you've got time?'

Anna had the afternoon off, and she was due to head up to the Red Cliff Hotel to run over some plans with the event coordinator. Tamara was one of her most vulnerable patients, though, and she'd never forgive herself if she didn't go and check on her first, and something bad happened.

✉ Hi Luke, it's Anna Jones here. I got your message and I'll be over in twenty minutes.

'Enjoy your afternoon off.' Toni barely looked up from the

desk as Anna stopped off at the staffroom to pick up her bag. Ever since the joint stag and hen night, Toni seemed to have retreated into herself, as if any conversation with the other midwives might run the risk of them bringing up her relationship with Bobby.

'I'm going out to see Tamara Scott first. Her husband called to say he's worried about the severity of the Braxton Hicks she's having, and I just want to check it's not the start of labour. With her history, the consultant's really keen that she's in hospital to deliver, in case the baby needs any extra help.'

'Isn't she the lady with the eating disorder?' Toni finally looked up, the dark circles under her eyes suggesting it wasn't just volunteering to cover extra on-call shifts lately that had been keeping her awake at night.

'That's the one. She's quite fragile in a lot of ways. If things don't go according to the birth plan she's worked out, she'll find any kind of adjustment quite difficult to take. She'll probably need some extra support if she is in labour.'

'Aren't you supposed to be going up to the hotel to talk about the wedding?' Toni must have seen the look of surprise as Anna's eyebrows shot up. 'I overheard you telling Ella about it.'

'I am, but it can wait. I need to make sure Tamara's okay first.'

'I'll come with you. That way, if she needs someone to go to the hospital with her, I can take over. I've met her once in clinic and, when I'm not being awkward and prickly, I can be really quite empathetic.' Toni gave an apologetic smile. 'I'm sorry I've been a bit of a nightmare lately, it's just that things are... complicated.'

'You're a brilliant midwife and that's never once slipped.' Anna put a hand on her shoulder. 'As for the rest, your personal life is just that – *personal*. But I want you to know that you can always talk to me if you need to. The ball's in your court, though.'

'I know and it means a lot. I just don't want to have to think about it at work as well as at home.' Toni stood up, putting a full stop on the conversation. 'Let's get going.'

'Absolutely.' Anna nodded. All she could do, as a boss and a friend, was offer the opportunity if one of her team wanted to confide in her, but it was up to Toni in the end.

* * *

Anna stood on the step outside Luke and Tamara's house and, even with the limited view she had as Luke pulled back the door, it was obvious the place was immaculate. It was like stepping into a glossy magazine shoot and she immediately felt as if she looked like she'd been dragged through a hedge backwards as a result.

'Shall I take my shoes off?' Anna turned to Luke, who must have been hovering by the front door, judging by how quickly he'd answered it.

'Sorry, I hate having to ask people, especially in circumstances like this, but it freaks Tamara out a bit if she thinks the house might get messed up.'

'It's not a problem, lots of people ask us to do it.' Anna kicked off her shoes and Toni followed suit. All either of them cared about was checking that Tamara was okay. She'd been asked to do far more unusual things, anyway, including putting a crystal in her pocket to welcome one couple's baby with the right energy. 'How's she doing?'

'She's bracing against the back of one of the armchairs and the pains seem to be coming pretty fast.' Luke furrowed his brow. 'She keeps insisting it's just practice contractions, but I really think this might be it.'

'Does she know we're coming?' Anna followed Luke as he turned to head down the corridor, with Toni close behind her.

'She said I shouldn't have called you, but then she started

crying and asking when you were going to get here. So I'm sure she'll be okay about it.'

'Hi Tamara, are you okay if we come in? I've got Toni with me. I think you met her before, at one of the clinics?' Anna walked towards Tamara, who was bent at an almost 90-degree angle, with her stomach facing towards the floor.

'I've got a confession to make.' Tamara lifted her head to look at them. 'My waters broke two hours ago.'

'Why the hell didn't you tell me?' Luke visibly paled. 'We could have been at the hospital within half an hour. I've practised the route three times, just to make sure we didn't end up in a situation like this.'

'I didn't want to go to the hospital. It'll take away all my choices. I just thought, if I could somehow make it through until it was too late, I could have the baby here.' Tamara started to sob and Luke crossed the room to put his arm around her.

'It's okay, I understand. I'm just scared, that's all.'

'Me too.' Tamara was crying hard now.

'Okay, let's have a look at you and we can see what our options are.' Anna forced herself to keep a relaxed tone, despite the flicker of panic that made the skin on her face too taut to offer Tamara a reassuring smile. There was no particular reason to think she was going to have a difficult time, but with first-time mums it was always unknown territory. Then there was the fact that she was very underweight and physically and emotionally vulnerable, as well as the fact there was a high chance that the baby would have a birth weight on the low side too. All of that meant a hospital would be the safest bet, but if they had to do it here, she was more grateful than ever that Toni had decided to come along too.

'We need to go upstairs. Everything's in the wardrobe ready, there's plastic sheeting and it can all be thrown away afterwards.

I'm not even getting on the bed until it's laid down.' Tamara must have been planning this for a while. Even if the arrival of the baby didn't look imminent, Anna had a horrible feeling it would be almost impossible to persuade Tamara to transfer to the hospital.

As soon as they got upstairs, Toni swung into action and transformed the bedroom with the supplies Tamara had stored in the wardrobe. Anna's first check of Tamara's blood pressure had shown it to be higher than she would have liked. But once every possible surface was cleared or protected with the disposable sheeting, her blood pressure started to drop and she finally agreed to lie on the bed for an examination.

'How long have the contractions been this intense?' Anna had a strong suspicion what the answer was going to be.

'Since straight after my waters broke.'

'That explains it, because you're fully dilated, you're at ten centimetres already.' Anna exchanged a brief glance with Toni, who grimaced. Even if she'd been willing to go, there wasn't time to transfer Tamara to the hospital before the second stage of labour started.

'Does that mean the baby's coming now?' Luke was wringing his hands together.

'It means it's highly likely Tamara's going to have the urge to push at any moment.' Anna was still keeping her tone as light as possible, but that didn't stop a look of sheer panic washing over Luke's face.

'Shall I call an ambulance?'

'No!' Tamara was already trying to get up off the bed.

'It's okay, I think the baby will be here before it arrives anyway.' Anna took hold of Tamara's hand. 'If everything goes okay, we can do it here, but if you or the baby look like you might need any extra help, we'll call an ambulance then, okay?'

'Uh-huh.' Tamara suddenly slumped back against the bed, dropping her chin to her chest. 'I think I need to push.'

'Then go with it, let your body do what it was designed for.' Anna never ceased to be amazed by the strength of women in labour. As tiny as Tamara was, she was soon pushing with a power that was difficult to quantify, unless you'd seen it in action for yourself. Less than twenty minutes later, the baby was crowning.

'Okay, I think she'll be here with the next couple of pushes. You can do this.' Anna encouraged Tamara, as Luke and Toni supported her legs, giving her something to push against.

'You're so amazing, Tam, I can't believe you're doing this.' Luke blew his wife an air-kiss and she gave another groan.

'Oh my Godddddddd!' As the baby emerged, Anna caught her breath and not just because she was witnessing a new life come into the world. She'd seen a baby born with this condition before, several times, but not without the parents knowing in advance. It was never as bad as people feared, but there was no doubt it was going to be a shock. Especially to someone like Tamara.

'Is she okay?' Luke was beaming, just like a new dad should, as Anna lifted the baby up to lie her on Tamara's chest.

'She's absolutely fine, but she does have a cleft lip.'

'No, no, she can't have! It would have shown up on the scan.' Tamara's eyes flashed and she recoiled as Anna lifted the baby towards her. 'Get it away from me! It's not mine! My baby was perfect, they said so when they scanned her.'

'I don't understand. How could they have missed it?' Luke turned to Toni, as Anna held the baby in her arms.

'It's fairly unusual, but it happens sometimes if the baby's in the wrong position when it's scanned and it's especially common if the baby doesn't have a cleft palate too, as that's much easier to spot on the scan.' Toni answered Luke, but Tamara was silent, staring straight ahead of her. Anna had to look twice to check she was still breathing in and out. She'd expected tears or hysterics from Tamara, but the total silence was far worse.

'It's just her lip that's affected, her palate is fine, which is great news. It means you can even feed her yourself if you want to.' Anna looked down at the little girl, her almost navy-blue eyes wide open. She needed her mum.

'I don't even want to look at it. Take it away.' Tamara turned her head to the side and then she was silent again, closing her eyes, only the tears trickling down her face and dropping off her chin giving any indication she was still awake. When the baby's mouth started to move, searching around for her first feed, Anna felt like her heart was in danger of breaking too.

* * *

'I've spoken to the consultant and they're going to want to admit the baby to hospital.' Anna put a hand on Luke's arm, as he cradled his daughter to his chest.

'Her name's Belle.' He turned to look at Anna, his voice catching in his throat. 'Although Tamara said she doesn't want to call her that any more. She still won't even look at her.'

'I think she's in shock.' Anna had gone downstairs to make the call to the hospital, and Luke had followed with the baby, while Toni monitored Tamara. She'd barely spoken since the delivery and every attempt to get her to hold Belle, or even acknowledge her existence, had been rebuffed.

'I understand that, but Belle's beautiful, even with her lip the way it is. If I can see that, why can't Tamara?' There was a muscle going in Luke's jaw. 'A mother's love is supposed to outweigh anything and she knows better than anyone what it feels like when that's not the case.'

'Giving birth can be hugely traumatic in itself, and you know Tamara struggles with a lack of control. So Belle's condition being undiagnosed is all the more difficult for her to deal with.'

'Why do they need to admit her to hospital? She's going to be okay, isn't she?' Luke knitted his eyebrows together, his concern for the baby obvious.

'They'll run some hearing tests and a paediatric check, just to make sure there aren't any other issues, but all Belle's initial checks look fine. They'll also help you to get to grips with feeding, and Tamara might still be able to feed Belle herself, if she wants to.'

'That'll be a struggle if she won't even pick her up.'

'I know it's difficult for you, but I've seen mums have problems bonding with their babies before, and things usually work out in the end. You just need to give her time.' Anna wanted to promise that it would all be okay, but Tamara's existing mental health issues were complex, and there was no way of knowing how long it would take before Tamara was able to interact with the baby in the way that Luke expected her to.

'Belle's going to need me in the meantime, isn't she?' Luke looked down at his baby daughter. 'I've got a catering business. I can't just take time off, especially not at this time of year with loads of weddings coming up.'

'Try not to worry about all of that for now. We'll give you as much support as we can, but friends and family often rally around at a time like this.'

'My family will help if Tam lets them, but she's funny about letting people get too involved. And, as for her own family...' he shook his head, 'you probably know all about that?'

'She told me things are difficult.'

'Things with Tam are always difficult.' Luke sighed. 'But I love her and we'll get through this somehow, just like we've got through everything else.'

'She's lucky to have your support; not everyone in her situation has that. I'm sure it'll make all the difference.' Anna silently prayed she'd be right, wishing she could relieve some of the burden resting on Luke's shoulders. 'Shall we go back up and let Tamara know the ambulance is on its way to take Belle in? And that she can go with her, if she wants to?'

'Okay, but I can't see her being willing to leave. Can you?'

'Maybe not, but we've at least got to give her the option.' Anna followed Luke, who was still carrying the baby, up the stairs. Tamara might not have bonded with Belle, but her dad already looked like an old hand.

'The hospital need to take Belle in, Tam, and I think we should both go with her.' Luke's tone was gentle, but his wife kept her head turned away. 'You can't keep pretending not to hear me, or that she isn't here. I know the thing with her lip is a shock, but if you look at her properly, you'll realise it's not that bad and Anna's been telling me all the things the hospital can do to help.'

'But her face, it's so... I can't look, because that's the one thing I didn't want for her, to go through what I did. I wanted her life to be so much happier than mine and now it isn't going to be. Maybe it's my fault, something I did, and I'm so sorry if I've done this to her. But I can't bear it, I can't! I won't watch her be bullied and tortured by other kids the way I was.' Tamara was still looking in the other direction. 'I went through all of that at school, the name calling and the taunts because I didn't look the way they thought I should. There was always something they found to hate about me, right from the moment my parents dumped me at that school. I just wanted to go home and not have to face the constant taunts. Now the baby's going to have to face that too and it's going to be even worse for her.'

Anna desperately wanted to reach out and comfort Tamara, the way she should have been comforted when she was facing those taunts at school; taunts that in truth had nothing to do with how Tamara had looked, but the vulnerability other kids had seized upon because of her sadness at being sent away. It was that vulnerability that enabled them to convince her that the taunts about the way she looked were true. She wanted to tell Tamara that it would be different for Belle, because *she did* have parents who would fight her corner and support her when life wasn't fair. She wanted to say that everyone had times like that, times when they needed their mum and dad, regardless of anything else. But it would be easy for Anna to say, because she'd always had it. There'd always been someone to pick her up from a party when she'd been teased about her far-too-short ankle-swinging jeans that looked like they'd had a row with her shoes after a rapid growth spurt, and she just wanted to go home and have someone tell her that the other kids were only jealous when they called her carrot top and Duracell. That wasn't Tamara's experience, though, and she'd have to learn its power by being there for Belle. For now Anna had to take it slowly and help her see, bit by bit, that it was going to be okay.

'Luke's right, just look at her and you'll see how beautiful she is.' Anna slowly approached the side of the bed. 'The problem with playground taunts is that the kids will always find something to pick on, just like you said. Especially if it gets a reaction from you. I've got red hair, so you can imagine the ammunition that gave them, but most of it was pretty much water off a duck's back, I was so used to it. Then one lad in the year above picked up on the fact that my feet were really big, the biggest out of every girl in the year. It didn't matter that I was the tallest too, it gave them something new and he started calling me Sideshow Bob, you know, from *The Simpsons*? I lost my temper and launched myself at him in the playground. He'd probably have got bored eventually if I hadn't, but because he knew how much I hated it, and everyone else realised I did too, it pretty much stuck for the rest of the time I was at school. I swear, if I saw some of them now, they'd still call me Bob and find it hilarious.'

'What she's got is a million times worse than that! It's a deformity.' Tamara screwed up her eyes. 'I can't bear it. All I wanted was for her to be okay and not inherit my issues. Now there's no chance of that.'

'There's a lot the hospital can do to help minimise the impact of the cleft in the short term. Then, when she's between three and six months, they'll be able to operate.' Anna reached out and touched Tamara's arm, heartened by the fact that she didn't snatch it away. 'You might find this difficult to believe now, but a lot of people say they actually miss the gap when it's closed up, because it changes their baby's smile.'

'It's true. My second cousin's little boy had the op when he was six months old and she felt exactly like that. To look at him now, you wouldn't even know he'd had a cleft lip in the first place.' Toni reached into her bag, which she'd left in the corner of the room. 'I'm not sure if she's got any pictures on her Facebook account, but I'll have a look. If not, I can send you some later.'

'So she'll still be able to smile?' Tamara looked directly at Anna for the first time.

'Absolutely and, like I said before, if you want to, you might even be able to feed her yourself, with the support of the specialist staff at the hospital.' Anna took a deep breath. 'One thing we already know about Belle for certain, is that she loves a cuddle. She's been snuggling into her daddy's arms for the last twenty minutes, but I bet what she'd like most is a cuddle from her mummy.'

'I don't know if I can.' Despite her words, Tamara turned

slightly, towards where Luke was still holding the baby in his arms.

'Yes, you can, you're going to be fine and so is Belle.' Anna kept speaking in the same gentle tone, as Luke leant down and carefully placed their daughter in her mother's arms.

'I'm scared to move. What if I knock her and make it worse?' Tamara's eyes widened as Luke stepped back, leaving the baby resting in the crook of her arm.

'You can't hurt her lip. It's not painful for her either, it just stopped forming very slightly earlier than most babies, before the gap had fully joined up.' Anna still felt as though she was holding her breath as Tamara ran a finger very slowly down the side of her daughter's face.

'Apart from her mouth, she looks exactly like the baby photos your mum showed me of you. She's got the same brow line and her nose is just like yours.' Tamara smiled. 'I'm so glad she looks like you.'

'Look at her watching you, she hasn't taken her eyes off your face since I put her in your arms.' Luke was beaming and Anna shot Toni a look. They both knew a newborn baby couldn't focus on much more than light and motion at first, but Toni gave an almost imperceptible nod. They'd seen Belle come into the world, but now they were witnessing the birth of a family. Whatever helped Tamara to bond with her daughter was fine by them.

'When the ambulance comes, they're going to want to take Belle to the hospital, just to check her over and give some advice on how to manage the cleft until she can have the operation.' Anna smiled. 'I think she looks really comfortable lying in your arms and they'll probably suggest you go with her. Is that something you think you could do?'

'Can Luke come with me?' Tamara's eyes suddenly widened again, but her face visibly relaxed as Anna nodded.

'Absolutely and I can follow on in the car too, if you'd like. In case one or both of you needs to come back later, because they'll probably want to keep Belle in for a night or two.' Anna would have to text Brae to let him know what was going on. It was already far too late to make it to the hotel, but none of that seemed important any more.

'I can follow them to the hospital. You've got loads to be getting on with.' Toni gave her a pointed look.

'It's fine. I can do everything I need to do via an email. I'd rather be there to make sure Tamara, Luke and Belle get all the support they need.' Anna didn't often lay down the law as the unit's most senior midwife, but occasionally it came in handy. 'Anyway, you're on duty tonight, aren't you? So I need you back up at the unit, in case we get any more call-outs for home deliveries.'

'One of the other midwives could cover that.' Toni sighed, seeming to realise it was pointless to argue. 'Okay, I can stay and sort everything out once the ambulance comes, so you can come back to a nice, tidy house.'

'That would be brilliant, if you're sure?' Relief flooded Luke's face and Anna could have kissed Toni. She knew enough about Tamara's mental health to realise that coming back to the house and seeing any reminders of the trauma of Belle's delivery, could present a trigger.

'It's no problem. If you've got a spare key you can leave me, Luke, I'll just post it back through the door when I go.'

'I'll go and sort one out now and grab the hospital bag I'd packed for Tamara.' Luke caught Anna's eye for a split second. She hadn't missed the fact that he'd been the one to pack the bag. Tamara had never had any intention of going into hospital to have the baby. Sometimes, though, even with the sort of control issues Tamara had, life had a way of taking things out of your hands.

16

Gwen was talking so quickly Anna wasn't sure if she'd heard her right, which wasn't helped by the fact that Gwen was also jumping up and down on the spot.

'Did she just say what I thought she did?' Anna looked over at Ella, who was furrowing her brow as Gwen let out another whoop.

'If it's that we've won the lottery, then yes.' Ella grabbed hold of the older woman's arm, in a vain attempt to stop her leaping up and down again. 'Keep still for a minute, Gwen, and say that again but about ten times more slowly.'

'We've got five numbers on the EuroMillions and I'll finally be able to send Barry's bags packing!'

'Does that mean we've won? How much?' Ella was still trying to hold on to Gwen as she asked the question, but Anna couldn't work what all the excitement was about. Her ex-boyfriend had insisted that they stop doing the lottery when they'd matched five numbers on the UK version and got a payout of less than fifty pounds. Not even enough to cover a decent meal out, according to Greg. Admittedly the EuroMillions had a much bigger prize pot, but five numbers was still a long way off the jackpot.

Despite what had happened with Greg, when Gwen had set up a syndicate, Anna had been happy to join in. They each put in four pounds a week; half went towards the tickets and the rest went into Ella's lifeboat station fund. Most of the midwives were members of the syndicate, along with some of their partners, including Brae and Dan. Gwen's husband, Barry, had refused, although he still gave two pounds towards the lifeboat station fund each week. He'd said he was more likely to win *Britain's Got Talent* than the EuroMillions and he wasn't entering either of them. Although, according to Gwen, if they ever wanted someone with the talent to turn toast into the consistency of roof tiles, or burn water, then Barry was their man. If she was talking about packing Barry's bags, then it looked like he was paying the ultimate price for refusing to be part of it all. Whatever they'd won, Anna was already wishing they hadn't if it meant the end of Gwen and Barry. They'd always seemed so perfect together and the idea that it might just have been a facade was really horrible.

'We've won £19,873 – and twenty pence! Between the seventeen of us in the syndicate that's still over a thousand pounds each!' Gwen sounded every bit as happy as if there were three more zeros after that number and Anna felt a surge of relief. If they'd all become millionaires, everything would have changed. Gwen might have been tempted to retire and most of the other midwives would probably have left the unit and maybe even moved away. It might be strange to value what you already had more than a substantial lottery win, but the thought made Anna smile. All this was just a bit of fun, an unexpected windfall they could enjoy planning how to spend. But it wouldn't change anything and Anna was glad. Although she still had no idea what Gwen had in store for Barry.

'That's brilliant, but what did you mean about packing Barry's bags?' Anna looked at Gwen, who was still jigging about on the spot.

'Not packing his bags, sending his bags packing!' Gwen laughed. 'He's got them under his eyes and they make him look like Droopy, the cartoon dog. He could carry the shopping home from Lidl in them and he looks miserable even when he's at his happiest, if you know what I mean. Barry always said if he came into any money he'd get them done. I've been saving up for it as a surprise. I didn't quite think I'd make it in time for our fortieth anniversary, but this little bit extra will top it up to what we need. Although it's going to cost him in other ways...'

'How?' Anna braced herself for the answer. Anything was possible with Gwen.

'He said we had no chance of the syndicate winning the lottery, but if we ever did, he'd do three laps of the harbour wearing my underwear!' Gwen did another little jig. 'Now if we can just drum up some sponsorship for him to do it for the lifeboat station fund, then everyone really is a winner!'

As Anna had predicted, the members of the syndicate had no end of fun deciding how to spend their unexpected windfalls. Plans ranged from weekend trips to Disneyland Paris, new sofas and a colossal eighty-five-inch TV. Ella, Dan, Anna and Brae had all decided to donate half of their winnings to the lifeboat station fund, which left them just shy of six hundred pounds each.

Anna and Brae had considered just adding it to the wedding pot, but in the end they'd agreed it would be nice to buy something with it, something they could remember their little lottery windfall by, even when the money was long gone. When Brae had suggested that they both do their own thing with their individual wins, Anna had been taken by surprise at first. It was so unlike him. But Brae never did anything for himself, so if he wanted to buy some new fishing gear, or put it towards saving to upgrade the boat he'd shared with Dan, that was fine with her. God knows she never wanted him to take any risks out at sea after the last time, although he'd sworn any boat trips in the future would be about enjoying leisurely time in the sunshine, rather than going out to try and catch fish in the depths of winter.

As for what Anna would spend her winnings on, she'd had the germ of an idea for a while now and it seemed like fate had the same idea, stepping in to convince her it was the right thing to do. Okay, so maybe the timing wasn't perfect, with the wedding and honeymoon coming up, but as soon as she'd made enquiries about the advert and been sent some pictures, she'd known she just had to find a way to make it work.

On the day she'd handed over her winnings in exchange for her purchase, she could hardly wait for Brae to get home. He'd walked to work, which meant she wasn't listening out for the sound of his car. So, when what sounded like a transit van pulled up outside the house, she'd assumed it was a delivery, until someone started beeping the horn. If it turned out to be a delivery driver who was too damn lazy to get out of his van to drop off the parcel, he'd be getting a few choice words.

'What on earth are you doing?' Anna spotted Brae at the wheel of the ambulance parked outside their house, with the driver's window wound right down, as soon as she stepped out of the door.

'Bringing Amber home.' He patted the steering wheel and then swung open the door. 'Come and take a look at her. She used to be an ambulance.'

'I can see that, the question is what are *you* doing driving it?'

Anna just hoped it wasn't what she thought it was. Brae had talked a few times about the possibility of getting a van to do mobile deliveries of fish and chips to some of the more rural villages inland from Port Agnes. She had to admire his entrepreneurial spirit, but anything that meant he was out of the house for even longer would cut down the time they had together between her shifts, and she didn't want to trade that for any amount of extra income.

'I saw an advert from this guy Chris, who buys decommissioned ambulances and does them up to sell to businesses. You know Jethro, the mobile mechanic? He's got one.'

'*The Carbulance*?' Anna didn't like the way this was going as Brae nodded. He'd have to be out most evenings if the business was going mobile.

'That's the one. Anyway, he bought too many of the old ambulances to have time to do up, so he put an ad out to sell on some of the older models that had been sitting in his yard for while, and Amber was one of them. He used to be a paramedic himself apparently, so he couldn't bear to see any of them going to waste.'

'Okay, but why did you buy one? And why do you keep calling her Amber?' Anna had never worried about Brae disappearing to spend his nights with another woman, but now it looked like it might well be on the cards.

'Because she'll be our version of Vanna, of course! She's going to need a lot of work and it's going to take a while before we can take her out on the road, but I reckon she could be perfect eventually.'

'Oh Brae.' Anna burst into tears and he was out of the old ambulance in seconds, wrapping his arms around her.

'What's wrong, sweetheart? I'm sorry, I should have talked to you first. I know she's not quite the same. I did think about looking for an old ice cream van, but I thought the similarities might be too much.' He pulled her closer to him. 'But if I've got it all wrong and you don't want her, I can ask Chris to take her back or sell her to someone else.'

'No!' The strength of Anna's response took them both by surprise. This was the nicest thing anyone had ever done for her and she needed him to know it. 'She's perfect, I love her so much and I love you even more. But I thought we were waiting, with the wedding and everything. You can't spend this much just because it's something I wanted.'

'Amber's for us. She's the family camper and, anyway, I got a really good deal. She's an old girl with a few miles on the clock and Chris only wanted twelve hundred for her, but when he found out you were a midwife, he knocked it down to an even thousand. So with the money from the lottery win, it was nothing to top up the rest.'

'She's the best present ever.' Anna was shaking as Brae relaxed his arms and she looked at the old ambulance again. They were going to have so many adventures in Amber and, even if it was a couple of years before she was ready for the road, the first thing Anna was going to do was order a road map – the sort that had been made almost obsolete by satnavs – so they could start planning their first trip. There was one other thing she had to tell Brae before that, though, because it wasn't just going to be the two of them heading out in Amber.

'I've bought something with my winnings too. It's another family purchase, but mostly it's yours, because I really wanted you to have it.'

'Now you've really got me intrigued.' Brae was grinning and she just hoped she'd read the situation right. If he loved her surprise half as much as she loved his, she'd be so happy.

'Why don't you lock Amber up and then come in? I'll be waiting in the kitchen and you'll find out what it's all about.'

Dashing inside, while Brae shut the door of the old ambulance and made sure it was safely locked, Anna picked up the present she'd bought him, holding it in her arms as he opened the kitchen door.

'Oh my God, you didn't, did you? Is it really ours?' Brae held out his arms to take the dog, which was already desperately squirming to get to its new master. 'What's he called? Is he a he?'

'Yes he is and his name's for you to decide.' The pure white boxer dog puppy was doing its best to try and lick Brae's face, making him duck and weave like another sort of boxer altogether. 'He's had a bit of a tough time; the breeders didn't want to keep him because he's completely white, so he's no good as a stud dog. Then they knocked down the sale price because his mum stood on him and managed to injure his left ear so much that he lost part of it. Someone bought him, but they couldn't cope with him because they didn't realise how much work a dog could be, so he had to be rehomed again and that's where we come in. There was another man interested, but he lives on the fifth floor of a block of flats, apparently, and he's out at work all day, too far away to pop home and take him for a walk, like we can. It just doesn't seem the right life for a puppy, even the breeder thought so, which was why she gave me first refusal. At least you'll be able to nip back from work during the day, even if it's just to let him have a run around the garden for ten minutes. I know it's not ideal timing, with the wedding and everything, but as soon as I saw his picture I couldn't say no.'

The minute Anna had seen the advert something had clicked. He was perfect for them; he needed to be a part of a family and they wanted to make their family bigger, one way or another. Everything she'd read about adopting a child had suggested that having a pet that the child could bond with first, was a great way of helping them to settle in. It also gave the child someone to share their problems with, someone who'd just listen, without judging them or even chipping in with their point of view, exactly as Jasper had done for Brae. She'd already booked the puppy a place at the doggy day care centre, which one of her former patients ran less than a two-minute walk from the fish and chip shop, so that he wouldn't have to be on his own when they were out at work. She just hoped Brae thought it was a good idea too.

'I'm thinking of Jones, as a name for him.' The smile on Brae's face wiped away any last little scrap of doubt she might have had. 'That way we'll have your old family name and our new one together, even after you've become a Penrose. What do you think? Jones Penrose, it's got quite a ring to it.'

'It's brilliant.' Anna slid an arm around Brae's waist, planting a kiss on top of Jones' head. All that worry about whether she'd done the right thing and in the end it had been so easy. And now there were three.

17

The Golowan festival in Port Agnes was one of the things that got Ella into the mood for summer when she was growing up. It wasn't quite as big a part of life in Port Agnes as the Silver of the Sea celebrations, later in the summer, but Ella wasn't going to miss out on it now that she was back living in her hometown. The Golowan festival had always fallen in the third week of June and had meant the long school summer holidays were just around the corner. It was an ancient festival to mark midsummer and there was a parade of lanterns, culminating in the lighting of bonfires on the cliffs above Port Agnes, with a fireworks display that illuminated the night sky. Nearly all the shopkeepers got involved and, ever since she could remember, her father had been on the organising committee. Each local business owner would choose a lantern bearer to represent their business and there was a competition to see who could come up with the best costume. Over the years, there had been everything from Spider-Man, to Neptune, God of the sea. One year, Jago had forced Ella to dress as a Cornish pasty, complete with fairy wings, to give her costume a slightly more Midsummer Night feel. Thankfully, this year he'd left it up to her.

As well as the contest for best costume, they were also requesting voluntary donations towards saving the lifeboat station. Ella was asking the lantern bearers to go all out with their outfits and make them as memorable as possible. The video of Brae pirouetting into a heap on the ice rink had got a few thousand views, and about 1,500 signatures to go with it. Now they needed to continue building on that success, along with the movie scenes that he and Dan were still working their way through. One way to do that would be by making the lantern parade the biggest and best yet. It always drew in the crowds, but they needed it to go wide on social media too this time round – and the best way to do that was for the lantern bearers to look as camera-worthy as possible. Suddenly Jago's Cornish pasty fairy seemed like a work of genius.

'I can't believe you've actually got us doing this.' Toni fiddled with the false nose she was wearing and smoothed out the long ginger beard that hung down almost as far as her waist. The new look she'd adopted for the joint hen and stag do had disappeared almost as quickly as it had arrived, and the hair she had hidden under her wig was back to a single shade of brown.

'We said we were going to do a Disney theme to give us a wide appeal.' Ella grinned. 'And correct me if I'm wrong, but I think it was you who suggested *Snow White and the Seven Dwarfs* in the first place?'

'I was stupid enough to think I might get to play Snow White, or at least the Wicked Queen. I mean, Grumpy. That's just type-casting!'

'And I suppose making me dress as Dopey is too?' Jess laughed. It was nice to see her happy; ever since Jess had told them about Dom putting pressure on her to meet up, she'd been really quiet and that wasn't like her.

'If we're typecasting, then I take it you're all suggesting I'm lazy?' Anna pulled on the droopy hat that completed Sleepy's costume, and got into character by giving a big yawn. 'Although I think we chose the person with the best legs for Snow White.'

'I want this noted on my performance review and I want to go up a least one increment just for wearing these tights.' Bobby pulled out the sides of the blue dress he was wearing and did a curtsey. Ella, who was wearing the Wicked Queen's costume, gave her best villainous cackle.

'You've got to get through the parade first, my pretty!'

'I still don't understand why I couldn't be Prince Charming and I had no idea how much tights can chafe.' Bobby grinned despite his words and Ella caught Toni watching him. However hard she tried to deny that they were more than friends, Toni's feelings for Bobby were written all over her face.

'Now you know one of the many agonies of being a woman!' Ella had to hand it to her colleagues. As well as her closest friends, four more of the team from the midwifery unit made up the remainder of the Seven Dwarfs. Dan was playing the handsome prince to Bobby's Snow White, and Brae made the perfect burly woodcutter. The parade was always guaranteed to get covered by the local and regional news, but if they had a sufficiently impressive array of costumes, with word spreading it was all in aid of saving the lifeboat station, they might get picked up as the feel-good story tagged on to the end of the national news, or make one of the tabloids. That would boost the chances of getting enough signatures to really make an impact. If the Just-Giving page Dan had set up managed to get enough donations through to contribute significantly to the rebuild, that might just sway things too. Either way, they'd feel like they'd given it their best shot.

'This singing we've got to do,' Gwen, who was playing Sneezy, pulled a face, 'will it matter if I mime? Only according to my husband, there are feral cats who'd object to the noise I make when I sing.'

'We've got a backing track for all three songs. But I've seen you hit the dance floor, Gwen, so you can give the moves your all instead.' Ella had arranged for their group to be followed by a couple of members of the lifeboat crew, who'd be pulling a small float with a hastily rigged up sound system. One of the crew was a mobile DJ, who was also involved in the Silver of the Sea festival parade that happened every August, and so he'd assured Ella he knew what he was doing. As a result, they'd be accompanied by 'Whistle While You Work', 'Heigh Ho' and 'One Day My Prince Will Come'. Ella could hardly wait to see Bobby giving that one his all. If that didn't make some good video footage, then she didn't know what would.

'Shall we get this over with, then?' Bobby adjusted the long black wig he was wearing, looking like he meant business.

'Let's do it.' Signalling for the others to follow her, Ella hoped everyone else had gone to as much effort as the midwives for this year's parade. If Port Agnes wanted to keep its lifeboat station, it needed to rise to the occasion.

'Not many women could pull off a long white beard, but somehow you managed it.' Brae wrapped an arm around Anna's shoulders, as they walked towards the community centre after the fireworks that had marked the end of the parade. Jones was at Claudine's; the woman who ran the doggy day care centre in town was more than happy to look after the little boxer whenever they needed her to. Ella had organised an auction, and she was hoping that a lot of the crowd from the lantern parade would head to that too. They couldn't miss it after all of Ella's hard work, but they hadn't wanted to leave Jones on his own for that long either. Her dedication to saving the lifeboat centre was incredibly impressive, but it came as no surprise to Anna. Ella's parents were part of the fabric of Port Agnes, and, whether she realised it or not, her best friend was a chip off the old block.

'I've got to admit I was glad to get the beard off at the end of the parade. It felt like it was made of fibreglass by then and it was every bit as itchy! I just hope you remember your passion for white beards if I turn into one of those old ladies who can cultivate whiskers of their own.' Anna moved towards him, somehow knowing that they'd get that far. She hadn't had one second of doubt about it since Brae had asked her to marry him. Being with him just felt like coming home; there was no other way to describe it.

'I'm looking forward to growing old with you, whatever that brings.' Brae dropped a kiss on the top of her head. 'Anyway, I'm happy to pluck out any stray chin hairs you get, if you promise to return the favour with my ears when I turn into one of *those* old men.'

'And they say Hollywood movies don't represent real love! But you've got yourself a deal.' Anna smiled. It might not be the stuff of romcoms, but this was *real* love. Being there for each other and seeing beyond the superficial. Unwanted facial hair could do its worst in the years to come; she couldn't wait to be Brae's wife.

'Anything in particular you've got your eye on at the auction? I'm struggling to find the perfect wedding present for you, so if there is something it would do me a massive favour.'

'I don't need any big gestures for the wedding, especially not after you buying Amber. It'll be enough for us to officially be a family. That bit of paper might not mean a lot to some people, but it does to me.' Anna looked up at him as she spoke.

'I'm so sorry I never got to meet your parents.' Brae's eyes locked with hers. 'I'd have thanked them for raising such an amazing daughter and I'd have promised I was going to do everything in my power to be the best husband I can.'

'They'd have loved you.' It wasn't just an empty platitude, she was sure it was true. Everyone loved Brae, but the only thing her parents had ever wanted for Anna was for her to be happy, and Brae ticked every box on that front. Wrapping her arms around his neck, she kissed him, only pulling away when a group of teenagers walked past making kissing noises, and one of them shouted '*get a room*'.

'I suppose we ought to go in and check out the auction to see who buys your lot.' Anna reluctantly stepped back. Brae had donated an auction item of a fish and chip supper for two, once a week, for a whole year.

'I just hope there's someone out there who's as relaxed as me about turning their six-pack into a dad bod, just for the love of fish and chips.'

'Ella seemed pretty confident it would go down a storm; she's made it one of the top lots.' Anna slipped her hand into his. Their relationship probably seemed like a whirlwind to anyone else, and they'd been together less than two years. The social worker she'd spoken to at the adoption agency had sent out some more information in the post and she discovered they'd have to have lived together for a least two years before they could even be considered to start the adoption process. It had been a relief in a way, taking the pressure off needing to make a decision until things had calmed down again after the wedding.

There was a big crowd inside the community centre, which

meant squeezing in along the back wall to get a spot where they could see the stage. Ella was up there already, microphone in hand. She might have hated the attention she got when the video of the wedding that never happened went viral, but she was getting really good at taking centre stage for events like these. The thought of having to do that made Anna's stomach churn. She'd been asked several times if she was planning to make a speech at the wedding, especially as her dad was no longer around to make the traditional father of the bride speech. But she wanted to enjoy the day, which wouldn't happen if she knew she had to make a speech.

'Okay, our first lot is an occasion cake of your choice made by Mehenicks' Bakery at any time over the next twelve months.' Ella looked out to the crowd as she extolled the virtues of her parents' cake-making, although anyone who'd ever tried one of their cakes would need no convincing. 'It could be for any event: a birthday, wedding, christening, or even just a good old-fashioned get-together. I've grown up having a Mehenicks' cake for my birthday every year and I can testify just how good they are.'

'Would it be wrong to bid on that, if we haven't got an event coming up when we could use it?' Brae patted his stomach. 'It was lovely of Ruth and Jago to offer to make a cake for the wedding, but the trouble is any day is a good enough excuse for me to want a Mehenicks' cake. The auction offer won't quite take us round to our first anniversary, but I think we should have one of Jago and Ruth's cakes every year to mark it anyway.'

'Me too, but let's bid on the cake in the auction too. I'm sure we can think of something to celebrate between now and next summer. At least I hope so!' Anna knew exactly what she wanted to celebrate, but she was determined not to say the words out loud. There'd be no more talk of adoption until they got back from their honeymoon and in the meantime she'd carry on taking the Clomid. Brae had got himself into a blind panic reading some research about the slight possibility of an increased risk of cancer with long-term use of the drug, so they'd agreed on six months as a maximum and even that had taken a lot of persuasion on her part. There was no way he'd agree to any longer, even if her doctors did.

'Right, I'll start off the bidding on the cake at thirty pounds.' As Ella called out, Brae raised his hand. Luckily, at almost six feet four, there was no danger of him being missed, even right at the back of the room.

'Brilliant, any advance on thirty pounds?' Ella had barely got the words out of her mouth, before someone near the front shouted a response.

'Fifty!'

'Great, Brae, can you counter that?'

'Let's go to one hundred pounds,' Brae called out and the offer was immediately countered.

'Two hundred!' Whoever it was at the front of the room really wanted that cake and, if the bids were going up by a hundred pounds a time, it might well turn out to be fifty pounds per slice. Brae turned to Anna and she shook her head. There was plenty of time for them to bid on other things and show their support, but there was no point paying a crazy amount for the cake. Just because they didn't get it, it didn't mean they wouldn't have good news to celebrate. Now wasn't the time to start buying into her mum's superstitions.

The rest of the lots received a similarly enthusiastic response, with Brae's year's supply of fish and chips reaching a very respectable £800. It was a pre-submitted internet bid on a commission of one of Dan's paintings that made the top money of the night, though, at a staggering £4,000. When Ella finally read out the total for the money raised by the auction, it was impossible for Anna to feel anything but delighted, even if she and Brae hadn't managed to secure any of the winning bids.

'Tonight we've made £7,980!' Ella couldn't keep the grin off her face either as she made the announcement from the centre of the stage. 'We've also added over a thousand signatures to our online petition to keep the lifeboat station in Port Agnes open, but we'll be posting pictures of all tonight's events on our social media pages. Please share them if you can, to help push the petition over the magic 10,000 signatures before Parliament goes into recess for the summer. Thanks again so much for coming tonight and especially to those people who were so generous in their bids, and those who donated items for the auction. I was lucky enough to be born in Port Agnes and tonight is just one more reminder of why it's the best place in the world to live, with the best people. Thank you again and goodnight all!'

'She's done brilliantly, hasn't she?' Brae raised his voice to be heard as people around them began to file out of the community centre and back onto the street. 'Do you want to wait and speak to her?'

'I think she's being mobbed by fans!' Anna looked towards the stage as she spoke, reaching down when she felt her mobile vibrate in her pocket and looking at the screen. 'Oh God.'

'What is it?' Brae's voice was instantly filled with concern.

'I don't know if I'm worrying for nothing, but it's a text from Luke Scott asking if I can go over to their place when I've got a minute and see Tamara and the baby, but he told me not to worry if it's too late tonight. They were only discharged from hospital today, and Toni was going to pop over in the morning as it's my day off.'

'Isn't that the lady whose baby had the cleft lip?' Brae was always there when she needed to offload after work, and it was obvious now that he actually listened to what she said. Being at

Belle's delivery had been difficult, because of how much it had impacted on Tamara. While they'd managed to persuade her to take the baby to the hospital in the end, Anna knew it wasn't that simple. The anxiety and depression that Tamara had suffered from over the years, which had contributed to her eating disorders in the past, couldn't just be flicked off like a switch. A thoughtless comment or a sideways glance from a stranger, could be enough to trigger a reaction from Tamara that would be beyond her control, or any rational conversation. Mental health was far more complex than that.

'Yes, that's her, but they seemed to be doing really well last time I saw them. I just hope they're okay.' Anna was about to ask Brae if he'd mind her popping over to the Scotts' place before they went home, despite it being so late and Luke telling her not to worry, but she didn't get the chance.

'Let me drive you over there on the way back. I'm not going to get Jones until the morning, so we've got no rush to get home, as long as they're okay with it.'

'Are you sure?'

'Of course, just text Luke to make sure it's not too late for them and I'll wait out in the car for you.'

'I know I keep saying it, but I love you so much.'

'Finally the woodcutter gets the girl, instead of the handsome prince!'

'You mean he gets one of the less memorable members of the seven dwarfs?'

'There's nothing forgettable about you.' Brae put his arm around her again, as they headed out of the community centre. Anyone who said happy endings were just for fairy tales had it wrong.

* * *

'Are you sure they don't mind me coming in?' Brae looked at Anna across the top of the car.

'No, Luke told me to bring you in. Unless you'd rather wait in the car?' Anna didn't have any worries about Brae saying the wrong thing. He was far too thoughtful.

'I don't often get the chance to see you doing your job, so I can't wait. I just wanted to make sure Tamara won't feel uncomfortable with me being there. Maybe we should have a code word if you think things are getting difficult for her, and I can excuse myself.'

'Most people have code words for entirely different reasons, you know.'

'I'm saving those for our honeymoon!' Brae laughed and followed her towards the Scotts' front door. It was almost impossible to believe that they'd be touching down in Florida in a couple of weeks' time. They'd been looking forward to it so much and Anna still couldn't wait to be alone with Brae, but she had to admit she felt more than a pang about leaving Jones behind. Luckily Ruth had offered to have him stay with her and Jago, so that their dog, Daisy, could keep him company. It had made Anna feel a lot less guilty when Ruth had said she'd take them to the beach every day and that it would be great fun for Daisy to have another dog to play with too. It would be like Jones was having a little holiday all of his own and, next time they went away, he'd definitely be coming with them.

'Thanks for coming.' Luke had a smile on his face when he answered the door, which had to be a good sign.

'It's no problem. We had to come past on the way home anyway.' Anna turned slightly. 'This is my fiancé, Brae.'

'Nice to meet you. Although I'm already a big fan of your fish and chip shop, so you might well have seen me in there.' Luke shook his hand.

'I'm sure I have, but it's good to meet you properly too and congratulations on Belle's arrival.' Brae followed Anna's lead and slipped off his shoes. Luke had requested it when Tamara was in labour, but he didn't have to ask this time.

'Thanks, it's been a bit of rollercoaster, but it's amazing. Come through to the front room. Tam's in there with the baby.'

'How's she doing?' Anna couldn't read the expression on Luke's face and his words didn't give much of clue either.

'Have a look for yourself. That's why I wanted you to come over.'

Anna almost pushed past Luke in her haste to see Tamara and Belle. She just wanted everything to be okay for the young family. Belle's condition was such a tiny thing compared to what some children went through and, more than that, it was eminently fixable. That didn't stop it being huge for Tamara, though, and scary if Belle was struggling to feed.

'Tam, Anna's here, with her fiancé, Brae.' Luke held open the door to the room, letting them go in ahead of him.

'Thanks so much for coming over.' Tamara looked up and smiled. 'I felt so bad for not thanking you properly when Belle was born, I wasn't thinking straight.'

'You don't need to thank me.' Anna couldn't stop smiling either, as she watched Tamara cradling the baby in her arms.

'Yes, I do. If you hadn't been so patient with me, I'd have closed down and refused to go to the hospital with Belle. Then I wouldn't have been around to listen to any of the information they gave me.' A flush of colour spread across Tamara's cheeks. 'I've been managing to feed her myself and she lost a bit of weight at first, but she's half a pound above her birth weight already.'

'That's brilliant and nearly all babies lose weight after they're born, so you're doing fantastically.'

'What's even better is that all the other tests came back clear

and the specialist said the cleft lip should be a relatively easy fix.'
Luke looked down at the baby as he spoke. 'There was another
family in there whose baby was born with a cleft lip and palate.
He had something called Pierre syndrome, I think it was. The
poor little thing had to have a feeding tube in his nose.'

'Pierre Robin Syndrome.' Anna nodded. It was linked to
babies born with both a cleft lip and palate, and it could cause
trouble with their airways. So Luke's gratitude about the relative
simplicity of Belle's cleft lip was completely understandable. 'And
how are you both doing?'

'I've restarted my anxiety medication because they've said it
won't affect the baby while I'm feeding her myself, and I've asked
the hospital to refer me to the postnatal mental health team.'
Tamara bit her lip. 'I'm okay at the moment, but I don't want to
take any chances, so I'd rather put the help in place before I let
things get on top of me this time. Belle needs me and I want to be
the best mother I can for her.'

'You're doing an amazing job so far.' Brae spoke before Anna
had the chance, and Tamara's face broke into a genuine smile.

'Thank you so much. Would either of you like to hold her?'

'I know I would, but I suppose I should let Anna do the
honours first.' Despite his words, Brae took a step towards
Tamara. It was obvious he was desperate to hold the baby and
Anna wasn't going to deprive him of the chance.

'You can have the first cuddle, as long as I get one before
we go.'

'You just need to support her head.' Tamara gave Brae the
instruction as she handed her precious daughter over to him.
She didn't know what a dab hand he was at holding babies, but
Anna had seen him with his niece when she was younger. He
was great with his sister's son too, and Anna had been Morwenna's midwife when she'd first met Brae. At the time, she'd still

been with her long-term partner and she'd never dreamed that one day she'd end up as auntie to the children she'd helped bring into the world. She'd known for a long time that things weren't right with her ex, but it had taken a catalyst to make her realise they'd never be right and it had broken her heart. It had made room in her life for Brae, though, and for that she'd be forever grateful.

'You're a natural.' Luke patted Brae on the back. 'It'll be a lucky kid that gets you two as parents.'

'We're hoping we get to be the lucky ones.' Brae smiled and he caught Anna's eye for a split second before looking back down at the baby. 'No matter how many times I get the privilege of holding a baby, they always amaze me. She's so alert already.'

'It's her tiny fingernails and toenails I can't get over.' Luke laughed. 'God, if my mates heard me talking like this, they'd laugh their heads off. But how can something so tiny be so perfect?'

'What a couple of men's men we've got ourselves involved with!' It was Tamara's turn to laugh. 'But I wouldn't have it any other way and I bet you wouldn't either? Which reminds me, we've got you a wedding present.'

'You shouldn't have done that, but thank you so much!' Anna took the large gift bag that Tamara passed her.

'Should we open it now, or wait until the wedding?'

'Open it now if you like.' Tamara waited as Anna pulled out the package wrapped in tissue paper, tearing it off to uncover an A3-sized box frame, with words spelt out in wooden scrabble letters. Anna and Brae's names were at the centre, with love, home, marriage, family and Port Agnes, all linked from them.

'I love it, it's perfect! Look, Brae.' Anna turned the frame towards him.

'It's brilliant and what a fantastic idea.'

'Tam won't tell you, but she made it herself.' The pride in Luke's voice was tangible.

'Really? You should sell these in Pottery and Paper, down by the harbour. They'd go down a storm.' Anna looked at the picture again. Somehow it summed up everything that marrying Brae meant to her. It really was perfect.

'It's just a tiny thank you for everything you've done.' Tamara obviously found it difficult to take the praise being heaped upon her, so Anna squeezed her hand, hoping it conveyed just how grateful she was. Ten minutes later she'd finally had her cuddle with baby Belle, and Tamara was looking worn out.

'Thanks so much for the gift and for inviting us over, and especially for the cuddles with Belle.' Anna turned towards Tamara as they said their goodbyes. 'Toni will pop by tomorrow and I'll be in to see you in a couple of days.'

'I thought you might be off now until the wedding?'

'No, I've got a few more days to go, then I'm off the day before to get everything set up, so I'll see you the day after tomorrow.'

'We'll look forward to it.' Tamara glanced down at her daughter as she spoke.

'Thanks again for inviting me in and letting me cuddle your beautiful baby girl.' Brae said the words without a trace of hesitation and it was obvious he meant every one.

'It was lovely to meet you.' Tamara looked as if she was desperately suppressing the urge to yawn. It was definitely time to go.

'I'll see you out.' Luke stood up, stopping as they reached the corridor and turning to pull the living room door shut behind him. 'She's doing well, isn't she? I'm just terrified that something might happen and she'll go to pieces again. She still won't even talk to her family and her brother is desperate to see Belle. I'm sure mending fences with them would help her let go of the past.'

'She's doing all the right things and the fact that she's asking for support from the postnatal mental health team before she hits any bumps in the road, is a great sign.' Anna touched Luke's arm. 'We can't predict what might happen, but you know where I am if you need me. The whole team at the unit is there for you too.'

'Thank you, that really helps.' Luke nodded. 'Which reminds me, I wanted to do something to contribute to the fundraising you're doing for the lifeboat station. If you ever need some catering for one of the events, I'm your man.'

'That's great, thank you so much. Ella has been far more involved in that than me, so I'll let her know. She'll be really pleased. I'll see you in a couple of days.' Anna smiled as Luke opened the front door.

'Great. Nice to meet you, Brae.'

'You too.' Following Brae out into the darkness of the street, Anna looked back at the glow of light in the front room where Tamara was still cradling her baby. Sometimes being a midwife seemed relentless and exhausting, but every once in a while there were nights like this when her job felt like pure magic.

18

The blue and grey pleasure boat, which ran tours from the harbour at Port Agnes, to spot seals on the rocky outcrops stretching along the coastline to neighbouring Port Kara, was chugging out to sea as Jess headed along the coastal path. It was almost seven o'clock in the evening, but still warm enough not to need a jacket. The last boat tour left the harbour at seven during the late spring and summer months, but there were private charters up until midnight when the weather was calm enough. It was how Jess had celebrated her birthday two years before, drinking champagne on deck under a canopy of stars. It had seemed too good to be true and that's exactly what it had turned out to be. But she could still remember the words Dom had written inside the card he'd given her.

Darling J-J

Happy birthday! This is the last year you'll get to party without having to be up with a baby in the morning. So we've really got to make it count!

Love you forever. Dom xx

He'd really pulled all the stops out, starting with breakfast in bed, lunch and cocktails at Casa Cantare, a wine bar in the centre of Port Agnes, and a private charter of the tour boat for a moonlit tour along the coast. It had all been topped off by a late supper and an overnight stay in the hotel on the Sisters of Agnes Island, which was cut off from the mainland at high tide. Dom had gone all out for a birthday that wasn't even a milestone and, when she'd asked him why, he'd said he just wanted to make it a special one.

He seemed convinced that a night in a five-star hotel would give them the little bit of magic they needed to finally achieve their longed-for pregnancy. They'd been trying for almost six months at that point and, when the hotel hadn't turned out to be the charm after all, it had been the beginning of things starting to unravel. Seven months after her birthday they'd finally had the tests to find out why it wasn't happening and the results had been life-changing in more ways than one.

Her birthday this year had been a lot more low-key, dinner with Anna and Ella had been more than enough and she wasn't going to give what had happened with Dom any more space in her head. It had been so sweet of Anna to fit it in with everything she had going on and the last-minute rush before the wedding. Jess had so many good friends now and she had so much to be thankful for, not least having miles of blue sea that seemed to stretch out to infinity five minutes' walk from her house. She'd never get bored of walking along the coastal path and taking in the view that nowhere else she'd visited had ever quite matched. It didn't matter if it was a beautiful day, with the sun kissing her skin and bringing her freckles out of hiding, or the sort of squally weather that blew spray straight off the sea making salt stick to her skin instead.

Over the winter, just after she'd split up with Dom, the

weather had seemed to reflect her mood – storms rolling in from the sea and icy winds making her jaw hurt as she took her daily walk up here. Her misery had seemed as unrelenting as the weather, but the discovery that Dom was already seeing someone else had actually helped. She'd been let down before and she knew the drill. It felt strangely familiar, almost comfortable, to pick herself up and put herself back together again.

Jess had come to the conclusion, at a scarily young age, that she was the only person she could rely on and it had stood her in good stead, although the other midwives had gradually chipped away at that belief. Anna and Ella had organised nights out and helped her find somewhere new to live, after the house she'd shared with Dom had sold within two weeks of going on the market. Her new flat, in a converted attic above the booking office for Port Agnes Boat Tours, was small, but she loved it. It was the first place she'd lived that had ever been all hers. After the student houseshares at university, she'd lived in nurses' accommodation at the first hospital she'd worked in, then in a rented house with another midwife and two of the radiographers from the hospital, before finally moving in with Dom less than a month after meeting him. Living on her own was something she'd always resisted, but it had been a revelation.

The wooden staircase that led up to Jess's flat probably wouldn't have passed a safety inspection, but it meant she didn't have to go through the booking office to access her front door. The same landlord owned the whole building and he'd given her a key to the booking office for when it was closed, just in case she'd preferred to go in that way, but she hadn't ever used it. Being falsely accused of stealing in her first foster placement, and overhearing her foster carers' neighbour saying it was all they could expect from a *kid like that*, had made her paranoid about putting herself in a situation where she could be accused of something she hadn't done. The cash register for the booking office might be locked away in an inner office that she couldn't access, but she didn't want the boat owner coming in and saying there were two less life jackets on the stand than there'd been the day before, and everyone pointing a finger in her direction.

Although the paint was peeling off the bottom of the front door of her flat where it had been lashed by wind and rain, seeing the little sign on the wall next to it always made Jess smile. The words 'Puffins' Rest' were written above a picture of two puffins sitting side by side on a rock. There was a certain way the key had to be waggled in the lock to get it to open, but it was all part of the charm; like having a secret code to access the flat that only Jess knew.

Being nestled in the eaves of the house made it feel cosy, too, and the skylights, on the right-hand side of the open-plan living room and kitchen, spanned almost the whole space from floor to ceiling. There were two small bedrooms at the opposite end of the roof space and, until Jess had moved in, it had been a holiday let. She was almost sure the landlord could have got more rent for it from holidaymakers, but Anna had delivered all three of his children. So, when she'd told him to let her know if a flat came up that one of the other midwives could rent, he'd offered up Puffins' Rest. He'd said he was having trouble getting it on the books of the holiday rental firm, because he couldn't let holidaymakers have access via the inside staircase in the booking office and the company's safety regulations wouldn't allow their guests to use the same entrance as Jess. He could have found a way around that if he wanted to, though, and it was just one more thing Jess had to thank Anna for.

'Luna, I'm home. Are you there?' Jess called out into the silence. There was no sign of the little cat, whose dark and light grey stripes made her look like she'd stepped out of a black-and-white movie.

Jess had never intended to have a cat. She adopted Luna when she'd first moved into the flat, although it was more the other way around if truth be told. Luna was a well-known character around the harbour, hanging out in the hope of being thrown a sardine by one of the fisherman, but no one seemed to know who she belonged to. After Jess heard her mewing loudly one night and took a tin of tuna down to soothe the little cat's hunger, Luna had decided that she'd found her new owner. Maybe it was because she recognised a kindred spirit in the little lost cat who'd been forced to fend for itself, but, whatever the reason, Jess had done nothing to discourage Luna from following her home. Eventually she'd had to confess to the landlord that she was no longer the only tenant living in Puffins' Rest and, to her surprise, he'd offered to put in a cat flap. So Luna had officially become a permanent fixture.

'Hey you, have you had a good day?' Jess leant down and rubbed Luna's ears when she finally appeared from behind the sofa, threading herself in and out of Jess's legs and purring loudly. Scooping up the cat she braced herself, never knowing whether Luna was going to nuzzle into her neck, or expose her claws and sink them straight into Jess's flesh. Thankfully Luna appeared to be in an affectionate mood, her whole body vibrating with contentment as she purred into Jess's ear. 'It must be your turn to make dinner tonight?'

This had to be the first sign of madness; talking to a cat as if there was a chance it might turn around and answer you. Opening the fridge door, she peered in. There were three Waitrose ready meals from the last time she'd been in Truro, and she was just trying to decide between the risotto and the tomato and pesto pasta, when her mobile started to ring. Fishing the phone out of her pocket, she half expected it to be a patient, but she didn't recognise the number.

'Hello, is that Jessica Kennedy?' The woman on the other end of the phone sounded as if she hadn't expected Jessica to answer either.

'Speaking.'

'Great, I wasn't sure if you'd still be at work. My name's Esther and I'm calling from the fostering assessment team at Cornwall County Council.'

'Oh, hi. Thanks so much for calling.' Jess immediately felt the urge to put on a posh accent, although there was every chance Esther was phoning to say she wasn't going to be recommended to move forward with fostering. Jess had expected to start the assessment process almost straight after her initial training, but the checks had taken longer than anticipated to come through and she'd become increasingly convinced that Dom had scuppered her chances.

'No problem at all, I just wanted to let you know that all your stage one checks are complete at last and we can go ahead with your assessment as soon as possible. If that's still what you'd like to do?'

'Absolutely.' Even as Jess said the words her stomach suddenly churned like she was on a fairground ride.

'That's brilliant, because we want to put you on a fast-track assessment with a view to getting you ready for panel as soon as October.'

'That sounds...' It had been on the tip of Jess's tongue to say 'terrifying' – it was only three months away – but somehow another word came out. 'Amazing.'

'Brilliant! Well I'm hoping you'll also be pleased that Dexter, the social worker who was at your Skills to Foster training, has confirmed he's happy to carry out the assessment.'

'That's great news.' For the first time Jess really believed what she was saying. The assessment was going to be hard; it needed to be for the local authority to make sure it got the right carers for children who deserved the best possible second chance in life. But knowing Dexter would be the one asking her the questions and taking her back to a time she'd rather forget, immediately made it feel less like her legs were about to give out from under her.

'I'm so pleased you think so! Although everyone loves working with Dexter, so I didn't expect anything else to be honest. I'll let him know you're happy to go ahead and he'll be in touch to set up your first meeting.'

'Thank you so much.' Jess's posh accent might have disappeared as quickly as it had arrived, but frankly she was amazed that she was still managing to speak at all. It was really happening. If she didn't totally mess up the next three months, then she was going to be a foster carer. Picking Luna up again, not even having her shoulders raked by razor-sharp claws could dampen Jess's mood. Forget the Waitrose ready meals, this called for a celebration dinner and only a takeout from the Yangtze would do.

* * *

Anna needed one more look around the room before she could bear to close the door. Along with Brae, she'd spent the afternoon at the Red Cliff Hotel putting the finishing touches to the ballroom where, in less than twenty-four hours, they'd be getting married.

The hotel had provided all the usual decorations, but they'd wanted to personalise the event and add something to each table that was more meaningful than the centrepieces the hotel had suggested. Anna had bought ornamental trees and decorated each one with things that represented the guests on that table and their relationship to Anna and Brae. It had taken hours online, finding and ordering just the right things, but it looked amazing and, with a relatively small guest list, everyone at the wedding meant something really special to them. Brae's parents were flying back from Spain for the wedding and his brother-in-law had gone to the airport to pick them up. Everything was in place at last.

'Are you ready?' Brae put his arm around her as she finally managed to turn away from the doors of the ballroom.

'Ready to leave, or ready to get married?' She laughed at the look that crossed his face.

'I meant ready to leave, but now I'm worried about what your answer to the other question might be.'

'I'm more than ready to marry you. I have been since about an hour and a half after I met you.'

'What took you so long?' Brae pretended to tut. 'I knew within the first ten minutes.'

'What was it that convinced you that I was so unbelievably perfect!' If he could tease her, then she was going to give as good as she got.

'It was the strangest thing. I wanted to find out everything about you, but at the same time I felt like I already knew you really well.' Brae cleared his throat, his jokey tone disappearing. 'This is probably going to sound like the cheesiest line ever, but it was as if the one thing I'd been looking for all my life was right there in front of me.'

'Luckily for you I love cheese almost as much as I love you!' She grabbed hold of his hand, which was draped over her shoulder. 'Can you believe that this time tomorrow, we'll be married?'

'You've got until seven o'clock tomorrow to jump into a car

and head out of Port Agnes without looking back. Otherwise you're stuck with me.'

'I'm not going anywhere.' Anna squeezed his hand. 'And don't you even think about going anywhere either. One Port Agnes midwife being jilted on her wedding day is more than enough, thank you very much.'

'Do you think this bothers Ella? Being so much a part of this wedding? I'd hate to think it brings back any difficult memories for her.'

'As awful as it was to be dumped so publicly, she's told me she's really glad that it happened now. She loves Dan much more than she ever loved Weller. I think the problem is she spent so long convincing Dan that she never wanted to do the marriage thing again, he's completely ruled it out now. One thing being involved in our wedding has done for Ella is to make her realise she would like to do it one day. Maybe not yet, but she definitely doesn't want it to be off the table for good.'

'Do you ever worry that we're rushing things?'

'Never. I was with Greg for years and we both know how that ended. Looking back, it just feels like wasted time, when I could have been with you.' Anna widened her eyes. 'Why? Do you?'

'No. That's exactly how I feel. I can't believe you know everything there is to know about me and you still want to marry me!'

'The more I found out about you, the more I fell in love with you.' Anna smiled. Some people needed surprises, but she was more than happy knowing Brae inside and out and understanding exactly where she stood. Anything else and he wouldn't be the man she loved.

* * *

Anna hadn't wanted the formality of a wedding rehearsal dinner, but having a meal with Dan and Ella didn't seem like making a fuss; they did it all the time anyway. They'd booked a table at the hotel on the Sisters of Agnes Island, where Brae had proposed. The island was opposite the harbour, but at high tide it could only be accessed by boat. The hotel had its own launch and they were due to catch it at seven-thirty to make their table at eight.

Even though it was still light outside, the hotel on the Sisters of Agnes Island had lanterns lining the path all the way from the jetty to the hotel entrance ready to illuminate the darkness. There were thousands of fairy lights strung up in the trees outside, which would be lit-up beautifully by the time they left, as well as a series of sweet-smelling flower arrangements mounted on podiums lining the corridors. No wonder it was booked out for weddings so far in advance. The hotel had won a series of awards over the past year and even getting a table there was a challenge now. If Anna and Brae had wanted to get married in the beautiful Victorian conservatory where the weddings at the hotel took place, they'd have had almost a two-year wait.

A huge ice sculpture of a cherub dominated the centre of the conservatory, where they were having pre-dinner drinks. It was in almost the same spot where Brae had dropped down onto one knee without any hint of the self-consciousness that Anna knew he struggled with at times. He'd looked up at her and she hadn't even needed to think about her response.

Maybe it was dangerous to trust him as much as she did. She'd been hurt often enough in the past to know that people were more than capable of causing pain to those they professed to love, but somehow she just knew that wouldn't happen with Brae. All her married friends had warned her to expect pre-wedding jitters, and Gwen, the matriarch of the midwifery unit, had reminded her that it was never too late to change her mind, not even on the day of the wedding itself; a comment that had earned her an uncharacteristically sharp look from Ella. All the advice was well-intended, and it was pretty much what her parents would have said had they still been around. She didn't need any of it, though.

'Champagne for the bride- and groom-to-be, or do you want a brandy to calm your nerves after that boat ride?' Dan looked at Anna and Brae as he stood at the bar. 'I'm still quite surprised you and Ella agreed to the boat trip over here, after what happened in the storm.'

'Nothing was going to stop me getting here to try the dark chocolate and clementine parfait we saw in that *Cornish Life* article about the hotel. My mouth waters every time I think about it.' Ella's stomach rumbled exactly on cue.

'I think you've made your point!' Brae grinned. 'Hopefully we can all forget that the storm ever happened and concentrate on all the good things. It seems really easy tonight, knowing Anna's going to be my wife by this time tomorrow.'

'Romantic, but the parfait is definitely the lure for me too!' Anna laughed, as Brae gave her a playful nudge. 'Luckily the hotel's boat is a bit less ramshackle than that thing the two of you set out to sea in. It might be the middle of summer, but that doesn't stop the Atlantic breezes hitting the coast hard, like they are tonight. So, it's a good job we could sit inside on the way over, otherwise I'd have been celebrating my first anniversary before I could get my hair back under control again.'

'I think an evening like this calls for champagne to toast our best friends on the eve of their wedding.' Dan turned away and spoke to the barman, and Anna couldn't help smiling. Brae and Dan were right, there was so much to celebrate, and not just the wedding. Ella was really close to hitting her target of 10,000 signatures and she'd raised a phenomenal amount for the lifeboat fund so far. Brae had been shortlisted for the regional final of the Fish and Chip Shop of the Year award, and Dan had just taken a commission for a painting that would pay his bills for six months, even if he didn't take on any more property renovations for a while.

'I know the two of you are probably going to laugh at this, but would you mind if Anna and I popped out for a second to Face-Time Claudine and check on Jones?' Brae looked towards Dan and Ella as the waiter went off to get their order. 'We're not going to get a chance to see him until after the wedding and I want to make sure he doesn't forget me!'

'Anyone who looked at you would never guess what an old softie you are!' Dan grinned. 'Of course we don't mind, just don't be too long or we might start the champagne without you.'

FaceTiming a dog from the gardens of the hotel probably was a bit ridiculous, but if Claudine thought so she seemed more than happy to humour them. Jones obligingly licked the screen of Claudine's phone when Brae requested a goodnight kiss from the dog they were both equally besotted with, but Anna wanted to make sure she wasn't completely upstaged on the eve of their wedding.

'I never thought I could be this happy.' Turning to him she took a step forward until their bodies were touching. 'I can't wait for tomorrow to come and to tell the world exactly how much I love you. I don't care how corny that sounds.'

'It doesn't, not to me, and I can't wait either. I just don't want to make anyone too uncomfortable when they tell me I can kiss the bride, so I'll have to rein it in a bit tomorrow. But, if you don't mind, seeing as there's no one out here but us, I'm going to show you exactly how I'd really like to kiss you.'

'I think I can handle it!' She was still grinning when Brae kissed her, the passion behind it more than living up to his promise. There'd been times in the past when Anna had considered herself incredibly unlucky, losing the two people she'd loved the most so quickly. Then she'd found Brae, and to have known so much love from three amazing people in her life made her the luckiest person there was.

When they'd eventually made it back inside the restaurant, the first bottle of champagne didn't stretch to toasting all the things they had to celebrate, so they shared a second bottle over dinner. By the time Brae went back with Dan to spend his last night as a bachelor at Mercer's Row, and Anna went back to the cottage, with Ella for company, she was completely exhausted, but happier than she could remember being in years. It might have been down to the champagne, but against expectations, Anna had fallen into a deep sleep as soon as her head hit the pillow. If only she'd made it all the way through the night, everything would have been so different and she might still have felt like the luckiest girl in the world.

19

Anna wasn't sure if she'd been having one of those dreams where you fall and jolt yourself awake, or if it was something else that had woken her with a violent shudder. Either way, she was instantly wide awake, her brain racing through a mental checklist of every aspect of the wedding – despite her attempts to drown out her internal monologue by playing sleep sounds on her phone.

It was one of those horrible sensations, like being certain you've forgotten something vitally important when you set off on holiday, but having no idea what it was. It was almost four a.m. by the time she realised what it was – she'd forgotten her parents. Not literally, of course, but her decision not to make a speech at the reception and not having anyone at the wedding who'd known them personally, other than Anna, meant their absence would feel all the more marked. She needed to acknowledge them properly, but not even sleep deprivation could convince her to make a speech. She could manage a toast, though, and now all she needed was the perfect quote to sum up everything they meant to her.

Brae had a whole shelf of reference books in the study, a room he mostly used to do the books for the fish and chip shop. But she'd caught him in there several times, poring over a book of quotes when he'd been preparing his vows and wedding speech. There had to be something in there that would help her come up with the perfect thing to say.

Creeping downstairs so that she didn't wake Ella, she stepped over the stair that always creaked the loudest and headed into the study. There were two books of quotations on the middle shelf and Anna picked one out. The first quote she saw said something about no one understanding parental love until they were parents themselves, and it was all she could do not to slam that book shut. For the next twenty minutes or so, she felt like Goldilocks. Some of the quotes were too bland and some were two flowery, but then she found it, the perfect quote:

> *'Remember me and a part of me will always be with you.'*

It was a quote from *The Heretic's Daughter* by Kathleen Kent, and it summed up exactly what Brae had said to her: that her parents would be a part of everything she did, and part of the lives of any children they might have – genetic or otherwise – for as long as she remembered them.

Sliding the books back onto the shelf, she breathed out. She was ready now, to toast her parents, to thank them for all they'd done for her and to acknowledge that they were part of her forever. For a whole ten seconds she was bathed in a strange sense of calm, and then her fingers brushed against the spine of another book, her eyes immediately drawn to the wording. It was a book of baby names.

Pulling it out, she opened the front cover and read the hand-written words inside:

Ideas for baby Penrose-Hart

Anna knew all about Julia Hart, Brae's former fiancée, who he'd been due to marry when he left the Navy. It hadn't worked out and, after everything Brae had told her, Anna had never felt threatened by his past relationship with Julia. Until now. She'd had no idea they'd got as far as talking about babies. But then didn't everyone who got engaged have that conversation to find out whether or not they were on the same page about wanting children? Of course Brae would have said yes and, at ten years younger than Anna, Julia would have had years to fulfil that dream. The idea that they'd had a baby name book, though, and that it had meant enough to Brae for him to hold on to it for all this time, made it feel as if it had been rolled up and shoved down Anna's throat.

She should have just shut it, put it back on the shelf, and carried on. Brae had told her a hundred times that all he needed was her, and she'd believed it, because in the end she'd realised that all she needed was him. But, confronted by the book of names he'd looked through with his fiancé, imagining what their child might be called, she couldn't help turning the pages.

She got to the Cs and the name Cameron, before she saw the first writing in the margin. The words '*Yes or No?*' were written in black next to the name, in handwriting she didn't recognise. Below it, in red and in Brae's distinctive handwriting, were the words '*love it!*'

The tears that sprung into Anna's eyes might have been irra-tional and even self-centred, but she couldn't stop them. Brae had picked out baby names with another woman that he was never going to get to use. Even if they were selected to adopt, they'd never get to pick their child's name. It was stupid, such a small thing in the scheme of what it meant to be a parent, but it felt like just one more thing that Brae was being robbed of because he'd chosen her. Even as she tried to tell herself that was the most important thing in all of this – he'd chosen *her* – she didn't believe it. She needed to speak to him, to hear him say it didn't matter, that there wouldn't always be a part of him that grieved for the baby who would have been called Cameron, or one of the other names he'd told Julia he'd love to call their child. And he'd kept the book; that had to mean something, even if he never admitted it.

Reaching for her phone, she hesitated. How many times was she going to need Brae to reassure her before she believed him? She hated herself for it, but she loved him too much to stand in the way of what he wanted. They could get ten years down the line before the grief for those unfulfilled dreams suddenly got much bigger. Brae might be all the family she needed, but she couldn't bear to lose a second one. Losing her parents had been out of anyone's control and she could give up the chance of being with Brae for something that might never happen. She kept coming back to the one thing that was fact – he'd kept the book and the truth was staring her in the face. He'd wanted a baby, imagined it and even got halfway to naming it...

Her fingers were still hovering just above the phone, not sure whether to text him or just try to focus on all the things he'd already said to convince her that none of this mattered, when it started to ring – making her body jolt again, just like it had when she'd woken up. For a split second she thought it might be Brae, somehow sensing she needed to speak to him – which even without inheriting her mum's superstitious mind, she would definitely have taken as a sign.

'Hello.' The clock in the study said it was four fifty-seven. Never a good time to get an unexpected call.

'I'm so sorry to call you this early, Miss Jones, but we wanted to give you as a much notice as possible.' The woman's voice on the other end of the line sounded close to tears. 'This is Melanie Slater, the manager from the Red Cliff Hotel, I'm afraid there's been a fire.'

'Oh God, is everyone okay?' If anything was going to put Anna's worries into perspective, this was it. She'd chatted to a group of older people who'd been checking in for a short break while she'd been in the reception area the day before. They'd been excited to hear she was getting married and wished her all the best. The thought of them being caught up in the fire was the first thing that crossed her mind.

'We got everyone out and we're making arrangements to move all the guests to different hotels, which is the good news.' Melanie cleared her throat. 'But the fire started in the corridor between the main hotel and the ballroom, where the annexe bedrooms are. One of the guests lit some candles and left them unattended when they went to dinner, and the fire brigade think the curtains caught alight. By the time the smoke alarms went off the sprinklers didn't have a chance.'

'That's where my room is... my dress is in there and everything.' Anna was trying not to panic, but it was almost impossible.

'It's awful, the rooms in that corridor are completely gutted and there was nothing we could rescue from yours – it was right next to the one where the fire started. The ballroom itself is badly smoke damaged, but the water damage the firemen caused putting out the fire is even worse. I'm so sorry, but I don't think we're going to be able to salvage anything and obviously we aren't going to be able to host the wedding.'

'No one else is going to be able to do it at this short notice either, are they?' It was more of a statement than a question.

'I'm happy to ring around a few places for you, but what with it being one of the biggest weekends of the summer for weddings...' Melanie trailed off. They both knew it was impossible.

'I think it's better if I just accept it's not going to happen.' Anna screwed up her eyes to try to stop the threatened tears, but it was useless. 'There are so many people I need to contact, to let them know the wedding's not going ahead.'

'I wish there was something I could do.' Melanie sounded like she was crying now, too.

'So do I, but it's not your fault.'

'If you think of anything, this is my personal mobile number, just give me a call.'

'I don't think there's anything anyone can do, but thank you.' Anna stared at her mobile as she ended the call, her shoulders heaving as she started to sob. She hated herself for being so devastated when the important thing was that everyone was okay. It wasn't the end of the world, but that didn't stop it feeling like it. She might not believe in omens, but the wedding venue burning down hours before the ceremony was a pretty bad sign by anyone's standards. Maybe her mother had been right after all and things really did happen for a reason. After all, she'd have plenty of time to talk to Brae about the baby book now and find out exactly how much those dreams meant to him.

'Anna?' Ella pushed the door open before she had a chance to respond. 'Are you okay? I thought I heard crying.'

'The wedding's off.'

'What's happened? Is it Brae? Is he okay?' Ella crossed the room and sat next to Anna on the bed.

'It's not Brae, and I know I shouldn't be getting this upset when no one's hurt.' Anna's voice cracked, despite her best attempts to pull herself together. 'There's been a fire at the hotel and they got everyone out, but the room where my dress was hanging has been completely gutted and the ballroom's a write-off too. I know I can marry Brae as soon as we sort out another venue...'

'You've got every right to be devastated, anyone would be.'

'It's stupid when it's only a delay,' Anna sniffed, not sure whether to voice her fears to her best friend that it could be a sign she shouldn't marry Brae at all. Mentioning the book would feel like a betrayal of trust. It was a part of Brae's life that had nothing to do with her and if he'd chosen to keep it, in amongst the books with quotes of love, that was none of her business either. It had proved there were things she didn't know about him after all, probably hundreds of them. 'It's just that, for years, I haven't had a family. It might be old-fashioned but, for me, getting married signifies that we're officially a family. I wanted to get married on Mum and Dad's anniversary too, but now I can't help feeling it's a sign and I don't even believe in those!'

'No it isn't, it's just bloody awful bad luck and you and Brae are the last people who deserve that.' Ella hugged Anna tightly. When she finally pulled back, Ella took a deep breath. 'I don't think we should just give up on the wedding. There has to be some way of making it happen today. Maybe not with all the bells and whistles, but if the important part of it is being married to Brae and sharing your parents' anniversary, then I'm sure we can do it.'

'I love you for wanting to try, Ella, but we're never going to be able to find somewhere to hold it. Even the manager from the hotel said it's one of the busiest weekends of the year for weddings.'

'You've got the registrar booked, though, haven't you? So all we need is a venue.' Anna could almost see the cogs of Ella's brain working. 'Whatever you do, don't cancel the registrar, at least not until I've made some calls.'

'Even if we could find a venue. There's nothing for the guests to eat, the cake was already set up in the ballroom and I've got nothing to wear either, not to mention you or the other brides-maids. Fourteen hours is mission impossible, even for you.'

'We can wear jeans if we have to, and no one who cares about you and Brae will give a damn about the food, they can bring sandwiches if it comes to it. Just let everyone know that there's going to be change of venue and I'll post on the fundraising page when I've got more news. Everyone can access that, so they just need to look out for updates. As soon as it gets to a decent hour, I'll start making some calls. In the meantime, I think I ought to get you that brandy you turned down last night. It might be an ungodly hour of the morning, but it's supposed to be good for shock.'

'My stomach's churning like I'm on a rollercoaster, so I think we'd better stick to tea.' Anna was shaking, partly because of the shock and partly because a tiny part of her believed that Ella might actually be able to pull this off. And she still wasn't sure if she wanted her to.

'Tea it is then, I'll get it.' Ella stood up. 'After that, I'm going to start sending out some emails and messages, so people get them as soon as they wake up.'

'I don't want you to feel bad if we don't manage to rearrange everything, but I'll never forget the fact that you tried. It means so much to me.' Anna reached out a hand and Ella squeezed it in response. She was definitely going to need to speak to Brae now and, if they decided to call the wedding off, she wanted to be able to tell Ella before she ran herself ragged trying to rearrange a wedding that was never going to happen.

20

Ella was having trouble keeping up with the number of messages that had come in since she'd posted an announcement asking for help in rearranging Brae and Anna's wedding.

Some of the things had been a relatively easy fix. Luke Scott was one of the first people to get in touch, asking Ella to call him.

'Hi, is that Luke? It's Ella Mehenick, I'm ringing about your offer of help with the wedding?'

'Thanks for getting back to me. Anna was brilliant when our daughter was born recently and I just want to help out in some way. I run a catering business, and I'd been preparing and freezing canapés and desserts for another wedding I've got coming up, but I'd love Anna to have them for hers.'

'That would be great, but are you sure that's not going to cause you any problems?' As grateful as Ella was, she knew Anna would hate the idea of putting any stress on someone with a newborn baby.

'I was getting ahead because I thought I'd need to be with Tamara all the time to help her cope with Belle. But she's doing brilliantly and a lot of that's down to Anna. This is just a way of paying her back a bit.' Ella could almost hear the smile in Luke's voice. 'Just let me know where and what time we need to drop them off, and I'll be there.'

'That's brilliant.' Ella swallowed hard, not sure whether to admit the truth, but there was no point hiding it. 'The only problem is I haven't managed to confirm a venue yet, but I'm going to post the details online for everyone who offers to help as soon as I can.'

'Good luck! I'll keep checking back for the details.'

'Thanks and see you later.' Ella just about stopped herself saying '*hopefully*'. Without a venue, it didn't matter how many offers of help they got; this wedding wasn't going to happen.

Ella's parents, Ruth and Jago, had offered to make another wedding cake. It wouldn't be as grand, or have as many layers, but they were incredibly fond of Brae and Anna, so they'd do the best job possible. There wasn't time to make a rich fruit cake, but Jago would almost certainly include a Cornish hevva cake this time around. He'd told Ella it was going to be a deconstructed stack of various cakes to appeal to different tastes, and weaving in Cornish traditions whenever he could was her father's trademark. Ella just hoped they'd have somewhere to serve it.

Just after she'd spoken to Luke, a call came through from someone else who wanted to help. Miranda explained that Brae had taken over her stall at the Red Cliff Hotel's wedding fair when she'd been struck down with severe morning sickness. Apparently, Anna had taken Miranda to the hospital while Brae looked after the stall, and she offered Ella whatever she wanted from the stock she had made up, to help decorate the venue in lieu of flowers or centrepieces and, like Luke, she offered to drop it off. She even promised to make dried flower bouquets for Anna and her bridesmaids to replace the ones that had been lost in the fire. Ella had accepted the offer without really knowing what she was getting into, desperately hoping she wouldn't come to regret it until she'd had time to check out Miranda's website. She couldn't have hoped for more. The dried flower bouquets in the online gallery were stunning and the front page of the website was currently showcasing beautiful flower garlands, some of which were now destined to hang in Anna and Brae's wedding venue. If only Ella could find them one.

Anna had been despatched to get her hair and make-up done as planned, and Dan had been great at keeping Brae from getting too stressed about the wedding plans being thrown into chaos. He'd also promised to put in some calls to see whether he had any more luck than Ella in finding a venue. They agreed a deadline of three p.m. to find somewhere to hold the ceremony at seven, but the minutes were ticking past far too quickly. If she had to break the news to Anna that the wedding couldn't go ahead after all, Ella wasn't sure if she could ever forgive herself. Just before one p.m. she got another call.

'Oh, hi Ella, it's Beth Jenson. You and Anna delivered my baby on the day of the storm.' The voice on the other end of the line sounded tentative, as if Ella might have forgotten, but she'd never forget the day of the storm for as long as she lived.

'Beth it's good to hear from you. How's the baby?'

'He's great, thanks to you and Anna. We named him Stanley in the end, after both our granddads.'

'That's lovely.'

'Thank you, but I don't want to waste your time, I can only imagine how frantic things are there. I won't be offended if you say no, but I think I might have something to offer you for Anna's wedding.'

'Really, that's great!' Ella held her breath, hoping with every fibre of her being that Beth was about to magic up a wedding venue from somewhere.

'I got married last year and I had my dress and all of my bridesmaid's dresses dry-cleaned straight afterwards. I texted the girls and four of them have dropped their dresses back here already. If any of them are any good for you or the other brides-maids you'd be welcome to them, and I'm sure I was about the same size as Anna when I got married, before I acquired a mum tum!' Beth laughed. 'If you think the dress might be any good for her, you'd be welcome to that too.'

'That's so kind of you.' Ella desperately tried to keep some semblance of enthusiasm in her voice. It really was lovely of Beth to offer up her dresses, but without a venue to wear them in, it was nowhere near enough.

'It was the least I could do. I'd offer to drop them down, but Andy's got the car and I don't think I could get down there with the pram and five dresses.'

'Of course not, I've got to meet up with Anna when she finishes at the hairdressers in about an hour, so we'll pop in after that, if that's okay with you?'

'That's perfect. I just hope Anna likes them.'

'I'm sure she will, don't worry.' Ella glanced at the clock again, as another minute ticked past. She was already worrying more than enough for everyone. If they didn't find a venue in the next couple of hours, it would all have been for nothing.

* * *

Anna's heart was hammering against her chest. It was just as well that she didn't believe in bad luck, because she was about to do the one thing that brides weren't supposed to do on the day of their weddings – see the groom.

'Oh God, I'm so sorry you're having all this stress. I just wanted everything to be perfect for you.' Brae pulled her into his arms as soon as he met her at the beach hut, where she'd told him she'd be. She was already late for her appointment at the hairdressers, which Ella had sent her off to, but there was no point having her hair done if there wasn't going to be a wedding. Pulling away, she forced herself to look at him as she spoke.

'None of this is your fault. I want you to know that, before I say anything else.'

'Please don't say what I think you're going to say.' Brae's eyes were searching her face and she shook her head.

'I love you so much, it's not that I don't want to marry you.'

'Why does it feel like there's a but coming?'

'I was looking for the perfect quote this morning just before the call came through from the hotel, something I could say to toast Mum and Dad. But then I found this.' Ella handed the book of baby names to Brae.

'What is it?' Looking down at the book, there was no flicker of recognition of its meaning in his eyes.

'It's from when you were with Julia and you've both marked up the names you like.'

'Oh Anna, that was another life, it doesn't mean anything.' Brae looked back at her. 'I wouldn't swap anything for the life we've got together and I wish I could make you believe me.'

'I do.' Anna bit her lip, shaking her head again. 'At least I'm trying to, I really am. But, even if we get accepted to adopt, we won't get to choose our baby's name or go through all those things together. I focused so much on how I didn't want to lose the chance of having a genetic link to Mum and Dad, but you're losing the same thing. How can you give all of that up, when you could so easily have it all with someone else? I'm terrified you're settling for second best and that you're going to regret it.'

'I don't want anyone else.' Brae took hold of her hands. 'You think I'm settling for second best? Any life without you in it would be far less than second best. You're a brilliant, intelligent woman, Anna, so when the hell are you going to get it into your head that I love you? Not some future you who might be a mum, or some idea of a family life with you that might never happen. I love you for exactly who you are right now and, however much you might try and persuade me that you aren't enough, I know with one hundred per cent certainty that you are.'

'But you kept the book all this time.'

'When I broke up with Julia, we split all the books and DVDs we still had straight down the middle. Just before you moved in, I took all the books down from the loft and filled up the shelf in the study to try and prove to you that you weren't marrying beneath yourself with a buffoon like me who barely ever reads more than the cash and carry catalogue.' Brae laughed. 'I love you more than you'll ever know, but if this is anyone's fault, it's yours for being so amazing that I had to try and pretend to be well-read!'

Anna felt her skin go hot; she hated the idea that she might have made Brae feel like he needed to be anything different to what he was. There was no one like him and no one could make her happier than he had. 'There's nothing you need to change to try and impress me. I love you so much, but I don't deserve you.'

'That's true, but you're stuck with me anyway.' Brae laughed again, pulling her back into his arms. 'Now are we going to get married, or shall I tell Ella to stop trying to pull off the impossible?'

'Even though I've already had more luck than I deserve finding you, let's keep hoping for one more miracle.' If anyone could pull it off it was Ella, but it felt wrong to even hope for another miracle. Whatever happened, she was going to hold on to Brae's words until they could finally get married. The only reason the book had a special place on the shelf in his study was because he'd felt the need to convince her that she could love someone like him and that he was enough for her, not the other way around, but he was already perfect to her exactly the way he was and she'd never suspected he might have those sort of insecurities too. But it had made her realise how stupid she was being, thinking she needed to be someone else for him to keep loving her. Somehow the innocuous-looking little book that had accidentally ended up on a bookshelf had become the final piece of the jigsaw she hadn't even realised she'd been searching for. It had convinced Anna that she was enough for Brae too – just her – and that was more than enough of a miracle to be going on with.

21

'I feel terrible that you had to miss out on getting your hair done.' Anna turned to Ella, as they pulled up outside Beth's house.

'It's fine, I'll just pin it up and try not to let the side down!' Ella grinned. 'Your hair looks great by the way.'

'Apparently it's a fishtail braid, but she left it loose so some of the curls could escape and soften the look, or something like that.' Anna pulled a face. 'It's weird, because it's nothing like I planned when I was going to wear the tiara that's now probably just a charred mess, but I think I prefer this.'

'I love the wildflowers they've fixed in along the back.'

'Me too, but I'm worried about forgetting about them before the wedding, leaning back against something and instantly squashing them flat. I'm cut out for life as a midwife; all this dressing up feels really weird.'

'You'd better get used to it, because if Beth's dress is okay, you'll be going full bride in time for the ceremony.' Ella hoped the panic didn't show on her face at the mere mention of the ceremony. When Ella had met her outside the hairdressers, the first thing Anna had asked was whether they'd found a venue or not. She'd given a vague answer about it being narrowed down to two, and that she wouldn't be telling Anna where it was until it was all confirmed. Having to lie to her best friend was awful, but Anna had been through enough already. There was no point making her panic when everyone involved was doing whatever they could to find a venue. Ella wasn't going to confess unless she had to.

Beth met them at the door, with baby Stanley in her arms.

'Oh Anna, you look lovely.' She smiled and then glanced at Ella, the expression on her face saying more than words ever could.

'It's all right, you don't have to pretend. I know it looks like I've been out in a hurricane, but I've promised Anna I won't scare the children by the time I'm following her down the aisle!'

'Let's see if the dresses I've got can help with that.' Beth ushered them through to the front room, where a row of four maxi dresses in a delicate sage green hung next to a large black dress bag, which presumably contained the wedding gown. 'The bridesmaid dresses are a petite in a size ten, and two size twelves and a size sixteen in standard lengths.'

'That's perfect, thank you so much!' Anna clapped her hands together. 'Jess is tiny, so the petite one will be great for her. I ordered Toni's other dress in a size sixteen and you'll be fine with a twelve, won't you, Ella?'

'I'll wear two pairs of hold-it-all-in pants if I need to, even if it means I have to stand up all night!' Ella had no idea how Anna was holding back from unzipping the dress bag. If she didn't do it soon, Ella would.

'And now for the pièce de résistance.' Beth turned towards Ella. 'Would you mind holding the baby so I can get the dress out for Anna?'

'Of course I will.' Stanley gave Ella a quizzical look as his mother handed him over. For a moment the baby's mouth opened as if he was about to start yelling in protest, but then he relaxed into Ella's arms.

'It's a vintage dress I got from a shop in London. It felt like I'd traipsed all over the city by the time I found it. I just hope you like it.'

'Oh!' Anna made a strange, almost strangled sound and it was impossible to tell from the look on her face what she was thinking.

'Don't feel like you've got to wear it.' Beth ran a hand over the dress. 'If you only want to take the bridesmaids' dresses, that's fine. I just wanted to help if I could.'

'Oh no, please, I love it.' When Anna turned towards them, it was obvious she was trying – and failing – not to cry. The dress wouldn't have looked out of place in a 1930s Hollywood movie. It was vintage silk with a high neck and long sleeves, the silhouette looking as if it would hug her body in all the right places. 'It's just that if I could have worn any wedding dress, it would have been the one Mum wore when she married Dad. It was my Nanna's too. It got lost in one of their moves. I looked online for something like it before I thought I'd better just settle for a dress from Susie's shop. The dress I bought from Susie was a similar style, but I never dreamt I'd be able to find anything as close to Mum's dress as this.'

'Maybe it is your mum's dress?' Ella couldn't help hoping for the perfect fairy-tale ending, but even she knew that was a ten-million-to-one shot.

'It's not, but it's every bit as beautiful. Stupid as it sounds, it makes it feel as if Mum's having a hand in things. I don't know what's happening to me lately, but I'm seeing silly superstitions in everything, just like she did, except I'm only focusing on the good signs.' Anna took a deep breath. 'Are you sure you're okay with me borrowing it, Beth? It's really lovely of you, but I'd be mortified if anything happened to it while I had it.'

'It doesn't matter if it does.' Beth was struggling to get the words out. 'Just seeing the look on your face has given me a thousand times more pleasure than having it hung up in my wardrobe for the next sixty years ever could.'

'You two are killing me!' Ella laughed. 'Can you just put it on already, before we all end up soggy messes and Anna completely ruins her wedding make-up.'

Beth handed Anna the dress and the two of them disappeared upstairs, so Beth could zip it up for her. Ella was still rocking the baby in her arms and willing Dan to text her and say he'd found a wedding venue, when she heard one of the floorboards creak. So much for thinking that Anna putting the dress on would stop them all feeling so emotional. Seeing her in it was ten times worse.

'Oh Anna, Brae is going to sob as hard as I want to right now.' Ella's throat was burning. It was almost impossible to believe that the dress hadn't been made for her best friend, and that she hadn't spent months planning the perfect hairstyle to go with it. The long-sleeved lace bodice made Anna look like a Hollywood star from an old black-and-white movie.

'I want to hate you for looking so much better in it than I ever did,' Beth laughed, taking the baby from Ella, 'but I can't. You look absolutely fantastic!'

'Do you want to come along tonight? I'd love you to be there, to say thank you for this? Andy too, and the baby, of course.' Anna turned to Beth, who nodded in response.

'We'd love to? Where is it?'

'Your guess is as good as mine.' Anna nodded her head towards Ella. 'My chief bridesmaid over there thinks I need a bit more excitement in my life, and won't tell me what she's got planned yet. I feel like I'm trapped in an extreme version of *Don't Tell The Bride*.'

'I'm not deliberately trying to be difficult, I promise.' An internal battle was already raging in Ella's head, about whether to tell Anna they still hadn't found a venue. There was so little time left, she'd have to face up to it soon. 'It's just that—' Ella actually jumped as her phone started to ring, hoping against hope that someone up there had been listening to the silent prayer that had been running through her head all day. It was Dan's name on the display. He'd promised not to call until every option had been exhausted, or he'd found somewhere... Ella's blood was rushing in her ears as she snatched up the phone.

'Everything okay?' Her tone sounded falsely bright, even to her own ears.

'It is now. I think I've found somewhere.'

'*Think*?' Ella lowered her voice, knowing Anna would be able to hear every word she said.

'Okay, I *have* found somewhere. It's not exactly what you'd call conventional, but Brae thinks we should go for it and he's arranged for the registrar to meet us there. She's given it the okay too.'

'Great! So where's it going to be?'

'I need you to meet me at the harbour in twenty minutes with everything you need for the wedding, because you're not going to have time to get home again beforehand. If you can tell Toni and Jess to meet us there too, we can all head over together.'

'Okay, but where?' If they were meeting at the harbour, Ella couldn't think of anywhere it could be other than the Sisters of

Agnes Island. But the hotel had said there was nothing they could do, and she didn't want to give Anna false hope. The only other large venue near the harbour was the fish market, and surely not even Dan and Brae would settle for that.

'Is Anna with you?'

'Uh-huh.'

'Just tell her to be ready at her place forty-five minutes before the wedding. Bobby's picking her up and he'll get her to the venue. That's all she needs to know for now. I don't want either of you to worry about anything. If I tell you, you won't be able to keep it to yourself and then you'll both be worrying unnecessarily, because it's all going to be fine.'

'You better be sure, because she looks amazing and she deserves an equally amazing day.' Ella was whispering now and she wasn't even sure if Dan heard her.

'I'll see you in twenty minutes. I love you.' Not waiting for her response, Dan ended the call. Whatever it was that he and Brae had organised, there was nothing she could do about it now. She just hoped Anna could live with being in her own version of *Don't Tell The Bride* for another couple of hours, because the biggest part of the wedding was still a complete mystery to them both.

* * *

Anna's body shook as she stood on the edge of the harbour. It was half-past six and she was supposed to be getting married in half an hour, but she still had no idea where the wedding was going to be. Across the water, the lights of the hotel on the Sisters of Agnes Island shone like a beacon of hope. She wouldn't be going over there, though. The hotel was always booked solid in the summer and, in the five minutes she'd been standing by Bobby's side waiting to find out where she was going, a steady stream of boats had already made their way over to the island. Not just the hotel's own launch, but a mismatched collection that made it look like Port Agnes' attempt to recreate the flotilla for the Queen's Diamond Jubilee. There was probably a party going on at the hotel, but Anna wasn't even sure if Ella had really known where the wedding was going to be herself. When she'd taken the call at Beth's house, she'd said Brae wanted it to be a surprise for Anna and that she'd promised not to tell. But she hadn't exactly radiated calm, scooping up the bridesmaids' dresses and dashing off to meet Toni and Jess.

Anna didn't really care where it was, as long as it happened. Bobby had picked her up from the cottage, but he wouldn't be drawn on where they were going either, not even when she'd fired question after question at him on the drive down.

'I think your ride's here.' Bobby reached out and squeezed Anna's hand as she turned her head to look up the road that led away from the harbour.

'I can't see anything coming.'

'That's because you're looking in the wrong direction.' Bobby tugged her forward slightly and she looked across the harbour, where a lifeboat was powering through the water. It was strung with coloured lights, which were visible even though it was still daylight, and, as it got closer, she could hear music too.

'Your carriage, my lady.' Bobby laughed at the look that must have crossed her face as the boat pulled up to the jetty in front of them.

'Are we getting married on a boat?' Anna couldn't see Brae, but getting married on the boat that had saved his life and brought him back to her would have so much meaning to it. There'd be no room for guests and, okay, it would only be a blessing, but it was a reminder of the really important thing; that they were both there to get married at all.

'No, this is just how you're getting there.' Bobby took hold of her arm and led her to where the coxswain was holding out a hand to help her on board. 'But we couldn't think of any better mode of transport.'

'And we were happy to get involved after all you've done to help raise the profile of the campaign to save the lifeboat station.' Beth's husband, Andy, smiled as she stepped onto the boat.

'That's all down to Ella.'

'Listen, I've seen you dressed as Sleepy from *Snow White*! Not only that, you delivered my son, and most of the crew have got you to thank for bringing their children into the world. This was the least we could do.'

'Am I allowed to ask where we're going?' Anna still couldn't fathom it out. Maybe Brae had found a venue further up the coast and had wanted to make it even more special by organising the lifeboat. Wherever they were going, they now only had twenty-five minutes before the ceremony was due to start.

'Let's just say we'll be there in less than ten minutes.' Bobby tapped the side of his nose. 'That'll only give you another fifteen minutes or so to get yourself ready, so we'd better get you inside the wheelhouse to make sure your hairstyle stays intact. Toni warned me on pain of death not to let you down.'

'What's going on between you two?' Anna turned and fixed him with a look as he followed her into the wheelhouse. If she didn't get him to open up now, he probably never would.

'More than she'll admit to anyone, but less than I want there to be. I'd do all this tomorrow, if she'd say yes.' Bobby shrugged and Anna caught her breath. She hadn't expected a response quite that honest.

'You two would be so brilliant together, you already are. I've got to say I don't really understand the secrecy.' Anna locked eyes with him for a second. 'But I hope you can find a way forward.'

'Me too.' Bobby grinned, breaking the tension. 'I mean who doesn't want a crazy last-minute wedding, with a bride who has no idea where she's going and almost anything could happen!'

'Quite frankly, I'm surprised that *Hello* magazine isn't covering it.' She took a deep breath as the boat surged forward, heading out of the harbour into the bluey green water beyond. 'Here we go!'

* * *

When the boat pulled up on the dock at the Sisters of Agnes Island, Anna couldn't contain herself any more.

'Bobby, you're going to have to tell me what's happening, before the tension actually kills me!'

'You're getting married, that's what's happening.' He gave her another maddening grin, as some of the crew helped them off the boat.

'And you're in danger of me shoving you into the sea if you don't tell me in the next thirty seconds what's going on.' She was only half joking. 'The hotel told us they were completely booked up for the next two summers.'

'That was before.'

'Before what?'

'Before a crack team of midwives and their other halves got on the case. We've called in every favour and every thank you we've ever been given for delivering babies in Port Agnes to make this happen.' Bobby took hold of her arm again. 'One of the guests has even given up their room, so you and Brae can stay here tonight. You're not getting married in the hotel, though, that bit's a secret for a little while longer.'

'I don't understand.' Maybe they'd managed to erect a marquee or something in the grounds, but she couldn't see anything from where they were standing.

'Don't worry about that, let's head up to your room. Ella, Jess and Toni are waiting up there and all will be revealed.' Bobby nodded towards the lifeboat. 'You might just want to thank this lot first, because they've got another job to get to now.'

'Thank you so much.' Anna waved a hand to the crew. 'But please tell me I haven't held you up from a real call-out?'

'Don't worry, the crew in Port Kara are covering this evening, unless there's a major emergency, and nearly all the traffic in the waters around here at the moment is heading to and from the Sisters of Agnes Island anyway.' Andy dropped an expert wink. 'But your wedding breakfast relies on us doing our next job, so we'll see you after the ceremony. Good luck!'

'Thank you!' Anna had finally given up trying to work out what on earth was going on. The whole world had gone crazy, but they all seemed to be doing it for her benefit, and thank you didn't seem nearly enough.

* * *

Ella pulled back the door of the hotel room before they even knocked, and enveloped Anna in a hug.

'You're here! So what do you think?'

'I think you all look gorgeous.' Anna couldn't keep the smile off her face. They really did look great, especially Ella, who had been run off her feet all day, yet somehow managed to be glowing.

'Not a patch on you.' Toni, who was usually stoical, looked close to tears and she didn't flinch when Bobby slid an arm around her waist. Whatever magic spell had been cast to allow the wedding to take place on the Sisters of Agnes Island seemed to be rubbing off on them all.

'Here, have a glass of champagne.' Jess moved over to a silver tray on the table by the window that looked out onto the grounds. 'We're already a couple of glasses ahead of you.'

'I'd better not.' Anna shook her head to emphasise the point. 'My stomach has been a mass of butterflies ever since I got the phone call from the Red Cliff Hotel and I haven't been able to eat anything. One glass would probably knock me off my feet!'

'Well I'll have to drink it for you then.' Jess raised the glass she'd just filled into the air. 'Cheers to the best boss in the world and a wonderful friend on her wedding day.'

'Cheers!' Toni and Ella raised their glasses in response.

'I've got something I was supposed to give you from Brae, by the way.' Bobby held a closed fist out in front of him. 'But I wanted to wait until we were in the safety of the hotel room, so I didn't drop them.'

'Earrings?' Anna looked up at Bobby after he'd unfurled his hands to reveal a pair of pearl earrings.

'Apparently they're Brae's mum's. They were zipped into his coat when he got caught in the storm with Dan, but the coat washed up on the beach somewhere down the coast and the earrings were still zipped in the inside pocket. The coat had the Penrose Plaice logo on it, so the person who found it was able to track Brae down and send the earrings back to the shop. He wanted it to be a surprise.'

'That's amazing, they were supposed to be my something borrowed.' Anna's hands were shaking again as she reached out to take the earrings.

'So now Beth's dress can be your something old.' Ella smiled. 'Have you got something blue?'

'I went old school.' Anna lowered her voice. 'I've got a garter on! Gwen bought it for me, but I wasn't going to wear it so I didn't take it to the Red Cliff Hotel, but when everything else went up in the fire I thought I should use whatever I had left.'

'Now you just need your something new.' Jess shot Ella a sideways look.

'I think we can take care of that. Brae dropped this off earlier and said we all had to wear it today.' Ella took a bottle of Chanel N°5, still in its wrapper, out of her bag. Peeling back the cellophane, she took the bottle out of the box and held it out to Anna. 'You go first.'

'It's the perfume Mum always wore.'

'I know.' Ella's eyes had taken on a glassy look. 'He wanted you to have another reminder of her around you today. I hope it's okay?'

'Of course it's okay, it's much more than that.' Anna sprayed the perfume on and inhaled the scent, closing her eyes for just a second as she passed the bottle back to Ella. She might never be as superstitious as her mum had been, but Brae had been right again, it did make it feel like her mum was right there with her. She had her something borrowed, something blue, something old and something new. That covered all the bases and her mum would have loved it.

'Thank you all so much.' A lump formed in Anna's throat, as she tried to get the words out. 'Whatever is about to happen, I know you've all been working really hard so Brae and I could still get married today and I promise I'll never forget it.'

'Everyone I spoke to wanted to help. You and Brae are so well-loved in Port Agnes, it was easy to get what we needed. The trickiest part was the venue, but you're about to discover the solution that Brae and Dan came up with, and I just know you're going to love it.' Ella hugged her again, before pulling away. 'Are you ready?'

'As I'll ever be.'

'Let's get going then. You don't want to keep Brae in suspense, he's barely been able to stand still since we got here, and I don't think he can wait much longer.'

'Neither can I.' Anna stepped out into the corridor, taking the last few steps towards a new life that couldn't start soon enough.

22

There were petals sprinkled all over the path that led away from the main building to the chapel that had been deserted when the last of the nuns finally left the island, a few days after the start of the millennium. Anna had seen an article in the paper when the hotel had gained its licence as a venue for civil ceremonies the summer before, announcing that they'd got permission to use the conservatory and two other locations in the hotel. The article had said the conservatory would be available to book with immediate effect, and the other locations were scheduled for renovation over the next twelve months in readiness to expand their wedding services. The old chapel was one of them, but the last time Anna had seen it, it had looked dilapidated and a long way off being ready to host anything, let alone a wedding.

As they got closer, the glow from inside the chapel and the music drifting on the breeze left no doubt that it was where they were heading, and Anna felt like breaking into a run. She didn't care if the guests were sitting on piles of upturned bricks, or there was a chance of being dive-bombed by a pigeon during the ceremony, as long as Brae was there waiting for her.

'Good luck.' Bobby whispered the words and kissed her on the cheek, as he left her at the door to walk down the aisle on her own, just like she'd planned. Ella handed her a bouquet of dried wildflowers, roses and thistles, bound with twine, and an instrumental version of the Etta James song 'At Last' filled the air. If she hadn't known better, Anna would have sworn it was being played on a piano.

Breathing out, she stepped forward and everyone turned to look in her direction. There weren't any upturned bricks, or pigeons, as far as she could see. Instead, there were fairy lights and candles everywhere, illuminating the darkness inside the old chapel, which didn't seem to have any source of natural light. The pews were long gone, but there were rows of wooden chairs draped in garlands of dried flowers, and there were summer wreaths dotted along the walls. At the far end of the chapel, someone was playing the piano that Anna had thought couldn't possibly be there. It was beautiful; everything was a hundred times more perfect than she could ever have imagined, even if they'd spent fourteen months planning the wedding, instead of fourteen hours.

Looking up, Anna finally caught sight of Brae, who gave her a thumbs up and all she could do was nod. She was so much more than okay and she had to force herself to slow down her pace, as she walked towards him.

'You look amazing, I love you so much.' Brae wasn't waiting for anyone's permission and he kissed her before the registrar even had the chance to speak, let alone pronounce them man and wife, earning him a huge cheer.

'I love you too.' Handing her bouquet to Ella, Anna slipped one hand into his as they turned to face the registrar. Ten minutes later they were finally given official permission to kiss, and it took the guests even longer to stop cheering the second time around.

* * *

'I still can't believe you managed to pull this off.' Anna leant against Brae as he pulled her close to him. The hotel had brought in some agency staff, some of whom were busy serving canapés and champagne to the guests, while others rearranged the chairs in the chapel around fold-up tables, quickly covering them with white linen tablecloths and more tea lights.

'Ella was like a whirlwind. Luke donated the canapés and desserts. The tables and chairs were borrowed from the church hall and the people at the Red Cliff Hotel were able to supply the linens, lanterns and champagne, which were stored in an area of the hotel that wasn't damaged by the fire. Miranda and her contacts provided all the garlands and flowers. Jago and Ruth have made us another cake, and the boys from the lifeboat station sorted out the boats to bring the supplies and guests to and from the island. They're organising the wedding breakfast too.'

'So I've heard. What I really want to know is how you managed to arrange for the ceremony to take place here?'

'Apparently, last year you delivered the granddaughter of the guy who owns the hotel, and the year before that Ella stopped there being a full-scale emergency here when a woman whose pregnancy was high-risk went into labour and refused to leave the island.'

'I remember that.'

'When he read about what had happened on the campaign pages for the lifeboat station, he wanted to do something.' Brae smiled. 'At first, we couldn't work out how to make it work. It was too late to get a marquee put up, but then Dan asked about the chapel, because the hotel had already been given permission to hold weddings here, although they weren't going to do that until the renovations are complete next summer. When we looked inside it seemed impossible, but you know Dan. With his artist's head on, he could see the potential. Then it all started to happen and the hotel staff brought the piano over. Once the garlands were delivered, and the lights were strung up, I thought maybe we could make it good enough for someone as special as you. Ella, Toni and Jess were still hanging lights until about twenty minutes before you arrived. I'm still not quite sure how it all came together either, but it did.'

'It's so beautiful and even more so because everyone I care about has worked so hard to make it happen.'

'You deserve it, I just hope you can forgive me for the wedding breakfast. It's not quite as fancy as the menu we planned with the Red Cliff Hotel.'

'I don't care if it's hotdogs.'

'You're about to find out!' Brae laughed as some of the lifeboat crewman came in, carrying takeaway cool bags. 'It's fish and chips all round, I'm afraid. A couple of the weekend staff have been working at the shop all day to get it prepared and, maybe it's not haute cuisine, it's kind of fitting.'

'I couldn't think of anything better.' Anna's stomach growled at the prospect of a fish and chip supper and she couldn't help laughing. It really was turning into the perfect night.

* * *

An hour and a half later, the fish and chips had gone down a storm with the guests, and Luke's desserts had been served. Brae and Dan had both made heartfelt speeches, and it was almost time to cut the cake. Right up until that moment, the last thing Anna had planned to do was end up making a speech of her own. Doing any more than toasting her parents and her new husband had felt like too much. But looking around at everyone who'd worked so hard to make this night special, she just knew she had to do it. Before she had a chance to talk herself out of it, she was up on her feet, clinking a knife against her glass.

'Sorry everyone, I promise this won't take long and it's not really a speech, but I just have to say something to you all.' The butterflies were back as the conversation died down and everyone turned to look at her for a second time. 'Brae has already done a brilliant job of thanking everyone from Beth, who lent me this gorgeous dress, to the lifeboat crew for all their help. I just want to echo my thanks to all of you and especially my friends and colleagues from the midwifery unit and their other halves, who have gone above and beyond to make this happen. Particularly Ella, who's become like the sister I never had, and her wonderful partner, Dan. You're all amazing, and every single person in this room has got an important place in my heart.' Anna paused, glad of the chance to try and swallow her emotion, as the crowd cheered again.

When the sound finally died down, she cleared her throat. 'Some of you know that I desperately wanted to get married tonight, on my parents' wedding anniversary. As an only child of two only children, when I lost them I lost out on being part of a family too. I planned to toast them tonight, with a quote I found that summed up the fact that they will always be in my heart. It's from mother to a daughter and it simply says *"remember me and a part of me will always be with you"*. I know they're with me today and every day, because of that. Marrying Brae on their anniversary was so important to me, not only because I love him more than I've ever loved anyone, but because it signified becoming part of a family again – with his parents, and his lovely sister, Morwenna, and her family. Only now, looking around this room, I realise that's just the icing on the cake. I've been part of a family from the moment I arrived in Port Agnes. Only a family would go out of their way to do as much for me as you've all done tonight. Port Agnes has given me a family who've welcomed me into their community and it's given me Brae, who I know for certain is the one for me. So I wanted to wish you all, my Port Agnes family, every good fortune in your lives and to thank you once again for letting me be a part of your clan.'

For a second or two, there was silence, but then everyone got to their feet and started to clap. Any chance Anna might have had of holding back the tears was over. But if you couldn't cry in front of your family, when could you?

23

'Good morning, Mrs Penrose.' Brae smiled as Anna opened her eyes, and gently stroked the side of her face.

'Have you been watching me sleep?' Anna couldn't imagine it being a pretty sight. She'd probably had her mouth hanging open at best.

'Only for a few minutes, but I could have watched you all day.' Brae propped himself up on one elbow. 'Can you believe we're actually married?'

'After everything that happened, it's hard to! It really was the best day of my life.' Just thinking about it, she couldn't have kept the smile off her face if she'd wanted to.

'That speech you made hit me right here.' Brae slapped a hand against his chest. 'And I wasn't the only one. I think you caught everyone unawares.'

'If someone had told me I'd have to make a speech, I'd have dreaded it, but when I saw what everyone had done just to try and make things special for us...' She shook her head. 'I couldn't leave it unsaid.'

'Everything you said was true. The community here really are like family.' Brae pushed a strand of hair away from her face as he spoke. 'When people found out we were originally booked to have lunch at the Red Cliff Hotel today and stay another night before we went on our honeymoon, I lost count of the number of local pubs and restaurants that offered us lunch and dinner for free.'

'We could just eat at home. Last night's celebrations with everyone were so great anyway, I don't think we could top it.'

'We did get one offer you might want to accept. At Jago and Ruth's place, for a celebratory lunch with Dan and Ella, so you know we'll get fed like kings too.'

'What time do we need to be there?'

'Ruth said last night that lunch is at one, and we don't need to check out until twelve either, so we've got plenty of time. I want to give you your wedding present first, anyway.'

'You bought the perfume.'

'That was from your mum really. This is from me and I wanted us to be on our own when I gave it to you.' Brae got up and took a large wrapped package out of the wardrobe. 'I hope you like it.'

'Thank you so much.' Anna peeled back the paper. A painting, unmistakably one of Dan's, was revealed beneath the wrapping, making her breath catch in her throat. 'It's from the photo in my purse, isn't it? It's beautiful!'

'I hope it's okay that I got it done. I was the internet bidder on Dan's painting at the auction. I'd given Ella a pre-arranged maximum to go to, although knowing her she had something to do with ensuring it was the winning bid.' Brae stroked her hand. 'I scanned the photo when you weren't looking and Dan worked his magic.'

'I couldn't ask for anything better. It's such a grainy photo and, when I tried to get it blown up bigger, it just looked like a blur.'

Anna couldn't stop looking at the painting. The photo had been taken on a family summer holiday in Port Agnes, just before she'd started secondary school on their very first trip in Vanna. That holiday was one of her favourite childhood memories and it was one of the reasons she'd decided to settle in Port Agnes after her parents' death. The painting and Amber were the nicest presents she'd ever had, and nothing she gave Brae could even hope to match his wedding present to her.

'I thought it would look great above the fireplace.' Brae kissed the top of her head. 'I might not have had the chance to meet them, but I know they must have been amazing people to have a daughter like you.'

'They'd have adored you. I don't even have to question that. I've got you a present, nothing as amazing as this. But I left it at home, because I had no idea we were going to end up spending the night on the island.'

'It doesn't matter. I've got everything I need right here.' Brae smiled again. 'And the hotel launch isn't going over to the mainland until twelve-fifteen anyway.'

Anna glanced at her watch. 'Do you want to get some breakfast, then? They said they'd be serving it until ten.'

'I'm not hungry.' Brae trailed a hand lazily down the side of her body. 'Not for food anyway.'

'You're not going to be one of *those* husbands, are you?' She grinned again. 'You know, the sort who want to spend all day in bed.'

'Being married to someone as beautiful as you, Anna Penrose, I'm afraid it's a given.'

'Oh, go on then!' She laughed, as he pulled her towards him. Married life was off to a very good start and she had a feeling it was just going to keep getting better.

* * *

Brae pushed his plate away after polishing off a third helping of Sunday lunch and sighed.

'That was amazing, Ruth, and I think you may have finally beaten me. I'm just gutted that I might not be able to do justice to Jago's dessert.'

'I love to see people enjoying their food, especially when it's something I've cooked.' Ruth beamed. 'Are you okay, Anna? You're eating like a bird, and there's no need to worry about looking skinny on your wedding day any more!'

'True, you can let yourself go now, like my Ruthie!' Jago laughed, earning himself a playful punch on the arm from his wife.

'If I look half as good as Ruth, I'll be happy. And lunch was beautiful, thank you.' Anna smiled as Ruth blew her a kiss. 'It's just the last couple of days have been crazy and I think I'm still running on adrenaline. I keep getting that feeling, like when you're on the top of a rollercoaster, launching into a loop the loop and your stomach can't quite catch up with the rest of you. I think my body is still in the panic mode it went into the moment the call came through from the Red Cliff Hotel. Hopefully it'll catch up with my brain soon.'

'Well I'm with Brae. My stomach's stretched to the limit and I only had two, admittedly huge, portions of roast dinner.' Dan massaged his belly. 'I couldn't resist eating that second helping, but I think I could do with a break to fully do justice to Jago's magnificent dessert.'

'It's a gorgeous day.' Ella turned towards her parents. 'Maybe we could all take Daisy and Jones for a walk on the beach to work up an appetite again?'

'That's a brilliant idea. You youngsters head off and your

father and I will get things straightened up in here, ready for dessert.' Ruth looked at Jago, who nodded.

'We can't leave you to do all the clearing away, you've already done all the cooking.' Anna's protests were immediately waved away.

'You girls work so hard. And look at those two, they're like a couple of your patients, they've got to be at least six months gone.' Jago roared with laughter again, as Brae and Dan both patted their stomachs.

'I think Brae's further on than me.' Dan winked, and before anyone could offer another protest about helping out with clearing the table, Ruth was up on her feet, clipping Daisy's lead on. The dog had made the most of sitting under the dinner table, and being fed titbits by all of them, so she probably had a belly bulge of her own to give Brae and Dan a run for their money. Anna and Brae were still trying not to give Jones any human food, but there was a pretty good chance that Jago had already broken that rule.

'Looks like we've got our marching orders.' Ella stood up. 'We might as well head to the beach, because if there's one thing I've learnt from growing up in this house, it's that you'll never win when Mum and Dad make up their minds.'

* * *

The walk along the beach was breathtaking. If a Hollywood movie could paint the perfect scene, then Port Agnes offered the next best thing. The sunlight bouncing off the sand made it look like it was covered in millions of tiny diamonds. It was all laid out beneath a bright blue sky and the tide was so far out that it made the beach feel empty, even though it was the height of summer.

'I bet you can't wait to get on the plane and head off to the

States.' Ella turned to Anna as they walked towards the edge of the water, with Dan and Brae already trying to skim stones across its surface.

'I'm not sure anywhere can hold a candle to Port Agnes.' Anna smiled. 'Although it'll be nice to have a bit of a break and relax, now that everything seems to be covered. Jess texted this morning to say she's going to keep going to the infertility support group meetings, at least until she gets approved as a foster carer and maybe even after that. She's got her first session with the social worker next week and they're hoping to get her to panel by October.'

'That's amazing. How are the rest of the group doing?'

'Lucy's got her first scan when I get back from holiday and she's asked if I can go with her, because she's still terrified it might turn out not to be true.' Anna could understand that feeling and it was why both Lucy and Jess had agreed to stay in the group in the end. When you'd wanted something for so long, it was almost impossible to believe you might get it until it actually happened.

'How are you feeling about adoption now?'

'I think we'll definitely go down that route at some point, but we've decided to enjoy it just being the two of us for now. Who knows, we might find out we enjoy the freedom too much to ever give it up.'

'Maybe you will and who needs kids anyway, when we've got those two?' Ella laughed as she gestured towards where Dan and Brae were trying to push each other into the sea, in an attempt to be declared the victor in the stone skimming contest.

'Exactly! I think we better round them up before Brae ends up breaking his hand again, just in time for the honeymoon. I might have braved making a speech yesterday, but I'm definitely not up for driving the hire car in Florida!'

After the boys had eventually declared the contest a draw,

they carried on along the beach. When they reached the point where Titan's Head could be seen in the distance, where Dan and Brae had been rescued six months before, Ella stopped.

'Let's get a picture with Titan's Head behind us. Then I can upload it to the lifeboat station campaign pages.' Ushering them all into a line, she snapped a few photos.

'You're incredible.' Anna looked at her friend, as she selected the photo she wanted to upload. 'You've done so much with the campaign in such a short time and if anyone can stop them closing the lifeboat station, it's you.'

'Oh my God!' Ella suddenly sprang into the air, shoving her phone towards the others as she landed. 'Look at the number of signatures on the petition now!'

'There's over 150,000 there.' Dan widened his eyes. 'How on earth did that happen?'

'Someone's posted a link to an article that made them sign the petition. Hold on a sec.' Ella tapped the screen. 'It's about the wedding, look.'

Anna took the phone. The headline read:

Port Agnes Rallies to Save Local Midwife's Wedding.

It was an online article from a national newspaper and they'd used pictures from the social media pages for the lifeboat station campaign, including photos uploaded by guests from the wedding itself.

'That's brilliant!'

'You don't mind about the wedding being online and everyone reading about it?' Ella furrowed her brow. When they'd posted to let everyone know where the wedding was, the guests had just been told to meet at the harbour. Ella had told Anna she'd been terrified that random weirdos might just turn up at the wedding otherwise.

'If it helps, I don't mind what we do.'

'I got quite used to being recognised for having a wedding that never was. But is there room for two celebrity midwives in Port Agnes?' Ella grinned.

'If you can have your fifteen minutes of fame, then so can I!' Anna slipped an arm through hers. 'And at least it makes me feel as if I've contributed to the campaign in some way. If that number of signatures doesn't make them think again, then I don't know what will.'

'The JustGiving page has gone crazy too.' Dan turned the screen of his phone towards them. 'It looks like lots of people have donated as well as signing the petition.'

'Never mind all of that. Look at this photo someone took of me at the wedding!' Brae pointed to one of the uploads on Instagram. 'It might be the best photo of me I've even seen, I almost look like I've got a jawline in this!'

'You're gorgeous.' Dan grabbed hold of his friend's cheeks and planted a kiss on his forehead.

'Can we join the party?' Anna swung around at the sound of the voice behind them. It was Luke and Tamara Scott, with Belle all wrapped up in a baby sling on her father's chest.

'Of course you can!' Anna smiled. 'We're just celebrating Ella's lifeboat station campaign getting so many signatures. She's raised loads for the renovations too, if we can get the powers that be to agree to them. Thanks again for everything you did for the wedding. The canapés and desserts were amazing. I just hope you're not going to be overwhelmed catching up as a result.'

'That's brilliant news about the campaign and it was an absolute pleasure to help out with the wedding. Belle's such a good baby, so Tam and I have had plenty of time to get on with cooking together. There'll be no problem getting everything ready for the other weddings we're catering.'

'How's your first summer as a family of three going so far?' Brae moved to get a closer look at the baby.

'It's been really lovely.' Tamara smiled shyly. 'But actually, she's going to be part of a bigger family soon. I emailed my brother after you came over the other day, and asked him if he'd like to see Belle.'

'I'm guessing he couldn't wait to meet her?' Anna already knew the answer from the smile on Luke's face.

'He was so happy to hear from me and we talked for ages about the way Mum and Dad handled things when we were kids and he wishes things were different just as much as I do.' Tamara met Anna's gaze. 'What you said made me think. None of this was Rupert's fault and Belle deserves to know her uncle. So we're going over to see him and his fiancée tonight. I'm not ready to see my parents yet, but knowing that Rupert is on my side if I do might even make that easier eventually.'

'That's great.' Anna smiled, as Brae squeezed her hand; an unspoken understanding passing them between them. Things had a way of working out in the end, if you let them.

* * *

'This dessert is incredible, Jago.' Dan looked across at Ella's father, taking the words right out of Anna's mouth. She was finally feeling a bit better and more than ready for dessert when they got back from the beach, but what Jago served up far exceeded her expectations.

'It's a rocky road cheesecake pudding, Ysella's favourite.' Ella's dad was the only person Anna had ever heard call her friend by her full name. 'But watch out, because there's a silver sixpence in it somewhere and I'm not going on the hook for any dental bills.'

'I thought that was a Christmas thing?' Ella looked at her dad, who shook his head.

'I'd planned to put one in Anna and Brae's wedding cake, but I couldn't risk one of the kids getting a slice and choking. But the old rhyme goes, something old, something new, something borrowed, something blue, and a silver sixpence in her shoe. So I thought having it today was the next best thing.'

'The way I eat, I could end up swallowing it whole without even noticing!' Brae laughed. 'Luckily Anna and Ella are both trained in the Heimlich if I need it.'

'I think there's something in mine,' Ella chopped at the rocky road with her spoon. 'It looks gold though.'

Picking up the piece, Ella crumbled it between her fingers. The sound of the sixpence hitting her plate made Daisy bark and Jones followed suit. Except as Anna looked over, she realised it wasn't a sixpence, and a second later Ella finally realised it too.

'I don't understand, it looks like a really tiny bar of gold.' Ella stabbed it with her fork again.

'It's Cornish gold and there's enough there to make a couple of wedding rings if you want them, or something else if you don't.' Dan smiled, as Ella looked at him. 'I've been thinking about asking you to marry me for a while, but I want to make sure it's what you want and not just because I asked you. If and when you're ready, all you've got to do is get the gold made into rings. But if you never are, that's fine too. I just wanted you to know I'm ready whenever you are.'

'About bloody time!' Ella threw her arms around Dan's neck. 'And when the jewellers open on Monday, I'm going straight down there to see what they can do. But I'm telling you now, if you leave me standing at the altar, I'll hunt you down and kill you!'

'You'll have to get to him before I do!' Jago patted his future son-in-law on the back, Dan's response lost in a flurry of congratulations. If there was a better way of topping the weekend of their wedding, Anna couldn't think of one. Except it wasn't over yet.

* * *

'Are you okay?' Ella was waiting on the upstairs landing, as Anna came out of the bathroom. 'You looked a bit peaky downstairs and you've been up here ages.'

'I started feeling sick again after about two sips of the champagne your mum poured me.' Anna forced a smile, despite the churning in her stomach. 'How are you feeling about finding a gold bar in your dessert?'

'I still can't believe Dan and Dad cooked all this up. Dad had to make my dessert completely separately to make sure I got the gold. I'm going to have to watch those two together.' Ella rolled her eyes. 'Mum's already announced on Facebook that we're getting married. I've had so many messages, and Jess and Toni are offering their bridesmaid services again!'

'It was so lovely that Dan and your dad planned it together. I was nearly as excited as your mum.' Anna wrinkled her nose. 'I don't know what's wrong with me lately. All I seem to do is cry, but at least they're tears of happiness.'

'You know what all of this could be a symptom of, don't you?'

'I'm not pregnant.'

'And you know that for sure?' Ella raised her eyebrows, as Anna attempted a casual shrug.

'No, but the doctor told me how low my chances are, even

with the Clomid. He said I've got the fertility of a forty-four-year-old.'

'But not impossible, right? We've both worked with women of that age who've got pregnant.' Ella waited, until Anna nodded. 'I've got some tests in my bag, why don't you take one?'

'It'll just be a no.'

'At least then you'll be sure and, if your symptoms don't clear up, you can go and see the on-call doctor before you go on honeymoon. Now am I getting this test, or what?'

'Okay ,and when you go back down, can you send Brae up please?' Anna swallowed. 'Even though I know the chances are next to nothing, I can't help having a tiny bit of hope and if I'm going to cry my eyes out on anyone, I suppose it should be my husband.'

'Of course I will. Just wait here a sec and I'll be back up with the test.'

Ella was a good as her word, and she was back with a digital pregnancy test before Anna could convince herself to chicken out.

'I brought your bag up too. Text me if you need me. Otherwise I'll send Brae up in a few minutes.'

'Okay, thank you.' Anna didn't ask Ella to wish her luck. She needed something far closer to a miracle and she'd had more than her fair share of those already. Despite the warmth of the bathroom, she couldn't stop shaking. Three minutes later she was staring at the result through a blur of tears, jumping at the knock on the door.

'Anna, are you okay, darling? Ella said you needed me to come up.' Brae's voice was gentle and somehow she knew he'd make it all right.

'Come in.' Her voice was shaking as much as the rest of her, and Brae crossed the room to where she was sitting on the edge of the bath in two strides, crouching down next to her.

'What's the matter?'

Anna shook her head, unable to find the words, slowly unfurling her fist instead.

'I don't understand.' Brae picked up the keyring from the palm of her hand; a pair of silver and white baby bootees hanging from a silver chain.

'My parents gave it to me when I qualified as a midwife.' Anna's words came out in a rush. 'But now I want you to have it.'

'That's lovely, but I still don't understand. I know how much it means to you.'

'I'm pregnant.' Anna burst into tears the moment the words were out of her mouth.

'Really, are you sure?'

'Ella gave me a digital test. It's definitely positive.'

'But that's brilliant.' Brae scooped her into his arms as she continued to sob. 'Why are you so upset?'

'Because I'm scared.' Anna looked up at him. 'How can all these amazing things be happening to me? I can't help thinking something's going to go wrong and it's such early days. I had a couple of glasses of champagne the night before the wedding and another glass with the toasts. If I'd have known, I've never had done it.'

She'd thought about seeing the word 'pregnant' flash up on the testing stick a hundred times. It was going to come with a surge of pure unadulterated joy, she was sure of it. Only it hadn't, because she'd never *really* believed it would happen, not since they'd seen the fertility specialist. Every time she swallowed one of the Clomid pills, she'd seen it as just a stepping stone, something she had to try before she moved on to the next stage, mentally and physically. She hadn't truly thought it would work.

What she actually felt seeing the word 'pregnant' appear, was so much more complicated. She *was* thrilled, of course she was, but she was terrified of giving in to that feeling in case it was over almost before it had begun. Most of all, she still couldn't quite believe it was true; the same way she hadn't been able to believe it when Gwen had been jumping up and down telling her that the syndicate had won the lottery. Things like that didn't happen in real life.

'I know, but it was only a tiny bit of champagne and you didn't have a clue. You know better than anyone that thousands of healthy babies are born every year to parents who didn't plan it all perfectly. Even the fact that we've come this far is amazing and I think we should focus on that. Whatever else happens, we've got each other. So why shouldn't we get this miracle too, when I'm already the luckiest man in the world?'

'I knew you'd make it okay,' Anna sniffed, still clinging on to Brae. She had more to lose than ever, and she knew just how painful that could be. He was right again, though. She'd come to realise over the last few months that she was luckier than anyone she'd ever known for finding Brae. So it stood to reason that she'd surprised everyone, including herself, by beating the incredibly long odds the fertility specialist had offered up. The life she shared with Brae in Port Agnes had already given them more to celebrate than they could ever have hoped for, and, whatever happened next, no one could ask for more than that.

ACKNOWLEDGMENTS

Thanks as ever to all the readers who choose to spend their time reading my books and especially those who go to the effort of leaving a review, it means more than you will ever know and I feel so privileged to be doing the job I love.

I hope you have enjoyed the second of The Cornish Midwives novels. Sadly, I am not a midwife, or a social worker, but I have done my best to ensure that the medical and fostering details are as accurate as possible. I am very lucky that one of my close friends, Beverley Hills, is a brilliant midwife and I will be dedicating one of the future books in this series to her. I have also worked with foster carers and social workers for many years and so I have been able to draw upon this experience and their expertise in beginning to tell Jess' story. However, if you are one of the UK's wonderful midwives, providing such fantastic support for new and expectant mums, or indeed one of our amazingly dedicated social workers, I hope you'll forgive any details which draw on poetic licence to fit the plot.

My thanks as always go to the team at Boldwood Books for their help, especially my amazing editor, Emily Ruston, for lending me her wisdom to get this book into the best possible shape and set the scene for the next two books in the series. Thanks too to my wonderful copy editor, Cari, and proofreader, Shirley, for all their hard work.

As ever, I can't sign off without thanking my writing tribe, The Write Romantics, and all the other authors who I am lucky enough to call friends.

Finally, as they always will, my biggest thank you goes to my family – Lloyd, Anna and Harry – for their support, patience, love and belief.

MORE FROM JO BARTLETT

We hope you enjoyed reading *A Summer Wedding for the Cornish Midwife*. If you did, please leave a review.

If you'd like to gift a copy, this book is also available as an ebook, digital audio download and audiobook CD.

Sign up to Jo Bartlett's mailing list for news, competitions and updates on future books.

http://bit.ly/JoBartlettNewsletter

Why not explore the first in The Cornish Midwives series, *The Cornish Midwife*.

ABOUT THE AUTHOR

Jo Bartlett is the bestselling author of nineteen women's fiction titles. She fits her writing in between her two day jobs as an educational consultant and university lecturer and lives with her family and three dogs on the Kent coast.

Visit Jo's Website: www.jobartlettauthor.com

 twitter.com/J_B_Writer

 facebook.com/JoBartlettAuthor

 instagram.com/jo_bartlett123

ABOUT BOLDWOOD BOOKS

Boldwood Books is a fiction publishing company seeking out the best stories from around the world.

Find out more at www.boldwoodbooks.com

Sign up to the Book and Tonic newsletter for news, offers and competitions from Boldwood Books!

http://www.bit.ly/bookandtonic

We'd love to hear from you, follow us on social media:

facebook.com/BookandTonic

twitter.com/BoldwoodBooks

instagram.com/BookandTonic